MURDER ON
THE CORNISH CLIFFS

BOOKS BY VERITY BRIGHT

MURDER ON THE CORNISH CLIFFS

VERITY BRIGHT

bookouture

Published by Bookouture in 2023

An imprint of Storyfire Ltd.
Carmelite House
50 Victoria Embankment
London EC4Y 0DZ

www.bookouture.com

ISBN: 978-1-83790-766-3
eBook ISBN: 978-1-83790-765-6

Dedicated to my wonderful readers, without whom there would be no Lady Swift series.

Clifford,

Would I had any other option but to ink these words. And to you of all persons! However, my very life is in danger and I cannot countenance any public disgrace by going to the police. Thus my hand is forced. The truth can no longer be endured without recourse to the ignominy of this ungentlemanly missive.

Your urgent assistance is summoned, though what a man of your position can actually offer eludes me. However, I am aware that your former master, my good friend Byron Henley, often spoke of your 'hidden talents' so perhaps they may be put to use?

In expectation,

G. Cunliffe, Esq.

1

'My lady, I fear it may never come out.'

Pulled from her churning thoughts, Lady Eleanor Swift dragged her green-eyed gaze from the shivering swathes of Cornish winter-scarred gorse snaking past her side window. She swept the stray fiery red curl from her eyes and stared at her butler in the driving seat.

'The truth you mean, Clifford?'

His ever-impassive expression flinched as he wrestled the leviathan bonnet of the Rolls around a steep upward bend, evidently designed for nothing wider than an underfed donkey. 'I was referring to the deep crease in your forehead, my lady. The result of you frowning almost without pause since we left Henley Hall.'

'I have not,' Eleanor huffed, tugging on the holly-green velvet collar of her tweed travelling coat. Then her curiosity won. She peered at her reflection in the polished walnut dashboard. 'Have I?'

'Suffice to say, it is one thing to embody the behavioural traits of one's wilful bulldog, but quite another' – he gestured a leather-gloved finger mischievously at her forehead – 'to adopt his more unbecoming features.'

'Take no notice, Gladstone!' she tutted, stroking her bull-dog's soft wrinkled face as he lay next to his inseparable feline companion, Tomkins. Scooping up the letter that was the cause of her frown, she waved it in Clifford's eyeline. 'Well, you can hardly blame me for being disturbed by this. It's clearly a desperate plea for help from Mr Cunliffe whom I've never met, as you know. Even though he was a good friend of my late uncle's, his worries do strike me as rather far-fetched. And you seem sure he's, well, exaggerating, shall we say?' She shook her head. 'And what's more, the letter was written to you person-ally, rather than me. When did you last see him, anyway?'

He cleared his throat. 'Unfortunately, at his lordship's funeral.'

'Which I missed,' she said sadly.

'Not a matter that could have been helped since you were uncontactable, deep in the South African bush, commendably building a life of your own. One which his lordship entirely approved of, independence of spirit being precisely that which he admired. Especially in his favourite niece.'

Her heart swelled with affection for the kind-hearted butler she had inherited, along with her uncle's country estate, Henley Hall.

'Thank you. Even though, as I point out every time, I was his only niece, as we both know, Clifford.'

In truth, his words felt more comforting than a soft woollen blanket, as her uncle, Lord Byron Henley, had been her last surviving relative. Thoughts of his passing always threatened to leave her feeling horribly alone. Clifford on occasion stepping respectfully into the role of surrogate uncle meant the world to her. Especially as she tried to master the social pitfalls of being an English lady of the manor. Something that did not come easily after spending most of her formative years living a some-what bohemian lifestyle abroad with her unorthodox parents.

Her frown deepened as she peered again at the imperiously inked strokes of the letter.

'But that's what makes Mr Cunliffe's missive all the more upsetting! I can't approve of his tone to you at all, Clifford. It's bordering on rude. To actually put in writing that he felt forced to turn to you for help against his better judgement. Outrageous! It's almost as if he considered you—'

'Only a servant, my lady?' he said matter-of-factly. 'And rightly so, since he holds me entirely in the correct regard. That of being a mere butler.'

'Nonsense!' she cried, making Gladstone sit up with a whimper. Tomkins unfurled himself and slid lithely up Clifford's suited arm to curl around his stiffly collared neck like a velveteen ginger scarf. She nodded pointedly. 'See! Even Tomkins has worked out you're so much more than "a mere" anything. To me, certainly. Just as you were to Uncle Byron. He even implored you to leave the army with him so you could maintain your association. And friendship.'

Clifford bowed his head, obviously remembering his days as Byron's batman. 'His lordship was always beyond gracious. Not entirely unlike his niece.' He threw her a teasing look. 'At least in public.'

She smiled. 'I get it now. You think I've been too blunt a brick to notice your previous attempts to goad me into our usual squabbling to pass the miles on a long trip? And you might be right. Because I've been completely caught up fretting over what I'm going to say to this Mr Cunliffe about his obvious misapprehension that someone is trying to kill him!' She grimaced. 'At least I sincerely hope he's mistaken. And not only because it's supposed to be the season of goodwill to all men!' She sighed. 'He certainly wouldn't explain in any more detail over the telephone.'

'Indeed. Though regrettably, that was not my entire rationale for trying to distract you, my lady. It was, rather, an attempt to ease your floundering thoughts sufficiently to find not only a decorous, but also an expedient way to dispel Mr Cunliffe's, ahem, delusion. Expediently enough so as not to miss Christmas back at Henley Hall with your still only recently betrothed.'

The image of her dreamily handsome fiancé swam into her thoughts, lighting up her face.

'Your betrothed, for whom,' Clifford continued, 'the battle to gain any days away from his burgeoning police files is no easy task.'

She groaned. 'I know. Poor Hugh, he was fearfully disappointed about my dashing down here even though he understands and supports that I'll always be loyal to any friend of Uncle Byron's.'

'And, being a gentleman,' Clifford said, his eyes twinkling, 'Chief Inspector Seldon is well aware that he has unavoidably let you down on several similar occasions.'

She nodded ruefully. 'Don't remind me! Anyway, we've a few days yet before Christmas Day itself. So, we'll enjoy being guests of Mr Cunliffe for one night, reassure him that his fears are unfounded, and then hightail it home in time for all the planned celebrations!'

He held up a finger. '"Guest", my lady. In the singular. As on previous occasions, my presence at Gwel an Mor needs be scarcer than the Cornish pixies of folklore.'

'No, it jolly well needn't, Clifford!'

'My lady, at the risk of offering a contrary opinion, I believe your stay here will run a lot smoother if a better picture of the gentleman is painted ahead of your arrival. Which is imminent as, impossibly, the cliff road is now narrowing further, indicating we are almost at Gwel an Mor.'

'I'm perfectly capable of forming my own impression of him, thank you.'

'As you wish.'

'I do.' She tried to focus on enjoying the windswept plateau of fiercely resolute grasses clinging to the grey rocky cliff and the ocean of churning smoky-green water beyond.

'Dash it!' Her frustration broke out again. 'I know you're deviously plotting something to bring me around to your way of thinking, Clifford, but I can't fathom what.'

'Devious, indeed,' he tutted, easing the Rolls gingerly right onto a patchily repaired cobblestoned track. 'Perhaps, my lady, we might simply enjoy the last minutes of our journey? This is the final stretch around the headland, the other turning leads down the tortuous slope into the local village of Lostenev.'

As the car bumped along, she coaxed Tomkins back into the safety of her lap and tightened her grip on Gladstone. 'You win. I'm too curious about Mr Cunliffe. Maybe forewarned *is* forearmed. I assume from what you've hinted that his character is markedly different to Uncle Byron's?'

'Indeed. The very chalk to his lordship's cheese. Not only in stature, but even more distinctly, as you said, in character.'

'Well, I guess then, that's why he didn't understand that Uncle Byron considered you his butler, confidant and close friend, all in one impeccably suited, if often infuriating, package?'

Clifford's lips quirked at her mixed compliment. 'More a case of Mr Cunliffe wholeheartedly disapproving of such.'

'Gracious!'

'And, furthermore, disapproving of other, shall we say, similarly unorthodox relationships?'

She inhaled sharply. 'You mean Hugh and me, don't you?'

He nodded. 'A mere policeman, if you will forgive my referring to Chief Inspector Seldon in such a manner, being engaged to a titled lady? It would not be countenanced by a man of Mr

Cunliffe's traditional values.' He see-sawed his head teasingly. 'Although maintaining at least a modicum of traditional decorum may not always be a bad thing.'

'I shall deal with you later, you rascal,' she said, hiding a smile. 'In the meantime, I'm seriously beginning to wonder why Uncle Byron considered Mr Cunliffe a friend at all.'

She waited until he'd negotiated a near vertical slope that was so steep all she could see ahead was the Rolls' sweeping polished bonnet and beyond it, the sullen December sky.

'Dash it, Clifford. You know I wasn't born with much, if any, patience.' She ignored his mischievous nodding. 'And if you asked Mrs Butters to pack any in my travelling case, she must have forgotten. So, before I scream, tell me, what made the two most dissimilar-sounding men ever born stay friends?'

He tore his gaze from the road to hold hers momentarily. 'A heartfelt appreciation of that which each believed was inherent only in the other.'

'Go on,' she urged, now too intrigued to wait and work it out for herself.

'His lordship held Mr Cunliffe's unremitting embrace of stability and security in all areas of life in the highest esteem. Conversely, Mr Cunliffe was in awe of his lordship's unbridled bravery in the face of the unrelenting danger and uncertainty which became synonymous with the very name Lord Byron Henley.'

She flopped backwards in her seat, dumbfounded. 'I always thought Uncle Byron loved the freedom and derring-do of his adventurous bachelor life?'

'Unquestionably, his lordship did, my lady. But the quiet yearning for a degree of certainty is an instinct rooted to some extent in even the most intrepid of us, it transpires.'

Desperate to ask if that included him too, since she still knew so little about her oh-so-private butler's life, and even less of his loves, she curbed her runaway tongue. 'So, the flip side is

Mr Cunliffe has a dormant streak of wanting to be bold and spontaneous which rears up once in a blue moon?'

'Rather more that the gentleman often displays a tendency to gravitate to that which alarms him.' He hesitated. 'Obsessively so, if I might confide. And I fear his latest fixation that his life is in danger may be a case in point.'

'Poor chap!' She felt a deep wash of sympathy for the stranger she was about to meet. 'He must have worked hard to keep his nervous agitation under control, though. He was eminently successful in banking, you mentioned. A wonderfully supportive family, I imagine?'

'Regrettably not. Since similar neurosis runs widely through the Cunliffe family. Not that the gentleman would ever mention or admit to such. Hence, however, his fondness for your late uncle's company and reassuring good sense.' He pointed ahead as they cleared a set of formidable but weather-beaten iron gates. 'The stone tower and incongruous castellations around the last of this bend herald our arrival at "Sea View". Or Gwel an Mor as it is in Cornish.'

She rolled her shoulders back. 'Right then—'

Her jaw fell as the Rolls came to an abrupt halt. Blocking their way were several official-looking black cars.

'Clifford,' she whispered. 'Why do you suppose there is a huddle of police here in the driveway?'

A heavy-jowled face poked in through Clifford's side window, the salt-and-pepper moustache twitching.

'Inspector Trevilick's the name.' His strong Cornish accent elongated each vowel, taking the edge off his officious tone. His sharp blue eyes flicked between them. 'Now then, I'm hoping from my boots up you're not here to queer over the body?'

'Body!' She stared at her butler in horror. 'Clifford, Mr Cunliffe must have been right. And we're—'

'Too late, my lady!'

2

With its grey granite construction, Gwel an Mor struck Eleanor as resembling more a mausoleum than a home. Its imposing design stood to symmetrical attention against the sombre backdrop of the darkly clouded winter sky. Two regimental Doric columns flanked the black front door, while a row of tall windows on either side ran the length of the first three storeys of the early Georgian mansion. Even the awkwardly added castellations bolstered its formal air. Either side, tended lawns and shrubs stretched out like a neatly patterned carpet.

She took a deep breath and stepped out of the Rolls. Seeming to catch her sombre mood, Gladstone slid his portly form out after her with none of his usual exuberance, Tomkins slinking alongside like a silent shadow. Under the watchful gaze of the inspector, she gestured to Clifford. Before he could step over, both of them turned at the sound of sensible heels clipping around the driveway's swing-through. A harassed-looking woman with tightly side-pinned brown hair sidled along one of the police cars, hands clasped across the folds of her unassuming black dress. The stiff breeze flicked at the meagre fan of lace at her throat. She pressed it flat with a flustered hand as she curtseyed cautiously to Eleanor. Throwing Clifford an equally wary glance, she jerked her head behind her.

'House was expectin' you, m'lady. Though not with the ravens havin' marked out yer path.' She half turned. 'You'll have a drop of warm, all the same?'

Not waiting for an answer, she started back towards the front door.

Eleanor glanced quizzically at Clifford before setting off after this unknown woman, leaving Trevilick scratching his head.

'Mrs Liddicoat,' Clifford whispered, following his customary respectful two paces behind, with Gladstone trotting alongside and Tomkins nestled in the crook of his arm. 'Long-standing housekeeper. And, memory now serves, a staunch upholder of superstition.'

'Ah! Hence her reference to ravens as a portent of,' she lowered her voice, 'death! Though it didn't make for the warmest welcome. But hardly surprising, given the circumstances.'

Catching sight of the solidly built Inspector Trevilick hard on their heels, she raised her voice again. 'Poor woman, having to deal with such a tragedy.'

'Death comes to all,' the inspector called. 'The trick is to be ready for it.' She turned to see him running a hand slowly over his moustache. 'Wouldn't you agree?'

Finding only confusion, not comfort in his words, she increased her pace with a vague shrug in polite reply.

As she climbed the last pebble-inlaid step and entered the house via the massive oak door, her breath caught. A captivating candlelight- and bauble-covered Christmas tree dominated the hallway, rising to the second-floor landing and beyond. The tree's festively twinkling glass baubles, and fluttering gold-laced ornaments made the hand of death having struck at such a festive season seem even more cruel.

She offered the hovering housekeeper a sympathetic smile. 'It was remiss of me not to say out in the driveway, but I'm so sorry to hear the news.'

The housekeeper's eyes narrowed. 'Thank you, I'm sure.' Turning away, she called over her shoulder, 'Now, you're to go to the clutch parlour.' She shrugged. 'Though only friends of the house know the way, of course. So, I'll have to show yer.'

Eleanor noted her butler stiffen and flapped a discreet hand that this was no time for his exacting rules on how his mistress should be treated.

'Best behaviour, Master Gladstone. From you, at least,' she caught him mutter to her bulldog, who reluctantly stopped mid-stalk of the Christmas tree with a grumble of disappointment.

She had to admit, though, as she hurried along, the house-keeper's manner suggested the whole affair was no more than an inconvenience in her already busy day. Eleanor wished she could take her time through the house, since this was likely her one chance to glimpse the private world of her uncle's friend. And now, with his tragic death, that chance was lost forever.

She was, however, able to briefly admire the long passage-ways of waxed oak flooring, covered in parts by floral-patterned rugs of a seemingly universal dark pink and gentian blue. Through the passing blur of open doors, she picked up an over-riding hue of stolid green and dependable burgundy. Conservative ivory plasterwork ceiling roses, framed by Palladian cornices, presided over impressive fireplaces dressed with decorative friezes. The furniture was also formal in the extreme, with only a passing nod to comfort. The paintings adorning so many of the walls were exquisitely framed, the *objets d'art* set in myriad alcoves as delicate as the mouldings framing them.

All too soon the housekeeper announced at a half-open door. 'Visitor, sir.'

Eleanor stepped inside the room, her confusion deepening as she was now standing in what was surely some sort of museum? Waist-high glass cabinets lined three sides with more, smaller wall-mounted versions above, all set against the backdrop of turquoise silk bird-print wallpaper. All of them were occupied by a single egg of varying size and colour, the smallest being that of a pea and the largest, amazingly, a football! A rosewood table peppered with small, lidded baskets, a stack of plaques, a handwritten register and, most intriguingly, a quarter bale of straw, stood in the middle of the room. The faint strain of a piano filtered in from somewhere unseen, adding to Eleanor's feeling that she would soon wake to find this all just a feverish dream.

She nodded to Inspector Trevilick, who had somehow beaten her into the room. Then she noticed a man with thinning grey hair, his head in one of the many wall-mounted glass display cases. His black jacket and waistcoat with matching dove-grey trousers and tie struck her as a very businesslike combination, but rather overbearing for his diminutive stature. He turned around and frowned, causing his wire-rimmed spectacles to slide down his nose. 'Visitor? At a time like this?' His tone was taut.

Clifford motioned for Gladstone to stay put before stepping forward. He bowed from the shoulders. 'Sir, may I present Lord Henley's niece, Lady Swift? My lady, this is... Mr Cunliffe.' The cautioning look came too late, as her brows had already disappeared into her red curls.

'Mr Cunliffe! But I thought you were—'

'Ahem.' Clifford's quiet, but pointed, cough halted her words. Her gaze slid to the watching inspector.

'Umm, expecting me,' she ended, with what she hoped was a convincing smile.

Part of the letter that had brought them down came back to her; *I cannot countenance any public disgrace by going to the police.* And yet here they were, the heavyset inspector unnervingly jotting down notes without taking his eyes off her. Except, that was, for the odd flick of his gaze across to Clifford still nonchalantly holding Tomkins, Gladstone sprawled on the rug before him.

'Perhaps I missed your name?' Trevilick said to Clifford.

'He is Lady Swift's *butler*,' Mr Cunliffe said stiffly. His fingers quivered over a dark speckled olive-green egg in the nearest display case. 'Yes. Apologies, Lady Swift. An unfortunate incident has occurred. It has caught one quite' – his eyes darted to Inspector Trevilick – 'unawares.'

'Well, naturally,' she said, floundering as to how she might ask who had actually died since, to her relief, he was clearly still very much alive and breathing.

Before she could, the inspector stepped past the table. 'Mr Cunliffe, perhaps you'll be good enough to leave arranging your, one must say, most extraordinary egg collection, and explain?'

'Well, if I have to,' Cunliffe said waspishly. 'I had rather thought you were done with questions though, Inspector?' He adjusted his spectacles by their bridge. 'And that you had taken your leave.'

'So did I, sir,' Trevilick said. 'Until your still unexplained visitors arrived?'

'*Visitor*,' Cunliffe corrected, glancing at Clifford with a frown. It doubled as he seemed to take in Eleanor's bulldog and ginger tomcat for the first time. 'Lady Swift has journeyed down from her late uncle's estate, Henley Hall, to visit... briefly,' he added, rather pointedly to her mind but also to her relief, eager as she was to hightail it back to Henley Hall and spend Christmas with her fiancé. 'Lord Henley was a long-standing friend of mine.' His fingers ran down his jacket buttons as if fumbling through a glissando on the piano. 'He is sorely missed.'

Eleanor's annoyance at his cursory dismissal of Clifford's presence was somewhat soothed by the deep affection Cunliffe obviously still held her beloved uncle in. However, rather than his curiosity now being sated, Inspector Trevilick seemed even more interested.

'Very queer,' he muttered into his notebook.

Cunliffe scowled at him. 'I fail to see why. It is Christmas, in case you had not noticed. A family member of an old friend coming to visit is hardly of note.'

The inspector gave a polite shrug. 'In normal times, perhaps not. But at a time like this, as you yourself said? It just seemed likelier than not you would have telephoned the lady to postpone the visit.'

Cunliffe flapped a hand. 'It wasn't possible. The lady would have left long before. Besides, given who has... passed, it was not a call I necessarily would have felt the need to make.'

Inspector Trevilick turned to Eleanor. 'I'm sure you agree, Lady Swift?'

'Of course,' she said hesitantly, still totally in the dark over who it was they were talking about.

'Ah, so it won't spoil your Christmas, then?' His words sounded more like a statement than a question.

Cunliffe tapped the tops of his fingers together agitatedly. 'Why on earth would Lady Swift be upset by the death of my gardener?'

His gardener, Ellie? It was Cunliffe's life that was supposed to be in danger, not his gardener's.

She and Clifford exchanged a glance.

Cunliffe cleared his throat. 'Hardly a topic to discuss in front of a member of the opposite, er, gender. Apologies, Lady Swift.' He glared at the inspector. 'Nor with the police any longer, actually, since everything pertinent has been discussed.' He pointedly turned his back to the inspector. 'But yes, Lady Swift, my... gardener is no more. Dead at the bottom of the cliffs. Fell, you see?'

'Gracious, how awful!'

'Went over the edge of the path that meets the one leading

from the house,' Inspector Trevilick said. 'Dangerous spot, that main path is. No wider than a rabbit holding his breath. And it goes right along the cliff edge.' He rubbed a knowing hand along his generous jowl. 'Popular on a clear day, often enough. On account of being able to see the lighthouse. And the occasional dolphin or whale.'

'So maybe the poor fellow had been enjoying the view?' Eleanor berated her runaway tongue as the weather was about as clear as potato soup.

Trevilick raised an eyebrow. 'Possibly, Lady Swift. Up until an hour ago, that is. When he fell or jumped, maybe. Least, that's when he was found. Not a pretty sight, as you might imagine.'

'No,' Clifford said firmly. 'Her ladyship need not imagine, thank you, Inspector.'

Trevilick fixed him with a beady-eyed stare. 'Long drive in the lady's vehicle for you, was it, Mr Clifford?'

Her butler's ever-inscrutable expression didn't flinch. 'A few hundred miles, or thereabouts, sir. A mere jaunt to a machine as finely engineered as the Rolls.'

The corner of Trevilick's lips twitched. 'Thereabouts being?'

'Henley Hall, Little Buckford, Buckinghamshire.'

'Thank you.' The inspector closed his notebook and slid his pen into his inner coat pocket. 'Mr Cunliffe, I shall leave now. Thank you for your time.' Receiving only a dismissing nod from Eleanor's host, he turned to her. 'Lady Swift, I hope you enjoy your stay at Gwel an Mor. May Father Christmas have only treats in store for you.'

Deep in thought, she watched him leave.

Just the truth about what on earth is going on here would do, Ellie!

3

An icy wind whipped at Eleanor's red curls. Running his hand around the ebonised rosewood handle of the open front door, Mr Cunliffe bobbed his head awkwardly. 'Lady Swift, I do apologise since, rather rudely, you have been left attired in your outer wear. However, perhaps you'll excuse the unfortunate lack of good manners further and join me for the rest of my interrupted constitutional before the last of the light fades?'

With the inspector gone, she nodded in relief.

Maybe you'll get some answers now, rather than riddles, Ellie?

'Willingly. Even in late December, the outdoors always calls me.'

Gladstone bounded out ahead, followed by the skittish Tomkins. Cunliffe muttered something to himself and waited for Eleanor to join him before carefully closing the door. She tried to stop his rigid demeanour and obvious agitation affect her. Looking around for support, Clifford was nowhere to be seen.

She followed Mr Cunliffe along an uneven path towards the side of the house. As she turned the corner, her way was unexpectedly bathed in a stark yellow glow from the soaring bay window of what she took to be the principal drawing room. It illuminated the ornate terrace which ran along the back of the house and the knee-high box hedging lining a series of swirling paths.

Her host gestured right, however, before continuing hesitantly up a set of wide stone steps, each of which was flanked by an ornate Grecian urn. He stopped at the edge of the elevated grass expanse.

Too excited to wait for her to catch up, Gladstone lumbered ahead after Tomkins, who skittered between the low bushes at either end of the neatly mown lawn which, she realised, had been designed in such a way that it resembled a chessboard.

'How ingenious! And now I see the bushes are cut and shaped like chess pieces too!'

Cunliffe grimaced. 'An idea of my... late gardener. One of the only real pieces of progress completed before... well.'

At that moment a peacock appeared from behind one of the bushes and strutted towards a very unsure-looking Gladstone. Tomkins, who was made of sterner stuff, took it in his stride. Until he was met with a cautionary fan of feathers and loud screech. Deciding the bulldog, who was nonchalantly sniffing another bush, had the right approach after all, Tomkins skipped past and ran up the nearest tree as if he'd intended to all along.

Cunliffe watched the cat for a moment, then turned back to Eleanor with a deep breath. 'Lady Swift, I must apologise.'

'I really can't think what for,' she said brightly. 'I'm honestly just delighted to finally meet you. As one of Uncle Byron's long-standing friends, it was remiss of me not to contact you some time ago. Rather than wait for you to contact me, that is.' She tried to keep her tone nonchalant. 'Or Clifford, actually, as he was the recipient of your letter.'

He winced. 'Petitioning him, or your good self, was far from my finest hour, I admit.'

'Again, I fail to see why. Reaching out for help is no crime. Didn't Uncle Byron ever call on you for assistance?'

A flicker of wistfulness passed across Cunliffe's troubled eyes. 'Yes. But all too rarely. His visits to me in London, and here years later, were always such a highlight.'

She smiled. 'There you are then. You have simply called in one of his favours. And I am genuinely delighted to take up his mantle.'

'Hardly!' Mr Cunliffe stooped to pick up a stray twig from the lawn. He turned it between his thumb and forefinger. 'I cannot pretend I am comfortable with what I did, Lady Swift. It goes against every grain to ask a servant or a... a...'

'Woman?'

The twig snapped in his fingers. 'I did not anticipate that you would be informed of my letter. Nor particularly of its contents.'

She shrugged. 'It was absolutely right for Clifford to pass the matter on to me.'

His expression made clear his hearty disagreement. 'Still, my embarrassment aside, I appreciate the journey you made down here to Gwel an Mor.'

'Our pleasure.' She made a point of nodding towards her butler, now gliding over carrying a tray.

Her host seemed even more grateful for the interlude to gather his composure than she was to press her chilled fingers around the steaming cup Clifford had brought her.

'Seaweed, comfrey and ginger infusion, Mrs Liddicoat informed me, my lady.'

Cunliffe took his. 'An effective bronchial remedy.'

She took a long sip to hide her smile at Clifford's murmured, 'Hopefully more palatable with the dash of Dutch courage I added to yours, my lady.'

'Thank you, Clifford. Mr Cunliffe and I had just started discussing his unfortunate predicament.'

He half-bowed to Cunliffe. 'Most unsettling indeed, sir.'

'A gross understatement,' Cunliffe snapped. 'And now it is all the more concerning. A shocking state of affairs for a gentleman to find himself caught up in.'

Eleanor set her cup down on the tray to slide on her warmed mittens, which had magically appeared in the crook of her arm. 'Why don't we walk while you start from the beginning? Or jump to more recent developments and work backwards if you prefer, Mr Cunliffe?'

He stared into his cup. 'I know very little more than you do. Quite simply, I engaged someone who seemed bent on killing me and who himself is now dead.'

She gasped. *He must mean his gardener, Ellie!* She noted Clifford's raised eyebrow.

He nodded discreetly at her. 'Without success, sir, thankfully.'

'That we cannot be certain of,' Mr Cunliffe muttered darkly as he started down the path.

She grimaced at Clifford behind Cunliffe's back and then stumbled forward as Gladstone bowled into the back of her knees.

'Careful, old chum!'

Brushing her coat down, she caught up with Cunliffe. 'Perhaps I was wrong. Maybe we'd better start at the beginning. The person you are referring to was your... gardener, correct?'

Cunliffe hesitated. 'Yes and no.' He paced up and down, Eleanor following him. 'I took him on recently as head of the grounds staff. In the capacity of landscape architect.'

'Ah! So his role was to restore Gwel an Mor's gardens to their former glory?'

Mr Cunliffe shook his head. 'No. His role was to make these grounds the epitome of sophisticated modernity. Tear out the old and replace it with the new! Although now I'll have to find someone else and start from scratch again, I suppose.'

'Modernity?' She just caught Clifford's discreet, disapproving sniff. 'I meant, from what I've seen, the house itself seems such a... a perfectly preserved historic jewel.'

'*Restored*. Not preserved,' Cunliffe said frostily. 'A former family member had let it fall into a parlous state as he had squandered his time and money on... other matters. Anyway, a few years before my retirement, I realised that decades of working in the lofty world of finance had left their indelible mark upon me. I could not simply retire and waste away my days. I needed a project, a worthwhile pursuit. Well, I'd inherited this house some years earlier, but never imagined moving out of London. However,' he continued, waving a quivering finger, 'a sound investment opportunity must never be overlooked. So, I began to think of the possibilities.'

'How perfect. So you would have been on hand to oversee the works?'

'Yes, although as I said it was not my intention to move down initially, but to oversee them from London with the occasional visit. However, my physician was most insistent that my work in the demanding world of finance, as well as the years in our fair, if somewhat polluted, capital city had taken their toll. And, in consequence, I needed to retire somewhere where the pace of life was slower. And the air cleaner. I will admit quietly, Lady Swift, my... nerves and chest had suffered. And thus I moved here.'

'Well, the house is right by the sea. And the air couldn't be cleaner, especially with that wonderful sea breeze, as it's right on the edge of the cliffs.' She grimaced. 'Although they are the very cliffs your gardener, the poor fellow, fell from, I know.'

He looked up sharply. 'He was no poor fellow! And I wish with all my heart I had never heard of Jerome Withenhall St Clair!'

She stopped in her tracks, her brow furrowed. 'Wait a moment. St Clair? Why does that name sound so familiar?'

4

Before Cunliffe could respond, Clifford coughed respectfully. 'The Earl of Wickhamshaw's party you attended last summer, perhaps, my lady? His grand unveiling.'

'Of course!' She tapped her chin thoughtfully. 'Well remembered. St Clair was the chap who had redesigned the earl's gardens. Quite an ambitious and charismatic young man, I recall. If rather slenderly built and petitely proportioned.'

Her face reddened.

Like Mr Cunliffe, Ellie.

Clifford came to her rescue. 'Sir, perhaps it was on the recommendation of the Earl of Wickhamshaw that you chose to engage Mr St Clair for your own garden enterprise?'

'Actually, yes.'

'Mr Cunliffe.' Eleanor tried to keep the frustration from her voice. Having come several hundred miles and disrupted her festive plans, she was finding his offhand manner increasingly hard to bear. 'You haven't explained exactly why you thought St Clair was trying to... you know?'

'Murder me?' Cunliffe said grimly. 'Because I discovered he was not who he pretended to be, that's why!' His eyes clouded over. 'But he gave himself away. Yes, he did. Thought he was too smart for me, but I saw through him.'

Eleanor counted silently to three. 'Could you be more specific, please?'

Cunliffe sighed in exasperation. 'If I must.' He thought for a moment. 'For instance, he took to going into the village of an evening.'

She resisted the temptation to roll her eyes. 'The problem there being?'

He looked at her as if she were simple. 'Glaringly obvious! The only establishment he could have frequented at such an hour was the local inn.'

'He was residing on site then, sir?' Clifford said.

'He was. In the attic rooms above his office,' Cunliffe tutted. 'I should have insisted he do as the under-gardeners do, and find his own lodgings in the village.'

'Although he probably put in more hours because he was living on site?' Eleanor said, having sensed the financial benefits would no doubt have appealed to this retired doyen of banking.

Cunliffe's eyes lit up. 'Ha! That was his second mistake. He put in far *too* many hours!'

Now thoroughly lost, she could only stare blankly at him.

Mr Cunliffe's lips set in a thin line. 'I saw him creeping about the gardens in the dead of night, you understand, when any decent person would be in their bed.'

'Might he not have, perhaps... suffered with insomnia?' she said gingerly.

Cunliffe gave her a sharp stare. 'No! And that wasn't the worst of it. But it is hardly a topic for discussion with a... a lady.'

Clifford coughed again. 'Her ladyship has a distressingly robust mental constitution, I can assure, sir.'

Cunliffe nodded begrudgingly. 'Alright. I decided to check up on St Clair and his increasingly mysterious activities. He had shown me his master plan for my gardens, but never his workings out, his notebook, that I know every gardener keeps. So I searched his office one evening when I was sure he wasn't present and discovered some "discrepancies" in his supposed garden notebook. Symbols, in fact. Mysterious ones!' He ended in a wide-eyed whisper.

Probably just St Clair's own shorthand way of notating his landscaping projects, Ellie.

'And,' her host continued, drumming his fingers against his leg, 'that was around the time I started to feel increasingly... unwell!'

'Gracious! I hope the doctor was able to cure whatever it was?'

He sniffed. 'My symptoms are certainly not ones I would share with the local physician. The man is a fool. Fortunately,' he continued, tapping his temple, 'my mental faculties remained entirely unaffected. Which is why I was able to work out St Clair's true motive in coming here.'

Dare you ask, Ellie?

She did. 'Which was?'

'The gardens, Lady Swift! These very gardens.' He swept an arm around the lawn.

'Ah!' She shivered, only now realising how bitter the wind was. 'And why is that?'

'Lady Swift, I do not believe in fairies or pixies, Cornish or otherwise. But I do believe in *evil*. And St Clair was clearly an occultist! A satanic worshipper! Those symbols in his notebook were undoubtedly to do with black magic and the like!' He leaned in conspiratorially. 'He came here to gain control over the gardens and their own black magic! But to do so, he needed first to... to kill me!'

She risked patting his rigidly held arm. 'Mr Cunliffe, let's not dwell on that. Perhaps he wasn't actually trying to kill you?'

Cunliffe nodded slowly. 'True.'

Her mouth fell open. 'But... but you just told me he *was*!'

He regarded her as if she were slow of reason. 'I obviously drew that conclusion *before*. But now that he has been murdered—'

'*Murdered!*'

She exchanged a despairing glance with Clifford.

Cunliffe grunted. 'Of course. Someone *else* was obviously trying to kill me to gain control over the gardens. Who, I have no idea. But whoever it was mistook St Clair for me and pushed *him* over the cliff!' He gave her an aggrieved look. 'We were similar from behind. He and I were both of... modest stature and the wretch was always swathed in pompously immodest clothing for a person of his minimal standing. Aping the class he wished to impress, no doubt. That's why I knew it was him that was dead.'

Eleanor gasped. 'Oh goodness, I didn't realise Inspector Trevilick had asked you to identify the body.'

'There was no need. I was the one who reported it.'

'You found him?'

Cunliffe slid a handkerchief from his pocket and dabbed the corners of his mouth. '*Saw*, Lady Swift. I saw his... remains on the rocks down below during my habitual afternoon constitutional along the cliff path. It's very important for the lungs. And the digestion.' He closed his eyes momentarily. 'Most particularly the digestion, given the company at luncheon.'

'Someone else lives here with you, then?'

'Yes. Family.' He paused awkwardly. 'Two aunts and a nephew. All of whom came with the house. I simply don't have the... heart to remove them. And, of course, the staff live in. Except the two under-gardeners, that is. They reside in the village as I think I said. But the maid, the housekeeper Mrs Liddicoat, who you've already met briefly, and' – his mouth turned down – 'her husband, the handyman, live on site. Although the maid has been at her mother's since yesterday as the lady is ill, apparently seriously. Most inconvenient,' he muttered.

'Most gracious of you to continue Mrs Liddicoat in service, sir,' Clifford said. 'If you will forgive the observation.'

Eleanor caught his drift. 'Yes. Normally staff are asked to leave if they marry. At least in conventional circles.'

Cunliffe snorted. 'Like the family, the Liddicoats had also long been in residence when I inherited the house. I felt I could not ask them to leave.'

'And who would have inherited the house if you *had* died?' She clamped a hand over her mouth.

Why did you ask that, Ellie?

Oddly, Cunliffe seemed unfazed by the question.

'Unlike in some less orthodox families,' he said, looking pointedly away and then back, 'the male always inherits.'

She smiled sweetly. In her family, the eldest inherited regardless of sex. But her family had always been unorthodox, and she was proud of it.

Cunliffe cleared his throat. 'So, my nephew would get the house. Not that it matters as he lives here rent free anyway,' he added bitterly. 'Like the rest of the family!'

'And the staff? Would they get anything if...' She caught Clifford pinching the bridge of his nose and tailed off.

Cunliffe pursed his lips. 'They would get nothing! Why should they? I pay them more than I get work out of them already. Especially the husband.'

'And... and would any of them have known Mr St Clair would have been on the spot where he, er, fell from?'

Cunliffe snorted. 'Everyone in the house and grounds would have known! He always walked that way after he finished work and watched "the fading light of the day" as he put it, from the spot where he fell.'

'Speaking of your housekeeper, sir.' Clifford gestured his

head towards the door. 'I believe the lady is requesting your attention.'

'Oh, not again,' Cunliffe grunted. 'Lady Swift, please excuse me.'

'Of course. But first one last question. I appreciate you did not wish to involve the police, but if you originally thought St Clair was trying to kill you, why didn't you simply dismiss him?'

Cunliffe's brows shot up. 'Have you not been listening? The man was a satanist!' He blanched. 'I was afraid of what he might have done!'

Worse than murder, Ellie?

5

Back inside the house, even the festive decorations weren't enough of a distraction as Eleanor paced the hallway, itching for Cunliffe to reappear. At the base of the Christmas tree, Tomkins, however, sat mesmerised by the coloured-glass teardrops that spun slowly, throwing spiralling patterns onto the suspended porcelain cherubs. Gladstone, meanwhile, was in his element. Dislodging showers of pine needles with his stumpy tail, he lumbered around the lower branches, sniffing every lace-edged bauble as if hoping it might be edible.

Clifford arrived carrying her travelling cases. He tutted as she tugged him to a halt by his jacket sleeve.

'Clifford, how on earth am I going to carry on as Mr Cunliffe's guest?' she hissed.

He placed her cases on the oak floor with an admonishing look. 'The difficult conversation on the lawn notwithstanding, surely the gentleman still deserves the benefit of the doubt, my lady?'

Feeling abashed, she nodded.

'Then simply do as always. Devour unladylike amounts of fayre and, ahem, commit an indecorous number of faux pas.'

She rolled her eyes good-naturedly, knowing his mischievous teasing was to ease her fitful thoughts. 'It still amazes me Uncle Byron survived your razor wit for so many years.' She peeped over both shoulders. 'And Mr Cunliffe's... peculiarities, too.'

He raised a quizzical brow.

'Oh, come on! Devil worship. That's preposterous, Clifford!'

'If you say so, my lady,' he replied impassively.

'Well, of course I do. Like all right-thinking people would. But I know that is your respectful way of disagreeing.' She scanned his face. 'Are you feeling the full ticket, though, Clifford? Because, really, I think this bracing sea air may have numbed your faculties.'

'As your butler,' he said pointedly, 'it is far from my place to hold an opinion, contrary or otherwise, as I have oft said. However, interest in the occult, particularly regarding "black magic" and devil worship, is, in fact, not uncommon. Even among respected personages of learning, such as Mr Aleister Crowley, a gentleman born to not insubstantial means, who has published several books on the subject.'

'Gracious!'

He looked over her shoulder and shook his head wearily. 'My lady, when you said you would keep watch on the four-legged members of our party...'

She looked around, her tone indignant. 'What? I have. Neither has wandered anywhere... oh, Gladstone, no!' Her hand flew to her mouth at the sight of her bulldog's earth-streaked jowls, a glass bauble swinging from his front teeth. 'At least Tomkins hasn't—' A shower of pine needles pattered down onto her face. 'You, too,' she groaned. Straining up on tiptoes, she spotted her ginger tom in the higher branches. 'Honestly, how have either of you got to your age without learning the concept of acceptable behaviour?'

'I wonder,' she caught Clifford mutter as he stepped around her. While he extracted Tomkins from his perilous perch, she dropped to her knees and waggled a finger at her bulldog. 'Give me that, Gladstone! It is not a ball to play with. And it isn't yours.' With a low grumble, he shuffled backwards mutinously. She tried in a firmer tone. 'Mr Wilful. Give. It. Up!'

Finally having coaxed it from him, she bit her lip at the now soggy edges of the lace frill which ran around the centre of the sphere, ending in a loop for hanging.

'Maybe no one will notice,' she said with a wince to Clifford as she stood up. She paused in placing it back on the tree. 'Oh goodness, I hadn't noticed it's not a typical Christmas picture inside. There's a darling little portrait photograph of a child in this one.'

'Ahem.' Clifford swept his arm over the tree. 'As there are in a fair proportion of them, my lady.'

'So delightful. I haven't come across that before, have you?'

'Only in the most traditional of households. It was popular for a time during the early reign of Queen Victoria since it combined two new fashions. That of having a Christmas tree, which Her Majesty's consort, Prince Albert, is credited with having introduced to the nation. And the increasing accessibility to portrait photography. As treasured mementos of family past and present, the photographic miniatures were immortalised in glass baubles.'

'What a great idea,' she cheered extra brightly to hide the wash of longing for the family Christmas she hadn't had since her parents disappeared when she was nine. Even with her uncle having taken her in, he'd invariably been away on business throughout the rest of her childhood.

With a sigh, she fluffed out the lace on the bauble and hung it back on the tree in the nearest gap. 'Now, where do you suppose Mr Cunliffe has got to?'

'Your host is deep in discussion with Mrs Liddicoat in the

kitchen, I believe, my lady. Over the arrangements for dinner. Which, I understand, will commence promptly at eight o'clock.'

She stared at the grandfather clock as her stomach rumbled. 'That's still hours away!'

'Barely sufficient time to prepare. At least for a certain lady guest, perhaps?'

'Oh thank heavens, I'm not the only guest then.' Her shoulders hadn't finished relaxing before they stiffened at his knowing look. 'Dash it, I am, aren't I? Which means I'll have to dredge up all sorts of polite chatter to play the good guest.'

'And without having met your dinner companions beforehand.'

She cocked her head as the sound of music filtered into the hallway. 'Who else was it Mr Cunliffe said lives here?'

'Two aunts and a nephew, my lady.'

'Right. Then since it appears I'll need to entertain myself for some time, please stop Gladstone and Tomkins creating any more havoc. At least, while I go and introduce myself to my dinner companions to stave off the effects of starvation.'

'While leaving time to dress for dinner, naturally,' Clifford said stiffly.

'Pff! Five minutes is plenty.' She bit back a smile. 'And as you're kindly taking my cases up, have a rootle past my unmentionable frillies and hoik out a suitable frock for me to hurl myself into, would you?'

Leaving him running a horrified finger around his collar, she set off in the music's direction.

After all, Ellie, if by some absurd chance Mr Cunliffe is right and someone did kill St Clair thinking it was him, then everyone in this house is a suspect!

6

Eleanor retraced the route the housekeeper had led her along to the egg collection room. From there she continued following the tinkling of keys and marvelling at the impressive collection of portrait and landscape paintings. At the end of the corridor, she paused at the only door. She knocked. No reply. She knocked louder. Still no reply. Shrugging, she turned the handle and stepped inside, a confident smile and ready apology on her lips.

At a baby grand, two identical elderly ladies sat shoulder to shoulder. Hands rising and falling, their white-haired heads bobbed and rolled under their lace caps as synchronously as if they were one being. Given that they were dressed in the same shade of midnight-blue taffeta, Eleanor wondered if they were indeed twins.

Her arrival still seemed to have gone unnoticed as the music continued unabated. Hoping it wasn't on account of being unwelcome, she stepped up to the piano.

'Good afternoon,' she said loudly. 'Forgive me interrupting but I'm Lady Swift. Mr Cunliffe's guest.' She cringed as the last of her words boomed around the room, the piece having fallen to the volume of a fairy tiptoeing over the keys. 'I was hoping to meet you before dinner, you see,' she added more quietly, her cheeks burning with embarrassment.

'"Fantasia",' the one on the left said sharply, ear cocked towards what her fingers were expertly producing.

'Umm... delighted to meet you,' Eleanor said.

'No, no. Flora,' the other said, swaying.

'Schubert,' the first said, before bowing her head to the keys once more.

'In F minor, naturally,' her sister said wistfully.

'Naturally.' Eleanor was now wishing that she could back away until they had finished, feeling every inch an intruder in their clearly shared love of the piece. Or better still, that she hadn't come at all and had waited for the proper introductions around the dining table. But waiting had never come easily to her. However, she was there now, but conversation was difficult as the music seemed to burst into a frenzy without warning and subdue just as quickly. She sighed to herself. Had Clifford been on hand, he would likely know Schubert's 'Fantasia in F minor' inside and out and could have given her a helpful signal when to open her mouth. The ladies' alabaster faces gave no hints.

'Perhaps you knew I would be visiting Mr Cunliffe?' she said quickly during a lull in the tempest. 'I thought I'd say hello to you before dinner and then maybe meet the other, er, family member.'

'He isn't very much like him, you know?' the second sister said suddenly.

'Oh no, he isn't,' the other agreed. 'But more than he'd like to admit.'

'But that's nephews, you see,' they chorused.

Eleanor thought fast. 'You mean Mr Cunliffe isn't like his nephew?'

The two ladies glanced at each other with a slight frown. 'We are Aunt Flora.'

'And Aunt Clara.'

'And so adept at the piano.' Eleanor hoped their conversation might stay lucid for just a moment. 'Gwel an Mor must be such a lovely house to all live in together.'

'It means "Sea View",' Clara said. Like her sister, her paper-thin skin stretched with the animated smile that lit her face. 'Water, water everywhere, Flora, nor any drop to drink...'

'The very deep did rot... Oh...' They both clamped a bony hand fleetingly over their mouth before playing on. 'That ever this should be, Clara!'

'Yea, slimy things did crawl with legs, Flora...'

They stopped playing with a flourish and stared at Eleanor.

'Upon... the... slimy... sea,' Clifford's voice intoned.

'Oh, your man knows the rules! What fun!' Clara cried as the two sisters started playing again.

Eleanor looked quizzically at Clifford.

'I am guessing Miss Clara and Miss Flora challenge each other,' he whispered, 'to recite a line of verse from memory, or perhaps compose one on the fly to fit whatever they are observing or discussing. The verse in question was Coleridge's *The Rime of the Ancient Mariner*. I once knew a gentleman whose grandmother did similarly.'

At that moment, the sisters stopped playing and gave each other a generous round of applause. Eleanor joined in enthusiastically.

'Wonderful, ladies. Thank you for letting me stay for the end of your recital.'

Flora shook her head. 'No, dear. Sadly, it's a lost art.'

'Unlike the pianoforte, embroidery, cultivating, and thankfully, the art of good conversation,' her sister said earnestly.

The irony that theirs so far had been impossibly confusing, Eleanor would have found quietly amusing in any other circumstances. 'Cultivating? Perhaps like with roses or orchids?' She figured this was her one chance to take the conversation in a more helpful direction. 'Or gardening generally? But gracious, I hope that topic isn't upsetting for you? After the tragedy of the gardener, Mr St Clair, being found at the bottom of the cliffs this afternoon?'

Without a word, the two of them launched into another furiously busy piece of music.

It might have been a minute later or five, when Eleanor's now frazzled ears pricked up.

'Such uncouth boots, weren't they, Flora?'

The bass line increased in ferocity. 'Sounds like him stomping in.'

The sisters shuddered in unison. 'Horrible man.'

'Horrible!' Clara trilled.

Eleanor leaned across the piano's polished wood top. 'Who? Mr St Clair?'

'He'd never make a pianist,' Flora said with a glower at the keys. 'Those horrible big hands he kept gesturing through the window with.'

Eleanor feared the answer, but forged on. 'Gracious, why would Mr St Clair have been gesturing through the window to you?'

The twins shared another knowing look. 'Not St Clair. Trevilick, he told us he was.'

Something dawned. 'Ladies, are you talking about the inspector who came because the gardener died?'

They nodded.

'As if we were common criminals, wasn't it, Flora?'

'Questions, questions, all around. As if answers must be found, Clara.'

'But none so rude as where were you? Two forever by and by, only thankless we did spy, Flora.'

This seemed to ruffle them both as they added extra gusto to their playing.

Eleanor gave up trying to anticipate when the music would quieten and simply raised her voice.

'Did Inspector Trevilick ask you where you were this after-noon then, ladies?'

They both blanched. 'We feared he was going to ask to see... our room,' Flora said. 'Those horrible boots in our special space.'

'Unthinkable!' Clara added.

Eleanor silently counted to ten, thinking the inspector must have done a better job than she was if he learned anything tangible from these two. 'Were you in your room all afternoon?'

Flora nodded. 'From lunch. Save one short turn around the lawn to arrive at the table for consommé time. Chicken at lunch.'

'Beef at dinner,' Clara said emphatically. 'We've another there, you see. But it's upright. And needs tuning.'

'We've reminded Godfrey to get around to it. But that's the trouble. Especially those who cannot play the pianoforte without fumbling their parts!'

Ah, Ellie. So Godfrey is Mr Cunliffe's first name.

She joined in with their grimace, mostly because the relent-less piano music was making her head hurt. 'Perhaps Godfrey, I mean Mr Cunliffe, has been distracted by something?'

They both shrugged. 'Each to their affairs.'

'Although some more than others!' Flora said sharply.

'I'm intrigued,' Eleanor ploughed on, even though it seemed a thankless task. 'Who more than others, I wonder?'

'Edwin!' Flora said in a tight-lipped tone.

Clara shook her head sadly. 'Our great-nephew. And our misfortune.'

Evidently this Edwin fellow isn't beloved by all the family, Ellie. Maybe we'll find out why later.

However, not wanting to delve into unnecessary family disagreements, she opted for a sympathetic smile. 'So perhaps the inspector also asked if there were any witnesses to you being in your room all that time?'

'Horrible man! And foolish. We saw each other, of course.'

'We're always together. And we saw Edwin in the garden, silly boy.'

Eleanor's ears pricked up. 'Was he, perhaps, with Mr Cunliffe? Or Mr St Clair?'

The music stopped abruptly with one discordant note.

'He shouldn't have disturbed things,' Flora said frostily.

'The house doesn't like things being disturbed,' Clara said sombrely.

Who are they referring to, Ellie? Cunliffe or St Clair?

Before she could find out, the piano lid closed with a bang.

7

Eleanor spun around to find Mr Cunliffe's harried face staring at her from the open door.

Without a word, the sisters rose and passed Eleanor in a duet of rustling taffeta. Flora turned back. 'Beef consommé isn't served in here, dear. You need to look elsewhere.'

As the sisters closed the door without even acknowledging Cunliffe's presence, Eleanor shook her head and quickly slapped on a smile for her host.

'Mr Cunliffe. I've, er, been chatting with your aunts.'

'What did they tell you?' he snapped. Immediately, he coloured and cleared his throat. 'Apologies, but they are both, er, a little unnerving if you haven't met them before.'

Talk about the kettle calling the stove black, Ellie.

She had the unsettling feeling Cunliffe was watching her closely. 'And,' he continued, pulling out a handkerchief and wiping his mouth, 'they sometimes come up with the most absurd nonsense.'

More absurd than my gardener's trying to kill me, Ellie?

She bit her tongue and followed him into another room. A pea-green drawing room, as it turned out. The plum accents in the thick velvet upholstery did little to dispel the feeling of having stepped into a tureen of soup. The room was sprinkled with two sweep-fronted Chippendale settees, a couple of high-backed walnut chairs and a selection of elegant side tables. Grateful for her uncle having imbued Henley Hall with his warm, if somewhat eccentric, spirit she turned towards the sash windows and caught sight of the view.

'Oh, my!' she gasped. 'How simply spectacular.'

The sweeping vista of endless green-grey sea was unbroken from every angle, the flowing white horses mirrored in the floating white seagulls in the sky.

Mr Cunliffe stepped over, nodding. 'It still takes my breath away, Lady Swift.' His hand strayed to his chest. 'But the days are dark for me, I fear.'

She turned to face him, concerned by how suddenly he had paled. An idea struck. 'Perhaps some more fresh air would do us both good? I should like to see where Mr St Clair fell from, please.'

He jerked upright. 'A surprising request. Visiting the scene of a death, recent at that, is hardly an activity for a lady. Particularly, a titled one.'

She threw him an innocent smile. 'Perhaps Uncle Byron didn't mention he took me in at the extremely impressionable age of nine?'

'And instilled his unorthodox view of life in your unseasoned self most thoroughly, I have begun to suspect.'

'Which way are we going then?' She headed for the door.

'Goodness. I'm sorry, Lady Swift,' he flustered, 'but I have an urgent matter to attend to.'

She smiled sweetly. 'In that case, just point me in the right direction.'

Once alone in the tiled rear passageway by the glass-panelled door Mr Cunliffe had reluctantly shown her to, she frowned. Where on earth had her butler—

'Ah, hello, Clifford,' she said, sensing his presence behind her. Spinning around, she nodded. 'And in your warmest over-coat and stout boots, too.' She peered down at them in amaze-ment. 'Which are as immaculately polished as your butlering shoes, Clifford. How do you find the fortitude to bother? It's December in Cornwall. We'll be up to our knees in mud, and worse, in minutes, no doubt.'

He sniffed. 'I believe that is the singular, and not infre-quently courted, province of a certain lady of the manor. Whereas her butler...' He left that hanging.

She swept her hooded cloak from his arm and took the wellington boots he held out to her. 'Thank you, Clifford. For reading my mind on this occasion.'

He shuddered. 'Perhaps I might be excused further excur-sions into such, ahem, murky depths, my lady.'

'"Murky depths!" You terror!'

He arched a brow. 'Given the reading matter which fell from your handbag as I retrieved it from the Rolls, it must be entirely inhabited by the cast from scandalous penny dreadfuls.'

She folded her arms. 'And what, pray, is wrong with a cast-away damsel and a dashing pirate falling in love?'

'Everything, my lady. She should have held out for a chief inspector.'

She was still chuckling when a thought struck her. 'Oh no! We can't leave the terrible two alone. But they can't come with us along the cliff path either.'

'Fret not, my lady. Masters Gladstone and Tomkins are suit-ably ensconced, reflecting soberly on their grave misdemeanour with the Christmas tree.'

'Which means cosied up in their bed after you'd settled them into their new lodgings, you closet softie. Right, come on then.'

As they walked, she shook her head.

'Doesn't it strike you as odd, Clifford?' Distracted, she

stopped and pointed at a crumbling folly in the style of a Greek temple. 'Oh, what an enormous amount of work there is to do! St Clair obviously hadn't got very far before, well, you know.' She sighed. 'It all looks so sad and lost.' She looked up to see Clifford staring at her. 'Yes alright. Where was I?'

'If I am not mistaken, my lady, you were about to ask if I found it odd?'

She nodded. 'Exactly. Cunliffe asked us to come down, albeit begrudgingly, because he believed someone, originally St Clair, is trying to kill him. And he still very much does believe that, by the way. He made it abundantly clear only minutes ago. And yet—'

She paused by a small summerhouse trying to gather her thoughts. He stopped a few paces behind.

'He is resolutely resisting our efforts to help?'

'Yes! That's it. It's that infuriating thinking that a man can't, or shouldn't have to, rely on a woman's help, even though they have no one else to turn to.'

'Or a servant's, my lady?'

'Or a servant's.' She rolled her shoulders back. 'No matter, Clifford. As a friend of Uncle Byron's, we will ignore Mr Cunliffe's old-fashioned viewpoint.' At her butler's look, she grimaced. 'Alright, I know it's not exactly old-fashioned. Whatever, we will still help him, whether he wants us to or not. Now, let's... I say, who is that?'

Beyond the garden gate out onto the cliff path, a man wielding a golf club was hitting a line of balls. Dressed only in a thin white shirt and slacks, despite the freezing December air, he looked only a few years older than Eleanor. Seemingly unaware of their presence, he raked back the thick lock of black hair that fell over his eyes and whacked another ball out over the cliff. Without watching where, or how far, it went, he stepped to the next.

'Who is he?' she whispered to Clifford.

'Mr Edwin Marsh, Mr Cunliffe's nephew.'

'Ah, yes. Clara and Flora mentioned him. Excellent! I can ask him some questions. Let's just hope he's less flighty and easier to keep focused than his great-aunts.'

'Disappointment may await, I fear, my lady.'

'You've met him?' She frowned at his nod. 'In the short time since we arrived?'

'Not at all. He was living here with them during your late uncle's visits.'

'And you didn't warn me about *any* of them?' she hissed in disbelief.

'Tsk! You were most adamant on the way down that you were, what was it?' He stroked an imaginary beard. 'Ah, yes, "perfectly capable of forming your own impression, thank you."'

'Traitor!' she huffed good-naturedly.

'Besides, my lady, one of the two ladies was once quite an eminent amateur painter, I believe. Member of the Royal Academy of Arts. Successful exhibitions and suchlike.'

'Really? Maybe they're not quite as mad as they seem, then. Well, one of them, anyway.'

She pushed open the swing gate. 'Good afternoon,' she called cheerily to the man's back.

The whack of another golf ball was the only response.

She raised her voice. 'I said, good afternoon!'

'Heard you,' came the languidly clipped reply. 'Just thinking it over.'

'Your swing?' She dodged around his club as he swung it up over his shoulder again with a sharp swish. Now face to face, she couldn't help arriving at the uncharitable conclusion that he must have been drawn nose first, and then the artist had lost heart. 'Or is it stance that's most important?'

'Couldn't care less.' Another ball plunged to its fate on the rocks below.

Like St Clair, Ellie.

'About the swing, I mean,' he continued. 'It's your brash assertion that offends me.' A follow-up ball went sailing into the air. 'Good afternoon, indeed! Foul afternoon, I'd say.' He wiped his club on the back of his trousers before sending the next ball sailing. 'Foul. Much more like it.'

She glanced at Clifford, whose ever-inscrutable expression had faltered in outrage at the man's lack of manners.

'Mr Marsh,' he said pointedly. 'This is *Lady* Swift. Your uncle's guest.'

Marsh ignored him, tipping a second bucket of balls onto the path in a vague line. 'Delighted, I suppose.' He adjusted his grip. 'Confused, actually.'

She put her foot on his next ball, waiting until he looked up and made eye contact. 'Because of the timing with your uncle's gardener, St Clair, being found dead, Mr Marsh?'

He stepped around her and moved onto the next ball. 'Absolutely. Rather off, one might think, actually.'

'Which you evidently do.' She shrugged. 'Thank you for sharing your opinion.'

'Oh, pleasure. Genuinely.' He cajoled the next three balls into a straighter line with the tip of his club, nodding as she kicked him the one she had trodden on. 'Staying long?'

'Probably not. Unless you'd like me to, of course?' she said cheerfully.

He leaned on his club handle with a sigh. 'More to think over.'

Floundering to find something she could like in this chap, the thought struck that maybe he'd been brought up here at Gwel an Mor by his rather dotty great-aunts.

In which case, Ellie, that might account for his peculiar manner.

'Mr Marsh, can I ask how long you've been in the house?'

'Don't see why not. FORE!' She jumped at the rousing

whoop he'd given to the ball he'd just hit exactly the same as the others.

She tried again. 'Mr Cunliffe told me you live here with him and your great-aunts?'

'I do.' He grinned behind the unruly forelock over his face. 'Not that they like it. But why wouldn't I? It's my right. Despite what dear old Uncle Cunliffe might think!' he ended bitterly. The next ball sailed into the ether with even greater vehemence.

'Is that what you told Inspector Trevilick? I assume he must have questioned you about the gardener's death?'

Marsh's club missed the lined-up ball. 'Confounded cheek! Do you know he had the audacity to do just that? Question a chap in his own house!'

'Isn't that the usual job of a policeman?'

'Couldn't care less. Wanted to know where I was when that damn fool fell over the cliff.' She watched the next ball fly into space and then drop like a stone. Or a body.

'And what did you say? To the inspector. About where you were?'

'What any good boy would.' His tone sounded suddenly sly. 'That I was in my room. The truth feels good. Sometimes.'

'A cloth, sir?' Clifford offered Marsh a pristine handkerchief as he wiped his golf club on the back of his trousers again.

'I'll think it over.' Another streak of mud joined the others down his calf, accompanied by a childish laugh.

Already struggling not to wrench the golf club from the man's hand in frustration at his stilted and offhand answers, Eleanor gritted her teeth. 'Anyone see you there all that time?'

'No.'

'So you took your stroll alone, then?'

'Not much of a stroll around one's room.'

'I meant your stroll in the garden. Your great-aunts mentioned they saw you. They were in their room too, you see?'

He glared at her. 'Yes. But they didn't! Blind as bats, the pair of them. Couldn't hit a golf ball with an elephant, either one. And from their room, certainly not recognise anyone crossing the lawn. Even though they always play peeping Tom. Or Thomasina, I suppose, is more apt.' He shrugged. 'Besides, I know they couldn't have watched me, because I was watching them from my window, watching... *him*.'

'Him who?' she said as nonchalantly as she could.

'I don't know.'

Eleanor caught Clifford's arch of one brow. She took a deep breath. 'You just said—'

'I know what I just said. What I *meant* was it was one of those two lazy under-gardeners. Which one I don't know. They look too alike from a distance. Especially in the half-light.'

Eleanor spotted he was running short of golf balls.

'I didn't tell him,' Marsh volunteered unexpectedly. His next ball sailed high. 'The inspector. Obviously. None of my business.'

'But it might have a bearing on the gardener's death.'

'How so?' Marsh turned slowly to stare at her. 'Nothing suspicious about an accident. Happens all the time. Anyway, his own fault, you know.'

She stiffened. 'How so?'

'Should have left well alone.' She held her breath. For a moment, she thought he was going to walk off, but after a beat he muttered, almost as if to himself, 'Everything was getting on...' He dug the heel of his club into the earth. 'Getting on fine. Just fine. It always is. Until... strangers come.'

'What strangers, Mr Marsh?' she asked tentatively.

'Uncle bloody Cunliffe! Then that fool St Clair, that's who!' His face reddened. 'And now you!' He spun around and sent his last ball crashing through a pane in the summerhouse.

8

'Oh, do stop fuming about Marsh's lack of manners towards me, Clifford,' Eleanor said, stomping out her own irritation with each step along the narrow clifftop path.

'I do not fume, my lady.' He sniffed. 'I am a butler.'

'Oh, really?' She spun around, fighting with the luxurious wrapover front folds of her wool cape as she tried to slide her hand through the velvet-edged slit. Giving up, she shrugged. 'Then what, pray, are you doing?'

'Seething.'

She laughed. 'Good man! Delighted to meet him.'

Clifford's brows threatened to meet. 'Mr Marsh?'

'No, silly. The man lurking beneath your impeccable butlering togs. It's an extremely rare treat to have him ever actually surface.'

He bowed from the shoulders. 'Consider one's good humour restored, my lady.'

'Excellent. Because I might need your infallible logic here.' Turning into the biting wind to point only yards further on, she raised her voice as her hood was blown back over her head. 'That roped off area just ahead must be where St Clair fell.'

He nodded. 'However, if I might be so bold as to suggest you do not venture to the actual edge, my lady?'

She shuddered. 'Don't worry. I have no desire to go the way of poor St Clair.' Together they paused in sombre silence, staring out at the roiling grey-green water below in the fading light. 'Although, I would feel at peace forever,' she murmured, the salty tang in the air catching her unawares. 'Carried off by the currents. Wrapped in the perpetual embrace of the endless ocean.'

Having spent her first nine years of life sailing the oceans aboard her parents' yacht, the sea still called to her soul as longingly as her heart called for love.

'My lady, if we might not even fleetingly contemplate your demise?' Clifford said earnestly.

Snapping to, she nodded. 'On a less sombre topic then, I remember Trevilick said you can sometimes spot dolphins or whales on a clear day.'

'And, I believe, also see the Lostenev Lighthouse. An amazing piece of design. Lighthouses in general, that is.'

Arriving at the point St Clair fell, they took in the scene together in thoughtful silence. Given the fact a man had recently died there, she had expected the path to be closed off. Instead, three bent, rusty iron fence poles had been driven into the ground in a 'V' shape to support the four- or five-foot long rope ringing the spot.

She peered carefully over the rope. 'It's not exactly a crumbling edge, would you say?'

'Indeed not, my lady. On the contrary, given the number of abandoned shallow holes, I suspect Inspector Trevilick's men found the compacted ground rocky just below the surface.'

'Hmm.' She stretched just a little further for a better view. 'If he had tripped and fallen, however, I'd have thought he'd have grasped at every piece of vegetation within reach, but that wiry heather looks untouched.' She shrank back from the edge. 'Unless it was suicide. A possibility the inspector mentioned.'

'You're right. I did,' a strong Cornish voice said.

She spun around, clutching her chest.

'Inspector Trevilick.' She stared at the heavyset policeman who was fighting the wind to keep his brown trilby on. 'I thought you'd gone. You scared the wits out of me.'

His sharp blue eyes gave nothing away as he stepped over to her. 'No offence, Lady Swift, but some folk might be thinking that had already happened. Seeing as you're a titled lady, hanging about in a freezing December wind up here. The very spot a man fell to his death.' She opened her mouth but closed it again as he ran his fingers along his moustache. 'But I'm not one of those folk.'

She frowned in confusion. 'I'm not sure what you mean, Inspector?'

'Simple, Lady Swift. I've been in my line of work plenty long enough for this nose' – he tapped the side of it – 'to pick up the scent of bamfoozlery. You, and your Mr Cunliffe, are holding something back from me.'

She pretended to ponder this, trying to think on her feet. She held his gaze. 'You seem rather certain of that.'

He pursed his lips. 'Oh, I am. For one, Mr Cunliffe seems unnaturally perturbed over all this. For a gentleman of his standing, the loss of a gardener is usually considered no more than an inconvenience.'

She winced, unable to refute his remark. 'Fair enough. And why do you deduce I am holding something back?'

'Chipstone.'

Her frown deepened. 'But that's the local town near... where I live,' she ended falteringly, a sinking feeling taking hold.

Trevilick nodded knowingly. 'It is. And I had a most interesting telephone chat with one Sergeant Brice from the local

police station there.' A smile played around his lips. 'Most infor-
mative the sergeant was too. And complimentary about you,
Lady Swift.'

'How kind of him,' she said weakly.

Trevilick hooked his thumbs through the stretched top
buttonholes of his double-breasted black overcoat. 'Do you
know, he holds you in the highest regard for having, if I might
quote the officer, "the rummiest knack of things where solving
murders is concerned".'

Clifford stepped to her rescue. 'It is rather a long-winded
story, sir.'

'*Stories*, Mr Clifford. In the plural. But don't you worry,
Sergeant Brice as good as read me the whole bookshelf of cases
you and your mistress have been mixed up in.'

She groaned. 'Good old Sergeant Brice. But, Inspector, your
digging into my affairs aside, none of that is relevant because
there hasn't been a murder here.'

'You're right, again. Accident. Suicide possibly on the cards.
But you'd just come to that notion, I believe?'

She nodded sadly. 'But we're strongly hoping we're wrong.
And that the poor fellow just fell. St Clair was in the middle of
a prestigious garden project that might have made his name. He
had everything to live for. It's far less likely to have been suicide,
I think.'

Trevilick shrugged. 'I'm not saying it was. I'm not saying it
wasn't. But there are no proper tall buildings or high bridges
anywhere around here. Nor any fast trains. And not really
much in the way of traffic to be throwing yourself under. If St
Clair had decided suicide was the way out, cliffs would have
been easiest.'

'And surest,' Clifford added soberly. 'If the tide was out.'

'As it was.' Trevilick looked between them. 'Which is why
what he met was rocks and more rocks. That's mostly all there is
down there, save for the patches of shingle. But at high tide, it's

just water. Covers the lot completely. We'd never have recovered his body then.'

She stepped as near to the edge as she dared, Clifford immediately at her side.

Below, a near-endless field of jagged grey rocks jutted out around the occasional giant slab of wind-clawed, long-fallen granite.

'Gracious, it must have been incredibly difficult to recover the body as it was. How long until high tide now?'

'About an hour. No, perhaps half an inch longer.'

'An additional ten minutes, my lady,' Clifford translated. 'Inspector, where exactly did Mr St Clair, ahem, land?'

Trevilick warily stepped nearer the edge and pointed down. 'See where that big rock juts out?'

She strained her eyes. 'Just about in this fading light, yes.'

'That's where one end of him was.'

'Which end?' Clifford said.

'His head.'

'And which way was his body pointing?'

'Towards the sea.'

'Thank you.' Her butler glanced back up at the path. 'And was the gentleman found face up or down?'

Trevilick's moustache quivered. 'Up. Why?'

'Mere curiosity, Inspector,' Clifford said smoothly.

He looked between them. 'Maybe. But a sharp box of tools you two are and no mistake.'

Eleanor sighed. 'It's all the more tragic it happened so close to Christmas.'

'Mmm.' Trevilick folded his arms. 'Lady Swift, as your Mr Cunliffe has clearly called you down here to investigate, what with your reputation for such matters, I would like to know what's really going on.'

She bit her lip, her loyalties torn. On the one hand, Mr Cunliffe was her uncle's long-standing friend. On the other, even though Trevilick couldn't have looked or sounded more different to her own policeman fiancé, he was still just trying to do his job. She caught Clifford's eye. He nodded.

She flapped a hand at Trevilick's now poised notebook. 'I need you to promise it won't go any further.'

'Unless I'm called to court over whatever it is, no problem.' He slid his notebook into his pocket.

'Thank you. I can't believe it would ever come to that. You see, the truth is a very delicate matter. In short, Mr Cunliffe asked for our help because he thought, well, he thought Mr St Clair was trying to kill him.'

Trevilick's brows rose. 'Did he now?' He looked up at the darkening sky, rubbing his fleshy neck thoughtfully. 'Though that doesn't fit with his being so perturbed by Mr St Clair being dead now, does it? That should have come as a relief.'

'It would have,' she agreed, 'if Mr Cunliffe hadn't immediately concluded that St Clair was killed in a case of mistaken identity. And that he himself had been the intended victim to have met tragically with those rocks down there.'

'Ah! Evidence then, has he? That Mr St Clair was after trying to kill him? Or that it was a case of mistaken identity?'

'No. At least none he's passed on to me. And he hasn't explained why he thought St Clair wanted to murder him in the first place either really.' She grimaced. 'He hasn't actually said another word about it.' *None that makes any sense, anyway, Ellie.* 'It's most baffling, I admit.'

She blanched as Trevilick rolled his eyes. 'No offence, Lady Swift, but have you met Mr Cunliffe's family yet?'

'Er, yes.'

'Then, being a sharp-witted lady, you'll think like me, I'll warrant. Again, no offence meant, but your Mr Cunliffe is as touched as the rest of them!'

'Honestly,' she said, hanging her head, 'the jury is out on our side at the moment. However, Mr Cunliffe is a notable name in the area, I imagine? Being a retired eminent financier and the owner of Gwel an Mor?'

'No dispute with that, Lady Swift. His is the largest house and estate for miles about.'

'Then to cover your back, I would suggest you get a post-mortem done.'

Trevilick raised his eyebrows. 'But it will only show that St Clair died from falling!'

'No doubt. But suppose Mr Cunliffe presses on with his theory that St Clair was murdered? To the point of declaring it to some higher-up person. Maybe your superior? You'd have covered your back by showing you were taking his allegations seriously.'

He nodded appreciatively. 'Not a bad shout, Lady Swift. As a thank you, I'll share the coroner's result with you tomorrow.'

'Tomorrow? Normally they take ages.'

'In your area, maybe. Down here, it's very quiet in terms of bodies.' He gave her a sharp look. 'Which I hope isn't going to change now you're here!'

9

Eleanor watched the inspector stride off.

'Clifford?'

He nodded. 'Like yourself, I believe, I am minded to examine the spot where Mr St Clair's body ended its tragic fall.'

'Good. But dash it, talk about bad timing. It's going to be properly dark all too soon. And high tide is on the way. Plus, that path down looks ridiculously steep.'

He raised a brow. 'Could it be that a certain lady of the manor is finally succumbing to prudence?'

She set off, calling over her shoulder. 'No! You'll have to keep hoping on that score.'

The immediate steepness of the path to the sea was troublesome enough, it being little more than a thin scar down the cliff face. The extra hindrance of many trip-inducing rocks, however, was even more unnerving. As was the path narrowing further. The spiky gorse bushes sprouting overenthusiastically on either side were no help either, being too sharp to even think of using as steadying handholds. Something she was repeatedly reminded of as they clawed at her face and snagged her cape. On top of it all, she felt decidedly queasy. That comfrey, ginger and seaweed concoction of Mrs Liddicoat's really hadn't agreed with her.

But there's no time for picking one's way too tentatively, Ellie. The light is fading as fast as the tide is rising.

'Nature really might be just a tad more on our side at this moment,' Eleanor grunted over the ear-battering whistle of the wind.

'Well, it is not raining or snowing, my lady,' Clifford called from behind. 'A path this steep and rocky would be treacherous in such conditions.'

'Small mercies and all that then.' She turned sideways to slide between two particularly large gorse bushes, only to find that the path had become a series of eroded steps.

'This is painfully slow,' she shouted behind her. 'Trevilick's men must have had a heck of a job stretchering poor St Clair's body back up this.'

'I imagine they would have hoisted it up by rope from the top of the cliff.'

'Ah! Of course.'

She paused to look ahead. 'There's a chain fastened into the cliff side.'

'Indicating the way is even steeper from this point, I would suggest.'

'Marvellous!' she muttered.

But there was no denying, the roar of the wind was merging more and more with the increasing rush of the sea. They were getting closer to the beach below. Abandoning the fight with her hood, she pushed on.

Thankfully, the final slope was thickly ridged granite. Unfortunately, it was near vertical, causing her legs to run out from under her at the last moment. Losing her balance, she lurched backwards and landed on a patch of shingle.

'The more elegant approach of stepping on to the beach did

not appeal then, my lady?' Clifford said as he dropped nimbly down beside her. He offered her his hand.

'Nonsense.' She bounded up unaided, regretting it as her knees grumbled at the strain the tortuous path had put them through. 'I heard that arriving by rump is all the rage in Cornwall.'

Ignoring his tut at her mention of anatomy, she peered upwards, straining to identify the precise spot they had been standing with Trevilick. From their clifftop bird's-eye view the rocks below had looked easy to follow to the crucial spot. Now, down amongst them, those same giant boulders and slabs seemed more like the indiscriminate result of a giant's temper tantrum. The patches of shingle offered none of the waymarks she'd hoped they might. The tide was now also covering some of the rocks she'd seen from above. Off to the right, a narrow channel threw up an arc of freezing spray with every incoming wave.

'Dash it, Clifford! It looks so different down here. And the one reference point of the rope around where St Clair went over is hidden by the wretched cliff edge.'

She left him walking his fingers up the cliff face in the air and picked her way across the shingle and boulders to roughly the midpoint of the cove. Her stomach rumbled again. Clifford waved his notebook at her and called, 'My lady, perhaps I might spare you seeing the actual spot?'

'Perhaps you might not,' she called back. 'Though I appreciate your solicitude. The tide is charging in. Look! It's covered half the rock pools already. If we aren't quick enough, anything which might be significant will be washed away for good.' She moved on, scanning the next section of rocks before jerking to an abrupt stop.

'Oh!' Even in the gloomy light, there was no mistaking the patches of congealed blood. She cupped her hands against the bellow of the sea. 'Clifford!'

'Here, my lady!' In a blink, he was beside her.

She pointed at the blood. 'You can make all the fuss you like of me later, I promise.' She glanced at the advancing waves. 'For now, tell me you've got some wizardry up your impeccable sleeves that will help us?'

'Wizardry of sorts, hopefully. The principles of trigonometry.' He reached into his jacket pocket. 'Although, in this failing light, it will have to be rough and ready at best. Now, my lady, you described Mr St Clair's stature as being, ahem, less than average.'

'This is no time for tellings-off over an innocent, if insensitive, remark, Clifford.'

'Indeed not. I merely need to know how tall the deceased was. In your best estimation.'

'Oh, because I saw him at the Earl of Wickhamshaw's garden unveiling, you mean?' She thought for a moment. 'I'd say five foot five. Or six, very maximum. He really was Mr Cunliffe's double in that regard.' They shared a quick grimace. 'I can see why St Clair's death has bolstered Mr Cunliffe's belief it should have been him that went over the edge. From behind in the failing light, they probably did look quite similar.' She shook her head. 'But Inspector Trevilick was adamant it wasn't murder.'

'Hmm. Fingers crossed we agree with him after this exercise.' Clifford paced slowly backwards from the bloodied spot, his brow furrowed. He stopped, shook his head, and retraced his steps.

'I could lie down and be St Clair's body?' she said, swallowing hard.

'Categorically you could not, my lady!'

She took the slim pocket torch he held out. 'Right, then I'll be on incoming tide watch while scouting around in case Trevilick's men missed anything. Lucky for us, St Clair didn't fall at high tide. If he had, he'd have floated miles off.'

'However, unlucky for his murderer!' Clifford said. 'Should that turn out to be the case.'

She slithered down the non-bloodied side of the rock to find her boots were ankle-deep in water. Her first thought was to contour around where St Clair had landed, but that drew nothing useful except the unsettling realisation the tide was coming in faster than she'd expected.

'Clifford, we've probably got five minutes at the very most,' she called up to him.

'Noted, my lady.'

She swished on further with little idea of what she was looking for.

There can't be any clues, Ellie. The poor fellow simply tumbled through the air and...

She blanched at the image of St Clair's body lying on a freezing rock slab as if on a ready-made mortuary table, waiting for the waves to wash over him. Shaking it from her mind, she diligently swept the torch across the shingle. Looking up, Clifford's form was now only a silhouette against the blackening sky.

Will time or tide beat us first, Ellie?

Deciding neither would because this mattered too much, she turned towards the sea. The telltale yellow arc of a lighthouse beam sweeping across the water in the distance added to her sense of urgency. She took a step forward. It made sense that something might already have been dislodged by the tide and be floating teasingly back and forth with every wave.

'Oh my!' A wash of icy water filled her wellingtons. 'Clifford!' she shouted, the drag of her now soaking cloak slowing her down. 'Time to go!'

His outline jerked upright just as a wall of spray whipped over her head, drenching her.

As he dropped down beside her and straightened up, she

noted his trousers had a dark, sodden ring at the bottom of each leg.

Definitely time to go, Ellie, before the water reaches our knees.

Together, they slipped and stumbled back towards the cliff face. Waving the torch in an arc to light the way better for both of them, something reflected from the shingle. She bent, scooped the object up into her pocket, and accepted Clifford's hand. Hoisting her onto the start of the path, he led the way up the granite slope. At the first bend, she paused to pour the water from her boots.

'No sense carrying all that back to Gwel an Mor. Nor the rest of the ocean you're stealing there, Clifford. Tsk, aren't you even going to wring out your trousers?'

His horrified sniff cut through the wind. 'For more reasons than propriety permits me to articulate, no, I am not.' He waved a hand up the path. 'Shall we finish this undignified retreat, my lady? I, for one, have had enough of the delights of the seaside!'

10

The dramatic outline of Gwel an Mor finally came into view as Eleanor pushed through the last of the spiteful gorse and emerged onto the top of the cliff.

'At last!' she gasped, glad, at least, that the queasy feeling in her stomach had subsided for the moment.

Maybe it had been the dwindling light that made the return trek seem so much longer than the way down. Or perhaps the extra exertion on the steep uphills. Or the increasingly raw December wind. But Eleanor had another theory and was holding fast to it. 'I think you're disagreeing purely to be obtuse now, Clifford. Hunger causes fatigue, everyone knows that. And even though my wonderful cook's herbed sausage tarts and Stilton twists were too sublime for words, our lunch in the Rolls was precisely' – she glanced at her pocket watch – 'six or more hours ago.'

'Notably,' he said from behind, 'on account of the lady of the house having ravished Mrs Trotman's picnic hamper before Henley Hall had faded from view.'

'It was a few miles after that, actually.' She set off again. 'And, for goodness' sake, squelch along beside me this once.'

'Respectfully squelching alongside, my lady.'

She shone the torch at him, catching the twinkle in his eye. 'You total terror! You've contradicted me the entire way back up just to keep me distracted.'

'Indeed. After all, you haven't eaten a morsel for hours.'

She laughed. 'And you said we wouldn't be able to squabble while staying down here. How wrong you were.'

He nodded. 'True. However, once within sight or earshot of the house, it is a different matter.' He pushed open the swing gate into her host's garden. 'As of now.'

'I suppose you're right.' She lowered her voice. 'Mr Cunliffe has enough on his mind without being outraged by his guests.'

'Guest. Singular, if one might remember, my lady?'

'If I must.' She trod carefully across the chessboard lawn, the only illumination being the weak fingers of light from the rear of the house. 'Though somehow, we need to talk about your conclusions regarding St Clair's fall. But first, dry togs.'

As they cleared the first two lines of topiary chess pieces, Clifford fell back to his customary few paces behind her. 'I believe, my lady, dressing for dinner may be a wasted endeavour unless we hasten. It is due to commence in...' He broke off. A low rumbling came from the sloping grassed bank to their right.

'What is that shocking racket?' She shone the torch in the direction of the noise. 'Good lord! It's—'

The force with which Clifford knocked her forwards winded her. She rolled over and sprang back up, catching her breath at his nauseous moan.

'Clifford? Are you alright?'

'Better than I fear you would otherwise have been, my lady,' he groaned in a taut tone, holding one arm bent tightly against his middle. 'However, my abject apologies.'

'Don't be silly! You pushed me out of harm's way.' She shone the torch after the slowing rumble. 'What is that?'

'It is the extremely heavy barrel of a lawn roller,' he said grimly.

'Perhaps it was just an accident?'

'Having had its handle removed? I think not.'

'Then quick!' she hissed, setting off in the direction it had come from. 'Whoever set it rolling must be up there!'

At the top of the slope, her torchlight swept over a seemingly impenetrable ornamental thicket. Within it, however, she glimpsed the handles of what looked like an ancient wheelbarrow, so someone had obviously succeeded in breaching it at some point. A screech and flutter of wings made her jump. Above her head, a disturbed peacock flew across to another branch to perch for the night.

Clifford shook his head. 'My lady. If I might be so bold as to suggest this is a fruitless endeavour in the dark?'

'I'd already come to that conclusion,' she said, flashing the torch on his face. 'And you're in pain. Considerable pain, I'd say, as normally you wouldn't show a flicker of discomfort if you could help it. So, retreat seems the wisest choice.'

Her gaze darted left as a man she didn't recognise slid over the low retaining wall of the Liddicoats' cottage. Eleanor caught Clifford's eye and nodded. The man had most definitely appeared from the direction of the thicket they had just tried to search.

As they started down the grassed slope towards the cottage, she spotted a figure at the window. She paused, Clifford stopping a few steps behind her.

'It is Mrs Liddicoat, my lady. In her kitchen.'

'I know. Please stay close.'

She walked out from the shadows, crunched up the path to the paint-flaked front door, and knocked firmly.

'Too early, sir,' came the hissed reply from inside. The door opened a crack to reveal the housekeeper wearing a deep frown and her brown hair lying around her shoulders. She shrank back at seeing Eleanor. 'Oh, m'lady, didn't expect it to be you.'

Then who was she expecting it to be, Ellie?

With a peeved twist of her wrists, Mrs Liddicoat wrenched her tresses up into a knot behind her head and stared back. 'What is it you be wantin'?'

At her abrupt tone, Clifford raised one brow to her. Eleanor nodded slightly. *Okay, play it cool.* She smiled, trying to put the woman at her ease. 'Gracious, my curls are far too rebellious for me to attempt anything like that.'

Mrs Liddicoat shrugged. 'Lucky thing you've no need of makin' yer own butter. It's the red that does it. And dinner's a ways away yet.'

Before the conversation became any more confusing, Eleanor tried again to put the woman at her ease.

'In case I don't have a chance afterwards, Mrs Liddicoat. Thank you in advance for whatever delectable treat you have prepared.'

Mrs Liddicoat shrugged. 'Same as always it is. Broth is beef because the ladies insist on it. Followed by Mr Cunliffe's favourite roast.'

'Which is?'

'Seagull. But there's no chance for special requests at this short notice.'

Eleanor decided a direct approach *was* best. Especially as Clifford's arm obviously needed attention and the man responsible was very possibly skulking in the cottage.

'I wouldn't usually disturb you at home, but I was just returning to the house, you see?'

'Not a thing,' came the curt reply.

Eleanor glanced at Clifford, who arched a mystified brow.

'Not a thing what?'

'Not "what", Mr Clifford. Not a thing I saw!'

'Hardly surprising,' Eleanor said smoothly. 'What is there to see? It is quite inky black out here now.' She watched the woman's expression. 'However, I, or rather my butler, had a most unfortunate... accident. You might have heard—'

Mrs Liddicoat caught her breath. 'Not... water, m'lady? Say it isn't?'

Eleanor frowned in confusion, then noticed the housekeeper was staring at her soaked cloak. 'Oh, you mean because I'm a trifle... er, damp?'

Mrs Liddicoat shook her head vehemently. 'It's a sign. To hear water drippin' when there is none is a sure sign of... death!' she whispered.

Eleanor softened her tone. 'It's understandable to feel rather shaken after the news about Mr St Clair. Did he mention anything to do with water before he died?'

Mrs Liddicoat shook her head vehemently again. 'Not a thing!'

Eleanor nodded. 'Ah! That again.'

'Signs come in different ways,' the housekeeper blurted out, then bobbed a hasty curtsey. 'Mr Liddicoat'll need me now.'

She turned to go.

Eleanor held up a hand. 'Just a moment. Did you—'

'Enough!' a rough voice barked. A man sidled into view behind the housekeeper, who flinched like a scared rabbit. 'Enough talkin'. Get, woman, or you'll know the worst of it!'

Eleanor's hackles rose. 'I was the one interrupting your wife from her tasks, Mr Liddicoat. If you have any complaint, kindly direct it to me!'

Mrs Liddicoat grabbed her skirts and darted away as her husband stepped forward and glared at Eleanor. This was the first chance she'd had to see his features clearly. And it wasn't one she was relishing. There was something weasel-like in his grey-green eyes, the fix of his lips too reminiscent of a snarling fox. He ran the back of his hand over his mouth.

'You'll kindly keep away from my wife, m'lady. And stop

pokin' around, if you know what's good for you!' he ended in an angry mutter.

'Or what?' She held his dagger look. 'You'll try and run me over with a garden roller again?'

Mr Liddicoat's fists balled. 'Enough! I—'

'Indeed it is, Mr Liddicoat,' Clifford said firmly as he stepped in front of Eleanor. 'More than enough. If you know what's good for *you*. Which I'm quite sure you do?'

The door slammed shut.

Eleanor turned to Clifford. 'Sorry!'

'No apology needed, my lady. Perhaps, however, future diversions might be slightly more considered before being acted upon? If Christmas is to be survived, that is,' he muttered as they walked away from the cottage.

'Dash it! I'm really sorry, Clifford. Genuinely, I didn't intend to confront him at all. And certainly not by blurting that out. It was foolish, I know. My anger just suddenly got the better of me. He was so awfully bullish to his wife, I wanted to biff him on the nose!'

'With sincere apologies for speaking out of turn, but it is perhaps unwise to goad a wretch to step outside. Although, I confess, the result is far from a foregone conclusion.'

She laughed. 'Thank you for the compliment. And you can consider your mistress admonished. And rightfully so. Anyway, it's obvious there's no point in trying to talk to Mrs Liddicoat with her husband around. And, to be honest, I'm not sure she'd speak up if he wasn't.'

'Indeed. And I formed the impression that Mr Liddicoat is also rather reluctant to converse with us. Unless, of course, the exchange largely consisted of threats and curses.'

She nodded resignedly. 'You're right. I think we're better off following other lines of investigation for the moment. Now, let's get back to the house and get that arm of yours seen to. I fear it might be broken...'

11

'Come now, don't give me that stuffed goose look, Clifford,' Eleanor pleaded ten minutes later to her butler's averted gaze. 'I'm entirely changed for dinner underneath my robe. So step inside, for goodness' sake. And preferably before one of the terrible two trips you up.'

Her bulldog's front feet lifted off the oak floor with the force of his exuberant woof, while Tomkins ran along Gladstone's back to paw Clifford's jacket with a demanding meow. Her butler shook his head at all three of them.

'Collective emotional exhortations remain as ineffectual as they are inequitable.'

'This is no time for your stubborn donkey routine, Clifford.' She went to tug him inside the private sitting room adjoining her allotted bedroom but pulled back. With one hand, he was holding a long-handled kettle which was letting out wisps of steam from its stopper. The other hand poked out of a cheese-cloth sling.

'Regrettably, the maid is away, as you might remember Mr Cunliffe mentioned, my lady? That being the only reason for my venturing anywhere within the vicinity of your quarters.

And I intend to go no further than the threshold except to place your hot water down.'

'Perfect!' She slid past him and closed the door.

'My lady, please!'

'Relax! I hereby appoint you as surrogate maid. For me, only, obviously.'

'With the greatest respect, it is beyond breaking the bounds of decorum for me to be—'

'Clifford, would you like me to insist on the uniform, too? No? Good. So start by telling me honestly what hurts?'

He poured an inviting stream of hot water into a small painted-porcelain footbath she hadn't seen him produce. 'Merely a sprained elbow, my lady.' He grimaced in obvious pain. At her look, he added, 'Possibly fractured. Foolishly, I failed to stop the roller clipping me on the way past.'

'But only because you were occupied with making sure it missed me. For which, I am extremely grateful.'

'My pleasure. In as much as it should never have happened.'

'But a possible fracture? You should get it seen to.'

'If it is fractured, it is minor and will heal itself in a matter of weeks.'

She shook her head. 'You're incorrigible, Clifford, so I will abandon any attempt at persuading you to allow me to examine it, even though you know I worked as a nurse in the war. Just do take care and rest it if you need to.'

He bowed. 'Most gracious, my lady.'

She wiggled her still numb toes in her slippers as he added a generous dose of something aromatic to the steaming water.

'Mustard, cinnamon and powdered eucalyptus in lemon juice to aid circulation. And a few quietly liberated titbits from the pantry to keep the lady alive.' He slid a small waxed paper parcel from his pocket.

'Top-notch, thank you!' Gladstone's head jerked up as he

smacked his lips. 'But only one perfectly warmed brandy, you terror, despite my insisting you join me?'

'Sufficient infractions seemed inevitable without encouragement,' he said drily.

She tutted and shook out a selection of savouries from the waxed paper parcel.

'"Dormers" in the local parlance, my lady. Sausage meat rolls primarily. Plus, saffron and seaweed crackers with a soupçon of smoked eel pâté.'

'Nothing ventured.' She wrapped her robe tighter around the top of her ankles to spare what was left of his blushes before sliding her toes into the footbath. 'Mmm. Heavenly.' Tomkins curled up on her lap as she stared into her brandy with a frown. 'Unlike our visit here so far. What do you make of that roller incident?'

With a quiet tut, he slid a pair of tongs from his inner pocket to place each of the pilfered nibbles onto the side plate her glass had been resting on. 'Concerningly, I can only deduce it was a poor attempt to scare you or sideline you with an injury. Or worse.'

'Let's go with the first. Either way, we're both pretty sure something fishy is going on here. What did all your measuring earlier down where St Clair fell tell you? Anything helpful?'

'I shall require a moment to complete the calculations if that suits?'

She took another of the surprisingly moreish crackers. 'Absolutely. Only do them so I can watch. I've still no real idea what you were doing.'

'As you wish.' He opened his slim pocketbook at a page bearing a meticulously drawn triangle, but with a series of different length lines connecting each corner. Only the upright seemed to be set.

'Why is there only one line without any variations, Clifford?'

'Because that is the officially recorded height of the cliff.'

'Even you can't know that off the top of your head.'

'Fortuitously, I just happened to pass through the library—'

'So, with your usual devious sleight of hand, you could pilfer one of Mr Cunliffe's books?'

He gave her a withering look. 'Pilfering is for petty thieves. And unruly cats, evidently.' He pointed at Tomkins sliding a cracker off her plate.

She shrugged, pretending not to notice Gladstone already licking crumbs from the floor. 'Go on. Convince me they aren't learning their sleight of paw tricks from you, then.'

He tutted. 'I slid into the library, purely in the hope that the framed topographical map his lordship, your late uncle, presented to Mr Cunliffe would still be in pride of place. It was a housewarming present.'

'And was it? Still there, I mean?'

'Yes. And it confirmed the height of the cliff, near enough, was as I'd estimated from the rocks below. The longest of the horizontal bottom lines' – he pointed to his sketch – 'denotes Mr St Clair's *actual* point of contact. And its shorter counterparts, where he might have landed in certain circumstances.'

'Oh gracious.' She bit her lip, staring at the sets of lines. 'And those are the different courses he would have sailed through the air?'

'The hypotenuses, my lady, yes. One moment, please.' Clifford's pen inked more meticulously neat numbers to more unfathomable mathematical formulas below the diagram. A few moments later, he held his notebook back out to her. 'From the distance Mr St Clair landed from the base of the cliff, he would have needed to jump with a significant amount of force to land where he did.'

'Jump? Oh, gracious!'

'A straight fall would be expected to end considerably closer to the cliff. Also, normally, in cases of falling persons, they are found face down.'

'But Inspector Trevilick said St Clair was face up.' She see-sawed her head. 'Not absolutely conclusive though, hopefully?'

'Ahem.'

'Ah! There's more. Go on.'

'Victims of a fall usually fall forward. Thus they are also almost invariably found with their feet...'

'Facing the cliff. Not head facing it, as St Clair was. Clifford, is it me, or does that sound like he may have been pushed? Or jumped?'

'It does, but it still doesn't seem to tally... quite.' He shrugged. 'I can say no more without more knowledge of events.'

'Mmm. Well done anyway for being such an egghead of all things trigonometry.'

He bowed. 'And might one enquire what you found on the beach, my lady?'

'That the sea here in December is even colder than I could imagine!'

He shook his head. 'I meant, what did you scoop into your cloak pocket?'

'No idea. I forgot all about it. Hang on.' She whipped her feet out to go and look, but froze at his halting cough.

'If I might save your host's flooring from wet footprints and retrieve it for you?'

'Tsk, Clifford! My cloak is lounging somewhere in my bedroom.' She smiled and padded off.

A moment later, she was back with a shrug. 'It's just a plant naming stick. Although there's probably an official fancy word for it, which my infuriatingly knowledgeable butler knows?'

'Indeed. A "label", my lady.' He hurried on. 'Wooden. Painted white. Ordinarily plant labels are metal with the plant name etched on it for permanency. However, as Mr St Clair's plan was a work in progress, I assume he needed ones he could write on and easily paint over and reuse as his ideas evolved.'

'I see. So it must have slipped from St Clair's pocket as he... fell.' She shook her head, not wanting to dwell on that awful image. 'I don't recognise what these two letters refer to though.'

She passed it to Clifford who peered at the label before passing it back.

'"S.R.". It is not the initials for any Latin name or colloquial term for any plant I am familiar with either. But Mr Cunliffe's grounds are likely peppered with a wide variety of exotica. We can ask Joseph if need be.'

Joseph was her gardener back at Henley Hall. He'd been her uncle's gardener before that and she was quite sure he knew the name of every flower, plant and bush that had ever been planted in a garden.

'Well, it's hardly the most pressing matter at the moment. More importantly, something is definitely off at Gwel an Mor. Dash it, Clifford! It looks like we're stuck here for a while. I mean, I wouldn't forgive myself if anything unthinkable *did* happen to Mr Cunliffe, despite his somewhat unwelcoming manner.'

'Categorically not. Though it is not your duty to even think of preventing such.'

'I'm here in Uncle Byron's spirit, Clifford. So, yes, it is. And look at it the other way. If St Clair did meet his end due to foul play—'

'He deserves justice.'

'Agreed?'

'Agreed. However, we have overlooked a significant hurdle in our investigating this matter, my lady. Everyone in the house knows that you were invited here by Mr Cunliffe himself.'

'Reluctantly.'

'My point entirely. A most unlikely guest for the traditionally minded gentleman to have called down. And at such a difficult time.'

'You think they'll feel suspicious of me if I ask any questions?'

'Given the roller incident, I would conjecture someone most definitely feels that and more already.'

'What can we do about it, though?'

'Nothing concerning questioning those in the house. But if we need to question anyone in the village where the under-gardeners live and, according to Mr Cunliffe, Mr St Clair spent many of his evenings, we need an unknown. Someone who can ask questions without arousing too much suspicion. In short, we need a mole.'

'But I don't know anyone down here.'

'No. But there is a certain chief inspector who is kicking his heels back in Buckinghamshire waiting for his fiancée to return.'

She gasped. 'Brilliant, Clifford! No one down here knows who Hugh is. Or that we're acquainted, let alone engaged. And who better to snoop around for us than the best detective in the country!' Her face lit up. 'And, as an added bonus, we can finally have Christmas together!'

12

Breakfast had been a thankfully brief affair to Eleanor's mind. Ordinarily, the first meal of the day was her very reason to bounce out of bed each morning. But today she had quietly admitted to Clifford as he'd topped up her coffee that none of the breakfast fayre was sitting comfortably with the roast seagull from the night before. Its disquieting chicken-cum-fish flavour she'd found particularly off-putting, as she had its excessive oily and gritty aftertaste. Now, in the Rolls, her butler's less than customary stately driving style was not improving matters. She peered over at him as the car lurched again.

'Is this your attempt at early morning humour, Clifford?'

'Categorically not, my lady.' He stared out at the road from under the brim of his bowler hat. 'Though not only because it is long past an hour to which "early" could be plausibly applied.'

She leaned back in her seat, smiling at Tomkins and Gladstone, both of whose heads nodded as they dozed, curled up on the back seat together.

'Dash it, it's not fair! I'm too unsettled in stomach and thoughts to engage in a battle of semantics with you. And you should have let me behind the wheel. Driving one-handed is impressive, but as I said, a little too... unpredictable for my stomach this morning!'

He grimaced. 'I fear, my lady, that on this occasion you may be right. However, the road is fairly flat and straight from now on, so I will endeavour to drive more smoothly to better aid digestion.'

She laughed. 'Thank you. Anyway, I hope it's not too much further to this rather impromptu rendezvous? If only for the sake of your injured elbow.'

Clifford glanced at the neatly folded map in the purpose-made holder on the walnut dashboard and shook his head. 'Regrettably fewer miles than if the appointment had been arranged somewhere more appropriate for a titled lady.' He eyed her sideways. 'Such as the home of the gentleman you are coming to meet, for instance?'

'Nonsense! That would have taken all day. Besides, he's down this way. And it means we're about to witness living Cornish culture and history at the same time. Put on especially for Christmas, too.'

'Ahem, I believe the festive element might merely be a ruse to permit the grudge to be extended.'

'*Grudge*, Clifford?'

'Oh, my!' she muttered a while later as they turned into a field and stopped beside a flamboyant wine-red sports car. There was a smattering of farming vehicles parked in the field amongst a sea of horse-drawn traps, weather-beaten bicycles and several unwieldy-looking charabancs. It was, however, empty of people, the small field beyond already ringed four rows deep with expectant faces below tightly pulled down woollen caps and scarves.

'I had no idea outdoor wrestling would be so popular in late

December, Clifford. It's going to be a devilish job trying to find our man.'

He gestured to the ostentatious lines of the sports car. 'I believe the gentleman might be spotted without too much difficulty, my lady.'

With Gladstone in excited tow, Clifford carried Tomkins around to the boot of the Rolls.

'Oh, is there a picnic?' She hurrahed, hurrying after him. 'Let's hope my stomach gets...' Her hands flew to her mouth as she stared into the boot. Now inside a carpet bag, Tomkins was stretched out on a woollen blanket, his head poking out of a padded hole at one end.

'Oh, Clifford, that is too darling and perfect for words. You total softie!'

Clifford bowed. 'It includes a shoulder strap for ease in carrying and a ventilated waxed cover, as well as two outside pockets, separated into feline and canine treats.'

Gladstone spun in an uneven circle at the 'T' word.

'It's a kitty kit bag!' she cheered, catching Clifford's lips quirking in amusement. 'And you made this when?'

'After trying to hold one too many an undignified conversation whilst wearing Master Tomkins around my neck. Mrs Butters assisted and had it ready to pack with the rest of the luggage when the need to hasten here to Cornwall arose.'

'Thank you, Clifford. That was beyond thoughtful. Only watch out, or Mr Lazy there will use all his tricks to cajole you into making him a matching one.'

Clifford shook his head at her bulldog's eager woof. 'Regrettably not, Master Gladstone. Since it would need to be of the robust wheeled variety, given the portly results of your devotion to sausages.' He closed the top of Tomkins' new mobile home carefully and adjusted the strap to fit snugly over his shoulder. 'My lady, shall we?'

After fruitlessly searching the crowds around the arena for ten minutes, Eleanor broke off as Clifford tapped her wrist and nodded to the far side of the field. The Earl of Wickhamshaw was striding through the crowd, head and shoulders above the masses. His eye-catching burgundy and cream neckerchief fluttered in the numbing breeze, which was also playing havoc with his devil-may-care greying hair. Deciding that pushing her way through the throng to reach him would be futile, she settled on a more direct approach to get his attention. Preparing to give a piercing two-fingered whistle, she halted at Clifford's remonstrating look.

'If we might try another way, my lady?' To her astonishment, her ever quietly composed butler cupped his hands and bellowed, 'FORE!'

Lord Wickhamshaw jerked around looking puzzled, since there wasn't a golf course for miles. Catching Clifford's semaphoring, he waved a newspaper before continuing an animated conversation with two men who looked like gangsters or bookmakers, she wasn't sure which.

A few minutes later he reappeared, striding towards her. 'Ha! What a fine morning,' he called, still yards away.

She nodded, admiring his cherry-red sports jacket and matching plus fours. 'You were right, Clifford. He was easy to spot. Not a patron of the most conservative gentleman's outfitter, is he?'

He sniffed. 'Sartorial statements in plaid are traditionally made with a single bright accent in the minor stripe only.' He arched a brow. 'Not as the base colour itself.'

'I think it's very refreshing,' she muttered as Lord Wickhamshaw came to a beaming stop before her.

'Women at a wrestling match, you mean?' he said genially. 'Because I'm with you on that score, Lady Swift!'

'Refreshing and enlightening. Delighted to hear it. Good morning, Lord Wickhamshaw.' She offered her hand for him to shake. Something she then regretted as he nearly pumped her arm from its socket.

'Good? No, no. It's marvellous! But of course women should be encouraged. Because that is the very founding tenet of sport. It must be for all!' he cheered to the field at large. 'Class. Gender. None of that should have any bearing. Or be any barrier. Guarantees the best then. Levels the field, you see? Though this vaguely green affair behind us here looks like it could do with a jolly good beating with a spiked badger.'

She laughed. 'Lord Wickhamshaw, it's a pleasure to see you again. And very kind of you to agree to see me. All the more since I hadn't realised you were such a fan of the sporting life.'

'Aha, no.' He waved his newspaper. 'Not a fan, dear Lady Swift. A devotee. A fanatic. A disciple.' He looked down as Gladstone scrabbled up his plus fours.

'Sincere apologies, my lord,' Clifford said, trying to restrain her bulldog while balancing the bag on his shoulder.

'He's alright, man.' He ruffled Gladstone's ears with gusto. 'Not much use on a hunt though, are you, old chap? That belly wouldn't clear a bottom fence rung, never mind a stile.' Tomkins poked his head out of his window with a loud meow for attention, receiving a quietening chin tickle from Clifford. The earl waved an amused hand. 'What's his sporting use, then? Mousing out moles on your golf lawn?'

She smiled. 'No, he's my butler and a great many things besides. The less troublesome two have no claim to anything, except being overindulged and equally beloved.'

'Touché, my lady,' Clifford said impassively, despite his eyes shining with amusement.

The earl clapped his hands. 'Sparring with your butler, Lady Swift. Haha! I love it.'

'You were saying how much sport means to you, Lord Wickhamshaw?'

'In truth, I escape as much as possible this way. Cornish

sport is the finest, you know. Hurling, shinty and particularly their wrestling.'

'And yet somehow you still found energy and time enough for the astounding landscape project that has made your grounds the finest I have ever seen.'

'Thank you. Wealth and privilege are transient, brittle beasts of which any of us are mere custodians for as long as our tenure endures. To neglect such a creature is a disgrace, in my book. My various estates deserve the best I can provide, both in their upkeep and their development for future prosperity.' He gave her a wry grin. 'But when the bell rings, haha! It is play-time earned for the sports field.'

'Well, I don't want to keep you from playing too long. Would you mind therefore if I just come clean about why I asked to meet you?'

'Not at all.'

'It's about St Clair, the landscape architect.'

'Capital fellow. Has an extraordinary eye for form and pattern in garden design.'

'Had, actually.'

'*Had?* Thrown in the towel? What a crying shame.' He seemed to catch the gravity of her expression. 'Oh, I see. Fellow's up and snuffed it, you mean?'

'Went over a cliff. The one which borders Mr Cunliffe's grounds.'

'Poor chap.'

'How long have you known Mr Cunliffe, Lord Wick-hamshaw?'

'Oh, for years. On and off, of course. In that time, he's given me some useful financial advice. That's why I was delighted to pass the recommendation for St Clair onto him.'

'Can you tell me how you came to employ St Clair origi-nally, if you don't mind me asking?'

'Of course not. He came to my attention when I needed a

new head gardener for one of my minor estates. Original chap had a terrible accident with a tree. Fell on him, poor chap. Never been right since. So I needed someone new to step into his place.'

'Which turned out to be St Clair?'

'Yes. He'd been working for a pal of mine for some years. Had had a major hand in revamping his estate grounds.'

'Like he then did for you?'

'Precisely.' He adjusted his carnation. 'Ambitious for one so young. I admired that in him.'

'And you didn't find St Clair had any... odd traits? Or was maybe a touch secretive?'

Lord Wickhamshaw frowned. 'Quite the opposite. I found him very communicative. Kept me up to date on what he was doing. Methodical to a tee. Worked like a Trojan. All in all, a down-to-earth fellow you could rely on.' He paused. 'Although, truth to tell, there was a rumour that after leaving my service, he'd fallen foul of Lord Rathing when he was working for him. Although I never found out about what, as Rathing has been abroad since. Still is. But then again, between you and me, old Rathing is an easy bird to displease! Anyway, apparently, it rather hurt St Clair's meteoric rise in the landscaping world. Which is partly why I recommended him to Cunliffe. St Clair needed help back up, it seemed, and Cunliffe, well, he could get him at a bargain price. Not having quite the size of purse of Lord Rathing or I, you understand.' He shook his head. 'A hard man to replace. Still, at least Cunliffe's project can continue regardless.'

'Of course.' The earl's words filtered into her thoughts. 'But, you've just said St Clair will be hard to replace? So how can Mr Cunliffe's project continue?'

'Because Cunliffe can simply instruct a new fellow to follow St Clair's landscaping plan to the letter.' He spread his hands out. 'I could picture from the start how my gardens would look on completion. The detail in his plan of each and every section was remarkable. I've had it framed in my study. It's a work of art. Cunliffe really needn't worry at all. St Clair will have completed a landscaping plan for him just the same, I guarantee.'

A flurry of activity in the centre of the field made them turn. Three officials were remonstrating with two men dressed in thick white canvas tops and short black shorts. The two men seemed to be having a very loud and public disagreement.

'Ha! Let the sport begin!' Lord Wickhamshaw cried. 'Hancock and Sandow battle it out one last time. The ultimate grudge match!'

She nodded, remembering Clifford's words on the way down. 'So how do the Cornish wrestle?'

Lord Wickhamshaw's eyes glinted. 'Only by grip above the waist and not by use of the jacket collar. And with no wrestling upon the ground, though adroit use of legs and tripping up is the key. Hitches will be few in number today, I'll pledge. Three points ahoy!'

'Hitches? Three points?' She glanced at Clifford.

His hand strayed to his tie. 'My lady, in Cornish wrestling, a winning throw requires three points of the opponent's upper regions to make contact with the ground. Either both shoulders and one, ahem, hip. Or two of the latter and one of the former. A less than three-point landing is termed "a hitch".'

Lord Wickhamshaw nodded appreciatively. 'Knowledgeable fellow, your butler.'

She rolled her eyes. 'You have no idea!'

He offered her his elbow. 'Come and learn the rest of the rules up close, Lady Swift. I do believe you are a woman after my own heart.'

She smiled. 'A charming invitation, Lord Wickhamshaw. But perhaps another time. There is rather an important matter I need to attend to...'

13

'What is this untimely invasion?' Cunliffe's aggrieved voice grumbled out from his study. Eleanor rolled her eyes at Clifford and popped her head around the door with an apologetic smile. 'It's only me.'

Cunliffe shot up out of his chair. 'Ah, Lady Swift. I'm sorry, I thought you were... someone else.' He frowned. 'And some*where* else too.'

'I was. But now I'm back with a quick question.'

'Very well.' He gestured reluctantly at the seat opposite him.

'Quicker than that. I'm sure you're frightfully busy.' Looking relieved, Cunliffe stepped over to face her.

'I was hoping to peek at St Clair's plan for your garden works, that's all.'

'A strange request. But not one I can meet, I'm afraid. I haven't got it.' His face clouded. 'And neither do I know where it is.'

'Maybe in his office?'

'I looked. And no, it isn't.'

'Ah!'

So that's why Cunliffe said his project would need to go back to the drawing board, Ellie. 'Most unfortunate. But I assume you approved the overall design?'

'Well, of course I approved it. At least the initial stages. The project was to have been a legacy for Gwel an Mor. And that, Lady Swift, costs a great deal of money.'

'Then why only approve the first stages?' she said, swallowing her irritation over his condescending tone.

'Because much of the gardens have not been touched for half a century or more. Until St Clair had uncovered what was already here, he could not judge the exact extent of the works needed.'

'So he kept you informed of progress as he went?'

'In the beginning, yes.' His jaw tightened. 'But lately, he reported back to me less and less. He became increasingly secretive, as I explained to you.'

'You did. When did you last see St Clair's plan, by the way?'

'Some time ago. Right around when I started wishing I had never agreed to the idea of remodelling the gardens! In fact' – he reached for his handkerchief – 'I wish I had never moved here from London at all!'

Once she'd left Cunliffe's study, Eleanor waved for Clifford to follow her back down the corridor. Collecting Gladstone and Tomkins from the sitting room, she headed outside and across the path towards the chessboard lawn. She tightened her thick moss-green shawl around her shoulders against the raw wintry sea breeze.

'This way, chaps. Let's find St Clair's office.' She made for a gap in the tall hedge of vivid red berries which hid a similar gap in the stone wall behind. On the other side, there was a flagstone terrace with two smartly painted scrollwork benches.

'A favourite haunt of Mr Cunliffe's aunts in the warmer

months, perhaps?' Clifford said as he herded Gladstone and Tomkins along.

She nodded as they descended a set of granite steps, smiling at his inability not to point out his dismay over how inconsistently their cappings had been repointed. 'Very possibly, but rather more urgently, we need to unearth more about St Clair, Clifford. But from a different angle. Unhelpfully, all we've got so far are two completely opposing character references.'

'Indeed. Though both are from gentlemen of fine standing. Yet Lord Wickhamshaw appears to have experienced none of the reported disquieting traits which Mr Cunliffe recounted.'

'So, is that because St Clair's mental state changed? After all, it seems he had trouble with Lord Rathing. Or because Mr Cunliffe's mental state is even more fragile than either of us feared?'

Clifford waved for her to continue down the path. Lined with fulsome variegated bushes, its centre point was marked by a giant ornamental stone urn on a stepped pedestal. He lowered his voice. 'My lady, if we might refrain from commenting on our host? We are easily overheard in this part of the property.'

Appreciating the difficulty of his position, she nodded. 'Actually, let's go and grill those who worked most closely with St Clair first then. The under-gardeners.'

Clifford gave her a doubtful look. 'I fear they will not divulge much about him since he was their superior.' He sniffed. 'At least, one would hope not.'

'One hopes they will!'

Having identified the whereabouts of the under-gardeners by the sound of shears snipping, she was about to stride around the hedge to them when her sharp hearing caught a hissed whisper.

'But we can't do it now. It's too light. And there's a load more prunin' to do before day's end.'

'Sod the prunin'! More to the point, we've a load more stuff to shift out of here!' another voice answered.

Clifford frowned at the bad language and mimed for her to cover her ears. Instead, she craned her neck closer to their side of the hedge.

'How's that gonna work, genius?' the first voice said in a griping tone. 'With the police bootin' theyselves all over this place? They'd love to get their hands on the stuff, wouldn't they? And then how'd we explain how we come by it?'

'Keep yer voice down!' the other voice hissed again. 'And ain't the police as we needs mind. It's that woman ol' Cunliffe has invited down. Somethin' about her looks tell me she's the snoopy sort. And that butler of hers looks like a right beggar!'

'All the more reason to move it of a dark hour then. And prunin' still needs finishin' or ol' Cunliffe might ask questions hisself.'

A grunt of bad grace heralded the restart of shears snipping.

Eleanor gestured to Clifford they should wait a minute. After her limited patience gave up, she marched out backwards through the hedge's gap.

'It's only those working diligently at the coal face who really know.' She whirled around, pretending to be surprised to see the two men standing only a yard away. 'Ah, like these fine members of Mr Cunliffe's grounds team.'

They hurriedly raked off their caps, staring at each with a mystified look. Both somewhere between twenty and thirty, they wore rolled-up shirtsleeves and patched wool jerkins with earth-streaked workaday trousers tucked into stout muddy boots. The taller of the two nudged the darker-haired one forward.

'Good mornin', m'lady,' he stuttered.

Gladstone launched himself up the under-gardener's legs, receiving a rub of his head.

'Isn't it just!' She beamed. 'And, gentlemen, thanks to you, it has got even better.'

They exchanged a look. The slightly taller one nodded at a barrow a few feet away.

'We've no coal, m'lady. Only shearin's.'

'And Tomkins, my cat!' She pointed to the telltale twitch of a ginger tail snaking under the heap. 'But no matter. What I'm really after is your invaluable knowledge. The gardens, well, the immediate ones here at least, are beautiful. And that must be down to you two.'

'Us?' they chorused.

'Well, of course, you. Mr...?'

'Tristan Brae and Dewi Odgers is our names, m'lady,' the shorter one said. 'But—'

She waved at her butler. 'Notetaking, please, Clifford. I shall never remember everything I learn here by the time I get back to my own garden remodelling.'

Brae rubbed his hand along his cheek, leaving a smear of green. 'Learn, m'lady?'

'Yes. From watching you work. But I should probably warn you in advance, I'll likely bend your ears out of shape with my barrage of questions.'

'Watch?' Odgers said in a mortified tone.

'Not to check up on you,' she soothed. 'Goodness, no. Here you both are working away with no one supervising you. Highly commendable.' She frowned. 'Although, now I come to think of it, it's a little unusual, isn't it? I mean, before St Clair was employed by Mr Cunliffe, there were just you two chaps. What happened to the previous head gardener?'

'He died of pneumonia two winters back,' Brae said matter-of-factly.

Eleanor shook her head. 'Well, I'm sorry to hear that, but that must have been a while before Mr St Clair was employed here. Surely the original head gardener was replaced?'

Brae shrugged. 'Mr Cunliffe don't like to spend money unnecessarily. He told us he couldn't justify three gardeners any longer, so if he employed a new'un, one of us would have to go.' He glanced at his workmate. 'Me and Dewi been workin' here together since we were lads. So we suggested to him that we could cope perfectly well on our own and it would be cheaper for him to keep just the two of us on.'

'Well, poor Mr St Clair will hardly be coming to check your work now, will he?'

'Not unless he comes from the grave!' Odgers muttered.

Brae gave him a sly look and murmured, 'Wouldn't put it past him.'

Eleanor pretended she hadn't heard. 'But I should have offered my condolences, right at the start. It must have been quite the shock?'

The two of them shrugged and moved on to the next bushes. She tried a different tack.

'So is this winter trimming you're doing, gentlemen?'

'More as tidyin'. For keepin' the shapes after wind's been a batterin', m'lady,' Brae said, snipping away with his shears. 'Mind, if your own garden is a windy spot, try some skimmia. Him with the pink and white flowers still, even though it's December now.'

'Note all that please, Clifford.'

'Very good.' Her butler nodded, head down over his pocketbook.

Gladstone trotted back from further along the path and dropped a rotting crab apple on Clifford's impeccably shiny shoes. He shuddered.

'Why do I fear something may slither out and start a fight with my shoelaces?'

Brae speared it with the end of his shears and flicked it into the wheelbarrow.

'Thank you,' Clifford said weakly.

The two gardeners shared a quiet nudge before laying their tools on top of the heap in the barrow. Brae tipped his cap to her.

'Shearin's is finished here. So we'll be hurryin' on.'

Their shoulders both fell as she followed them.

'Do carry on, gentlemen,' she said brightly. 'I'm intrigued to see what I'm going to learn about next.' Tomkins skittered past to leap onto the front of the wheelbarrow and ride proudly like a ship's mascot. Eleanor shrugged apologetically. 'At least it's not Gladstone. He's rather heavier. I say though, I hope you're not frightfully behind on account of Inspector Trevilick keeping you back with too many questions?'

'No,' Brae said hesitantly. 'He dug us out after work in the inn.'

The gardeners carried on wheeling their barrow through a gap in the hedge.

'Gracious! Late in the evening then?' Eleanor said, doggedly following them.

'Not really,' Brae said. 'Dewi and me was let go early.'

'How generous.' She watched like an eager student as they set about more pruning. 'Seeing as Mr Cunliffe saw the poor fellow down on the rocks about three o'clock.'

Looking unmoved, Odgers nodded. 'We must a' been halfway to the village when he went whack on them rocks. Surprised we never heard him hit.'

'Ahem,' Clifford said pointedly. 'Images like that are not needed when her ladyship is present, thank you.'

Eleanor nodded gratefully to him and then turned back to the under-gardeners. 'How do you get to work here, gentlemen?'

'Boots, m'lady.' Brae pointed at his with a puzzled look. 'We come and go together, seein' as we share lodgin's in the village.'

'Walking. Gracious, that must seem a chore.'

He shrugged. ''Tain't too bad. Takes three quarters of an hour.'

'And did the inspector ask if anyone saw you on the way?'

Odgers leaned on his rake. 'He did. And they didn't. No one else walks that path. It only leads to here.'

Convenient, Ellie.

Brae nodded. 'Not until we reached the village. Course, then we met folks.' He rolled his eyes. 'All of 'em askin' why we'd snuck off early.'

'But we hadn't,' Odgers protested.

She did the maths quickly.

By the time they reached Lostenev, Ellie, St Clair would already have been dead.

'Mr St Clair let you go early as a reward, I imagine? For working hard?'

'The sea would turn to ale likelier than that,' Odgers grumbled.

Brae nodded.

She frowned in confusion. 'I'm sorry, but I'm sure you said that he let you go early the day he died?'

'Oh no. It was Mr Cunliffe what let us go,' Odgers said.

'Really? Was that usual? I mean, wouldn't that normally be Mr St Clair's province?'

'Yep.'

'So did you ask why Mr Cunliffe let you go early?'

They looked at each other blankly. Brae shrugged. 'Didn't ask, m'lady. We just scrammed when he said to.'

'I see. What did you think of Mr St Clair?'

'How's that then?' Brae said tentatively.

'To work with, I mean. Some people are easy. Some not always so. How did you find him?'

'He knew his business, fair no quibble,' Odgers said.

'Landscapin' was his thing, alright,' Brae hesitated. 'But it didn't come with, well, respect for the spirits of the garden.'

Odgers' eyes widened. 'Too right! Tore down an old folly in the first week!'

Brae nodded. 'And always pokin' around, askin' questions and comin' up on a man unexpected like.'

Odgers nudged his elbow. 'And turnin' up when you thought he'd left...' He tailed off at his colleague's warning look.

'I see,' Eleanor said lightly, shooting Clifford a quick glance. 'And on the plan he drew for the changes, were there lots of things like that planned? Tearing things down, I mean?'

'Must have been. But we only got to see the parts we was set to work on.'

'I see. Do you happen to know where Mr St Clair kept his plan? I'd love to see it to get some inspiration for my own garden project.'

'Mr Cunliffe's probably got it. If as not, it'll be in Mr St Clair's office, same as he kept it.'

Clifford looked up from his pocketbook. 'Did Mr St Clair consult the family in the house about his ideas? Other than Mr Cunliffe?'

'He never got involved with 'em as far as I know, sir. Best way, if you ask me.'

Odgers nudged him. 'Except him hittin' on Mrs Liddi—' He clammed up as his colleague elbowed him in his side.

'Actually, we gots to be goin', m'lady.'

And with that, they upped tools and left.

Once they were on their own, Eleanor turned to Clifford.

'So, it seems Mr Cunliffe was penny-pinching by not employing a new head gardener after the last one died. Which makes it even odder that he should then splash out and employ St Clair.'

'Possibly, my lady. Lord Wickhamshaw did mention that Mr Cunliffe may have secured Mr St Clair's services at a somewhat reduced rate, if the rumours that his lordship referred to were correct.'

'Mmm. Either way, I got the distinct impression that neither Brae nor Odgers were happy with St Clair hanging around.'

She shook her head. 'From what we heard, it seems they took the opportunity while there was no head gardener at Gwel an Mor to become involved in something they'd rather not have the police know about. Some small-time scam, perhaps? Or perhaps, something bigger?'

Clifford nodded slowly. 'And more deadly!'

14

Burying her desire to be deep in romantic festive preparations rather than another mysterious death, Eleanor ducked under the fingers of silver and white firs arching over the stone path. To her right, a small folly in the shape of a classical Roman temple was adorned with several fish sculptures just below its roofline. Clifford followed her gaze.

'The fish sculptures are, in fact, ornate gutter spouts, like church gargoyles often are, my lady.'

'Fascinating.' She looked ahead at where the path met seven others, all of which radiated out at the same angle, like the legs of a giant spider.

'Which one leads to St Clair's office, I wonder?'

Tomkins seemed excited by the path on her immediate right, so she followed it, any decision being better than the lengthy deliberations her butler would likely start in on if given the chance. 'Come on, Clifford! Maybe we'll find some evidence of whatever Brae and Odgers are up to. And the fresh air will aid thinking on the way.'

But after only a minute, she was brought up short. A series of steps flanked by a narrow ramp led down to a square arch in a high brick wall. The ornamental stacks protruding along its top seemed out of place with its otherwise functional air.

'Is there some sort of kitchen garden through there, Clifford?'

'I believe so, my lady. Given the selection of trugs just inside the entrance.'

'Well, dash it, that's no good. We're after St Clair's office, not rows of tragic-looking winter vegetables clinging to the idea someone has a penchant for frost-bitten mush.' She flapped a hand for him to turn around, frowning as he didn't move.

'The milder than average climate in this corner of Cornwall, my lady, allows some vegetables to be grown here later than elsewhere. Much of it would also be grown in greenhouses, as Joseph does back in Henley Hall. And, if memory serves, Mr Cunliffe mentioned that Mr St Clair had been granted the use of the previous head gardener's office and quarters. As such, it would almost certainly be sited amongst the year-round centre of produce, the kitchen garden.'

'Well done, clever clogs.' She nudged his arm, immediately feeling bad at his pained wince. 'Gracious, I forgot your sprained, sorry *fractured* elbow.'

Inside the walled quadrangle, various greenhouses sprouted out, like lean-tos, from the high stone wall. At one time, a couple of trees either side of the main path had been trained to grow their branches flat along a canopy of iron rods. Now, however, they were a sea of untended, overgrown gnarled knots and flaking lichen.

'Espaliers, my lady,' Clifford said. 'Fruit trees.'

'I've never eaten esp... whatever it was. Nice with custard, are they?'

His lips twitched. 'Apples and pears certainly are. Espaliers being the term for any fruit tree grown in such an easily harvestable manner.'

'Interesting. However, we're looking for St Clair's office, remember?'

'Over there, perhaps?' He pointed to a plaque on a green door set in the furthest wall.

'"Head Gardener's Office",' she read. 'Brilliant!'

Her immediate impression on entering was of earthy musk, overlain with decades of wood smoke. She stepped across the uneven cobbled floor to the shelves, but they were mostly filled with seed jars and little else. A woodworm-dotted roll-top bureau below a wonky window was set with a simple wooden chair, both discarded from the house, she surmised. To one side, a ladder disappeared through a narrow opening in the ceiling beams, suggesting the upstairs room was no larger than the cramped space where she was standing.

Clifford shook his head at her disapproving gaze. 'Unlike yourself, my lady, most employers are concerned only with outward show. An employee's title, or uniform, may be elaborate, but their wage and accommodation are usually far less... grandiose.'

She nodded, her eyes drawn to an iron-cowled fireplace with a meagre supply of firewood stacked in the narrow alcoves either side. She wished it was lit to stave off her shivers. A thick layer of ash peppered with a few charred pieces of charcoal suggested it had been burning not that long ago when St Clair had called this his office. Albeit far more temporarily than he'd expected.

Beside the desk, an architect's drawing board had been attached to a narrow wooden bench. Above it, a spooled pole bolted to the wall allowed the roll of paper it held to be pulled out and cut to any desired length on a toothed metal strip. Six clay pots sat on a tray, each holding a selection of mechanical pencils or fountain pens. A row of graded Indian rubbers stood in a groove along the carrier's front. And in pride of place was a wooden case monogrammed in scrolling carved script with the initials J.W.S.C.

'Jerome Withenhall St Clair,' she murmured sadly.

Clifford opened the case, raising an appreciative brow at the brass instruments lying on purple velvet. 'Drafting tools worthy of an architect or engineer. Scale dividers, ruling pens, callipers, compasses, protractors, set squares and a three-sided, varying scale ruler. Plus graded flexible wood splines. And the finest French curves I have ever had the pleasure of observing up close.'

She laughed. 'Steady on, Clifford!'

He eyed her sideways. 'If we might complete the rest of our regrettable task with even a shred of decorum, my lady?'

'Spoilsport. You know, I'm genuinely sorry you didn't get to meet St Clair. The two of you could have spent hours swapping notes on your obviously shared love of precision and design.' She stepped over to the desk, noting the thin film of dust across the top. 'He doesn't seem to have been a man for letter writing or keeping a journal, mind. Only for drawing out his garden designs. But Cunliffe said something about—'

'A notebook?' Clifford nodded. 'Which he believed contained mysterious symbols. Bravo, my lady.'

'Best save the bravo for when we've found it. And if it proves Mr Cunliffe's worries were unfounded.'

'Fingers crossed.'

The desk had only one central drawer, which contained nothing more than a trowel handle, two balls of twine and an unsprung mousetrap. Unsprung, that was, until she discovered it languishing at the back by feeling with her fingertips.

'Ow! That smarts!'

Clifford produced a miniature bottle of antiseptic from his pocket.

'Not necessary, thank you.' At his firm look, she accepted the handkerchief he had doused and pressed it gingerly across the red line running across the ends of her fingers. 'Why is that stuff so spiteful?' She held up a halting hand. 'Maybe answer that later. Right now, we need to rummage upstairs.'

'We?' Clifford said in a horrified tone.

'Yes, "we". Don't fret. You can search the parts you think I'll faint if I so much as catch a glimpse of, like St Clair's underthings. Meanwhile, I'll scout through the rest.'

'Scouting other areas will be expeditious, my lady, but uncomfortable,' he called over his shoulder as he cleared the last steps up through the hatch.

'Gracious!' she said, popping up after him.

The ceiling sloped at such a steep angle that, with her taller than average height, she was forced to stoop, and her butler was positively bent over. An iron bedstead filled the central space, which struck her as a waste. Had it been tucked against a wall, there would at least have been room for more than the minimal washstand and two clothes horses standing one in front of the other. A bowed shelf attached to the chimney breast held three oil lamps, a bundle of candles, a box of chalk, a couple of matches and a stack of spare lamp wicks.

She tugged at her fiery curls in confusion. 'Why did St Clair want so much light up here when there's nothing to read, or make, or... do at all? It's like he worked until he could barely make it up the ladder just to fall into bed.'

Clifford turned back from searching the pockets of the four pairs of trousers and jackets. 'Nothing. Save for some rather distinguished labels in his more formal outerwear. Mr Cunliffe remarked, I believe, on St Clair "aping" the titled classes in his dress. Other clothing comprises basic work shirts, woollen jumpers, and jerkins. Ahem. There is also a small wicker hamper. Of which a lady has no need of knowing the contents,' he ended hurriedly.

'Understood. Aside from the line of boots under his bed, there's nothing much else.' She pointed at the one drab concession to decoration, shaking her head. 'And that faded landscape picture just adds to the overall melancholy of the room. Do you know, I can't believe Mr Cunliffe was happy for any member of his staff to live somewhere this bleak.'

'Ahem. My lady, these are, in fact, commonplace quarters for a gentleman's staff. Household or grounds. The privileges you insist your staff enjoy are unusual, as I said before. But sincerely appreciated.'

She smiled. 'Well, I wish you'd let me do more. Now how about you ruffle under his brown wool blankets and the mattress in case there's anything I really shouldn't see there.'

To distract her wave of sadness, she tried to straighten the painting. 'I'd have taken this down and burnt it with delight, in truth. As you would have, Clifford, since it doesn't hang straight whatever you do. Mind you, it's probably covering some hideous patch of damp behi— Clifford!' she hissed. 'Not damp. It's an alcove.'

He took a single stride to join her. 'Containing a pocket notebook!'

Her elation, however, was short-lived as she flicked through the pages. 'Could Mr Cunliffe be right about St Clair being a satanist, do you think?'

He took the notebook from her and studied the pages.

'Not from the inked designs included here, my lady. The, admittedly few, occult symbols I have come across are nothing like those here. I imagine these are abstract patterns of bulbs or bushes and how they might be planted if' – he sniffed – 'one were to be a fan of the more modernistic approach to garden design.' Turning another page with the tip of his gloved finger, he shook his head slowly. 'But I do not recognise this as such. See this outline here, framed by a boxed square and set above a simple ellipse curve?'

'With what looks like maiden's hair flowing over it? What of it?'

'It has the hallmarks of a classical Greek urn, or lidded amphora. Save for the maiden's hair, as you referred to these long strokes either side and this peculiar long rectangle all but dissecting the middle.'

She peered closer.

'And here.' He pointed to another similar symbol. 'Definitely garden design, not occult related. Although I suppose someone of Mr Cunliffe's... excitable nature, might have misconstrued them as such after a hasty glance.' He frowned. 'I confess, I have no idea what they represent, though.'

'Well, whatever they represent, at least that part of Cunliffe's concerns seems unfounded. But it is intriguing. We should explore the gardens at some stage and find out what those drawings refer to. It might have nothing to do with St Clair's death, but then again...' She slipped the notebook into her pocket. 'Now I've no idea where to look for this wretched plan of—'

A crash followed by a triumphant woof made them dart for the ladder. In the room below, Tomkins sat innocently on the desk, his twitching tail clearing an arc in the dust as he licked his paw methodically. A trail of grey cat prints led across the desk. Eleanor looked around in confusion.

'Where's Gladstone?'

'I wonder, my lady,' Clifford said drily, stepping aside to reveal her bulldog standing ankle deep in the hearth. His wrinkled jowls were thick with soot, a perfect triangle of fine grey ash wobbling on his nose, and a lump of charcoal poking out of his mouth.

'Oh, Gladstone! You absolute monster!' She bit her lip, trying not to laugh at the ridiculous ghostly spectacle her supposedly pedigreed canine cut. 'It looks like he's wearing ash socks, Clifford.'

'Quite!' Her butler lifted the bulldog with one arm and deposited him, with a grimace, on the floor.

'Is it the state of Mr Wilful or your elbow that's paining you most?' she said in concern.

Having dusted off his gloves, he slid a pristine handkerchief from his jacket pocket in silent reply.

'Fibber.' She took it from him. 'I told you, you should get that injury looked at. But being an impossibly stubborn donkey, you'll have to put up with me doing a few more things until you see sense. Like driving. And cleaning up Mr Messy Chops here.'

She dropped to her knees and set to, wiping the grey-black soot from between Gladstone's wrinkled jowls. His stumpy tail wagged hopefully as he held on to his prize lump of charcoal.

'No chance, old chum. We are not playing ball with that, so... Give. It. Up!' She reeled backwards as she pulled it from his mouth. 'Ugh! It's covered in his...' She peered at it, carefully turning it around, much to Clifford's disgust. 'Look! There's something soggy on the back of it.'

Clifford bent down, lips pursed as he reached for his pince-nez. 'The last hope any vestige of refinement remains in the Swift household?'

'No, silly. It's paper. All... ugh... stuck together.' She peeled the folds apart tentatively and gasped.

'Bravo, Master Gladstone,' Clifford breathed, tracing his finger over the curving inked lines on the paper. 'The remains of Mr St Clair's plan for the gardens, I'd warrant.'

She nodded slowly, her brow furrowed. 'But why on earth would he have burnt his own plans?'

15

Eleanor tightened her gloves against her wrists, then flexed her fingers determinedly, nodding to Gladstone and Tomkins on Clifford's lap. 'Right, chaps.'

'My lady, if I—'

'Not now, Clifford.' She gripped the steering wheel. 'You managed to drive us to see Lord Wickhamshaw yesterday, but you finally confessed that your elbow gave you gip all night as a result. And the road there was fairly straight and flat, which this isn't.'

'Admittedly, my lady. But given that, then *when* may I offer a suggestion? When we actually plunge headlong into the sea?' He folded his good arm. 'I am merely asking for the sake of clarity.'

'Very droll. However, now I understand. You think I'll stuff the Rolls into a tree on the way down to Lostenev, don't you? In fact, you probably would have delighted in locking me in my room so I couldn't even try, wouldn't you?'

'Oh, happy thoughts,' he murmured. At her mock huff, he shook his head. 'However, I do not believe you will "stuff" the

Rolls on the way to the village. On the way back, possibly, because I fear the threatened snow will have arrived by then.'

She ignored his last remark and pulled smoothly away from Gwel an Mor's entrance steps. At least in her mind, she did. Clifford's pained look and hastily tightened grip on Gladstone and Tomkins suggested otherwise. Never one to be defeated, she hunched over the wheel, trying to concentrate over the unpleasantly harsh noise the engine was making.

Ah! The brake, Ellie.

Brake off, she tried again, this time with more success. And, despite having forgotten just how heavy the steering was in her late uncle's stately car, the end of the driveway came and went without incident. One small slide hardly counted, she decided. Dismissing a sharp intake of breath from her butler with a wave of her hand, she edged down the road pleased with her progress.

'Quarter of a mile to the first of the precipitous downward slopes,' Clifford said, staring straight ahead. In response, she sped up. 'Slower, if I might suggest...' He winced and pressed himself, Gladstone and Tomkins back into his seat.

A moment later, she folded her arms and glared at him, the car having come to a less than graceful stop.

'We just spun in a tiny circle on account of the road being spitefully greasy, that's all.' She graunched the gearstick into submission, hoping it was wide enough at that point to turn, as they were now facing the wrong way. 'Anyway, if I were to reverse to Lostenev, it would be the same distance as driving forwards.'

'I agree, my lady. Merely more alarming.' He waited until she had finally managed to turn the car around, then cleared his throat. 'Would it help if one pointed out the road is, in fact, icy, not greasy?'

'No, it wouldn't, thank you. And now I know you fancy doing it all forwards, I shall do so just to save you whining the entire way. You only had to say.'

'My lady, butlers do not "whine".'

'You're right,' she said, peering through the windscreen. 'I meant bleating.'

They both held their breaths, squabbling forgotten, as she started on the steep slope down. It passed rather more rapidly than she'd intended, but once they were on the relative level again, she risked a glance at her rigid passenger.

'It's your own fault, as you just admitted, Clifford. If you hadn't been so infuriatingly bashful and let me use my nurse's training, I could have attended to your elbow when it happened. Then I wouldn't have needed to insist on driving. Oh, sharp corner!' She avoided his gaze as the road straightened for a moment. Another tight bend appeared from nowhere. 'Dash it!' she muttered, wrenching the wheel hard. 'Perhaps we should have asked Mr Cunliffe if he has two bicycles?'

Clifford ran a hand over the impeccable crease in his suit trousers. 'Perhaps we shouldn't have!'

Risking a peep up at the sky, she shrugged over the unusually loud whine of the engine. 'I really can't fathom why you think it's going to snow, Clifford. The sky's been grizzly grey since we crossed the border into Cornwall, so why now?'

'Mrs Liddicoat informed me. Ahem. Perhaps the engine's excessive noise suggests a different gear, my lady?'

She obliged. 'Mrs Liddicoat? Clifford, please don't tell me she waved her seaweed at you as a portent of snowy doom?'

He sniffed. 'Seaweed is used to predict rain, not snow. In this instance, her big toe told her.'

Eleanor doubled over the wheel with laughter, jerking the Rolls to a halt while she regained her composure. She caught his admonishing look.

'Oh, stop it. I don't mean to be rude, but she also declared to me that a ginger cat is a charm against fire!'

He patted the cat. 'Ah! Master Tomkins you are a menace not entirely without purpose then.'

Eleanor shook her head. 'Clifford, Mrs Liddicoat's big toe predicting the weather? That makes her battier than Mr Cunliffe!'

He eyed her as if she were slow of mind. 'My lady, Mr Cunliffe's housekeeper does not hear voices whispering from within her slippers. She relies upon her rheumatics.'

'Oh, gracious! Poor thing.' She grimaced, feeling guilty for laughing.

'However,' he continued as she set off again, 'I prefer the traditional method of consulting my barometer. Which concurred exactly with Mrs Liddicoat, incidentally, since it dropped dramatically. Hence my concerns over this journey.'

'You brought a barometer with you?'

'The travelling one you so thoughtfully included in my birthday gift of two years past, my lady. It has accompanied us on every trip since.'

She was pleased that it meant so much to him, but it also reminded her how quickly Christmas was looming. She slowed as a sign pointing to their destination appeared. Peering down the turning made her blanch. Ice or no ice, quite how she was supposed to navigate anything so narrow and tortuous, she couldn't imagine.

'Clifford, all joking apart, kindly coax me down the next section for both our sakes. And I'm sorry if I've scared you so far.'

'Scared? Not a bit, my lady. Terrified, definitely.' He winked. 'Now, ease the wheel right, creeping forward and start to get a feel through your fingers for the unpredictability of the delicate creature you are in charge of.'

'Delicate, Clifford? You once rescued me in this incredible machine by driving through a barn while it was on fire!'

'Indeed. However, remember, in normal circumstances, motor cars are like ladies. They respond best to the solicitous touch. Boundary wall!'

'Silly place to put one,' she muttered, as it passed by inches from her side window. Taking the next bend at little more than a snail's pace saw them safely round. But the drop she could now see was even steeper, and the road even narrower than before.

'Will the Rolls actually fit?' she breathed, fearing the answer would be that reversing back to Gwel an Mor was her only option.

'It will. But barely. And then only if you can follow the road's exact line, which is far from easy, given the length of the bonnet.'

'Marvellous. No pressure then.'

Having managed it by less than a whisker, she allowed her groaning shoulders to relax for a second. Only to realise she now had to negotiate a series of hairpin bends.

'Clifford! Surely this is impossible!'

He nodded. 'Possibly. I have never attempted it myself. His lordship always drove us to the village, having borrowed Mr Cunliffe's motor car. It's a petite little thing. The Rolls, given its width, length, and weight, really is the worst vehicle to drive on these roads in these conditions.'

She threw her hands out. 'Then why on earth did you let me drive here in it?'

'Because, my lady, Mr Cunliffe would not have agreed to either you or I borrowing his car, being a mere servant—'

'And an even merer woman!' she muttered. 'No matter that we're trying to help him!' A shower of snowflakes splattered onto the windscreen. 'But dash it, why didn't you tell me driving this Goliath of a Rolls Royce down these tortuous roads has never been attempted before?'

'Because my mistress insisted on driving it. And it is not my place as a mere butler to argue otherwise.' He settled back into his seat. 'Shall we?'

16

Having decided by mutual agreement that the Rolls could go no further, Eleanor pulled into a small layby before the penulti-mate bend. They proceeded on foot, with Tomkins in his kitty kit bag and Gladstone straining excitedly on his lead. A series of centuries-old steps brought them into Lostenev High Street, with its low, whitewashed buildings lining the twisty cobbled road.

The soft frosted snowflakes pattering against her face made her feel all the more that she was in a Christmas picture postcard.

'Oh, Clifford, it's delightfully sweet. None of the front doors even come up to the top of my coat buttons. I wonder if Lostenev means "cosy" or "quaint" in Cornish.'

He shook his head sombrely. 'I believe it means "lost soul", my lady.'

St Clair, Ellie.

He nodded as if reading her mind. 'Perhaps a moment enjoying the harbour?'

The fishing village of Lostenev was built around a natural cove, many of the twee shops and terraced houses using the cliff face as one of their walls. Others simply sprouted out of the enormous boulders at all manner of angles, some coming to such a needle point, she couldn't work out how anyone could fit furniture into the rooms. Dominating the village was the harbour itself with its tiny, colourful fishing boats and giant reels of nets. Being low tide, the boats lay on their sides in the mud, accessed only by barnacle-covered rusty ladders set into the harbour wall. Seagulls perched on every available point, aboard and ashore, while a huddle of children lay sprawled on their stomachs despite the cold, staring down into the water, intent on their crabbing lines.

She wrapped her coat tighter around her middle. 'Well, I vote we give ourselves a quick break from everything morbid and instead, try to find at least a few small festive gifts. I left all my proper presents at home, having no inkling I'd be stuck here.' Her face lit up. 'And now, you-know-who will be here too, and I've nothing for him. Plus, I need suitable presents for Mr Cunliffe and each of his family. Oh, and little extra tree presents for the ladies. They'll just have to get them when we get back. Whenever that is.'

She paused to peer along the charming variety of festive decorations in each of the shops snaking on ahead around the harbour's curve. Instead of the traditional holly and fir wreaths and garlands which tended to proliferate in the rest of England, the finest of Cornish creativity was on display. Rope-thick swathes of dried seaweed of every verdant shade and variety were looped with all manner of crocheted angels, stars and snowflakes to frame almost every pane of glass. Candles twinkled among darling nativity scenes made entirely from large, artfully painted pebbles, all set on soft velvety moss tufts.

'Ten minutes to ourselves perhaps, Clifford?' she said airily, trying to hide her determination to find the perfect gift for her treasured butler.

'Ah! A Lady Swift's ten minutes.' Clifford counted on his

fingers. 'Let me see, factoring in her being let loose for the tantalising delights of shopping... perhaps, we might meet up again on say... Boxing Day?'

'Be off with you!' she laughed.

In fact, it was well over an hour later when she stumbled up the step into the last, and tiniest, of the irresistibly cosy shops strung out around the village. Already laden with a bulging festively embroidered sailcloth bag full of impromptu presents for each of the people who meant the world to her, she had one present still to get.

A wheezy laugh from behind the counter pulled her up short. 'Come along, now. No shirking, missy.' An untamed bush of grey hair above a face creased with laughter lines bobbed up into view. The late-middle-aged man waved a small tot of clear liquid at her. 'Shopkeeper's rules since it's festive tradition.'

She laughed. 'It's a delightful one. But I wish I'd known before venturing into every one of Lostenev's wonderful little stores. I'm awash with yuletide gin.'

'Nonsense!' He held up a plate. 'That's why our womenfolk make this saffron cake to soak it up.' Springing out in a spritely manner, he handed her a piece to go with her tot. As she drank and ate, he waved a hand at a display of leatherwork on two cloth-covered shelves. 'I have some fine items here, but if it's not rude to ask, what's a fine lady like yourself doing Christmas shopping in an out-of-the-way place like Lostenev?'

She hid a grimace. 'Well, I'm staying up at Gwel an Mor and—' She faltered as the shopkeeper's festive cheer seemed to disappear as quickly as a wink.

'Gwel an Mor, you said?' The man shook his head, eyes averted. 'Bad business, that. But only to be expected,' he added matter-of-factly, as if to himself.

She frowned. 'I'm sorry, but what do you mean?'

Instantly, the shopkeeper was all smiles again. 'Mean, missy?' He waved a hand. 'Oh, take no notice, it's the gin speaking.' He shifted a box from one side of the counter to the other and then looked up, rubbing his hands. 'So, shopping for someone in particular?'

She opened her mouth, but then slowly closed it.

Hugh will be down shortly, Ellie. It's better if he talks to the locals.

Instead, she groaned. 'Yes. Someone infuriatingly particular! I thought my fiancé was tricky to buy for, but I finally found the perfect gift for him. But my butler.' She rolled her eyes. 'He's impossible! And too learned for words. Everything he finds fascinating strikes me as unfathomably complicated or tedious in the extreme.'

'Hmm. A history man, perhaps?' She nodded eagerly. He beckoned her behind the counter. 'Then maybe my little hobby might interest him...?'

Ten minutes later, carefully wrapped package in hand, she hastily descended the shop step into the street and bumped into something bony.

'Gracious, sorry!' She spun around. Seeing no one, she adjusted her gaze downwards. A pair of piercing eyes glared back at her. 'I'm sorry,' she repeated genuinely to the diminutive woman, who was wrapped in a variety of purple wool shawls and hugged a huge woven-grass basket to her chest. Incongruously, her face was comprehensively overrun with wrinkles, yet her waist-length wiry hair was raven black without a wisp of grey.

'Well? Do you want 'em, or not?'

Eleanor looked over the woman's shoulder, then over hers. She shrugged. 'Want what?'

'Them, that's who!' The woman shook her basket at her so hard the lid slid half off.

Eleanor reluctantly peeped inside the dark interior only to be all the more confused by its contents. 'Umm... fish?'

'Indeed, my lady.' Clifford's measured tone came from behind. She turned to catch his eyes shining with amusement. He took her package and bag and doffed his bowler hat to the woman with a charming smile. She looked away bashfully, clucking at Gladstone, then Tomkins, whose head poked eagerly through his kitty kit bag window. 'Her ladyship has been hankering to purchase half a dozen from you since she started shopping, dear lady.'

'Six, yer say!' The woman's head and shoulders disappeared inside her basket with a raft of unintelligible muttering. A moment later she placed six shimmering silvery green- and blue-tinged creations into Eleanor's hands.

'Oh my, they're beautifully embroidered keepsake bags in the shape of fish!' Eleanor breathed, admiring the silky-threaded scales she had mistaken for real in her haste.

As the woman popped her head back in the basket, Eleanor tugged at her butler's sleeve.

'Clifford,' she hissed. 'How long had you been watching me flounder with her before wading in to bale me out?'

'A lady's ten minutes.' He winked. 'Forgive my not formally introducing you to "Addled Aida", as the lady is locally known. She's been dogging your footsteps the entire length of the high street to make a sale. Now.' He examined his pocket watch. 'If we are to catch that train and have you back at Gwel an Mor in time for dinner, we—'

'What's that you say?' The woman's head shot out of the basket, eyes boring into Eleanor's. 'You the lady from the big house on the cliffs?'

Eleanor sighed quietly. *Oh, dear, here we go again, Ellie.*

She nodded. The woman shook her head vehemently. 'Why did yer come? Those eyes of yourn is greener'n emeralds. But what's the point, if they ain't put to use? Answer me that!' the woman snapped.

'Erm, well...' Eleanor recoiled slightly as the woman clutched at her shoulder.

'Nothing good that ever went into that place came out, I tell yer! 'Tis a place for fortune hunters and fools, not the souls of good men! Let what's buried in the past, stay in the past!'

Eleanor gently removed the woman's hand. 'Er... absolutely. I—'

The woman spun around and pointed out to sea. 'Be like him! Alone, incorruptible, in a sea of wickedness!'

Snatching up her basket, she nodded to Eleanor. 'Thank you kindly for your purchases, miss.' With a coy smile to her butler, she shuffled back the way she'd come.

17

Shaking her head, Eleanor set off in the opposite direction and, once she was sure the woman was out of earshot, stopped and threw her hands up. 'What exactly was all that about, Clifford?'

He stroked his chin. 'I assume the lady has heard of the demise of Mr St Clair.'

'And the "Be like him!" part?'

'I can only assume she was referring to the Lostenev Lighthouse, my lady. Personifying it, as it were, as a guiding beacon?'

She looked down at the embroidered bags in her hand. 'Well, I suppose it was worth putting up with. These really are rather lovely.' An involuntary shiver ran down her spine. 'Let's just hope she's better at making bags than prophecies!'

She looked up at a creaking noise. Above her head a blue and white sign swung in the December breeze.

'Kerensa Come Quick.' She shrugged at Clifford.

'I believe, my lady, "*kerensa*" is Cornish for "love".'

'With stargazy best or cracky finest.' A cheery plump woman poked her head out of a window made from a salvaged brass porthole. 'Dependin' whether pie or stew is yer tipple?'

'Well, both, definitely,' Eleanor said. 'But sadly, we haven't much time.'

'Then step inside and toast yer bones with a taste of the first. I've a few little 'uns ready.' The woman glanced at Clifford. 'Both of you, mind.' With a throaty chuckle, she gestured at the stone path running alongside and disappeared.

At the end of the path, a low door led into what Eleanor recognised as a 'snug', a backroom of a pub reserved for women with their male partners. Or butlers, she mused. Inside, five tables were spread with blue and yellow anchor-patterned cloths. All were empty except one, which was filled with ruddy-cheeked women and a few elderly white-whiskered men. A flickering fire beckoned, particularly to her bulldog and now released tomcat it seemed, as they bounded over together and settled down. Strings of shells painted in festive red and green served admirably as decorations along with a three-tiered stack of bottles on the deep mantelpiece, each bearing one letter of the painted message 'Merry Christmas All!' Amusingly, the surrounding chairs were upholstered in cast-off fishermen's woollen jumpers, the chairs' arms ending in a ribbed cuff.

She sat down at the spare table by the fire, enjoying her butler's bright-eyed interest in the lovingly crafted model fishing boats adorning the walls.

Their hostess bustled in with a tray. 'How's that for quick?'

'Very. Allow me, madam,' Clifford said.

'Anytime yer like, sir. Anytime at all, in fact.' She bumped her hip against him, which set the other women off into rounds of mischievous giggles.

'I think we shall need to come here lots, Clifford,' Eleanor said with an innocent look as the woman left him with the tray.

'If we might not, my lady,' he said firmly, putting it down.

She flapped an insistent hand for him to sit.

'Stargazy pie sampler, I believe.' He waggled a stern finger at the plaintively meowing Tomkins and the keenly sniffing

Gladstone. 'This is not for you two. You'll get yours in a moment!'

He passed her one of the two small oval dishes topped with golden brown pastry from which four silvery sardine heads protruded, staring glassily at her. She dived in.

'It's delicious! The filling is like a rich mustardy sort of custard with potatoes, eggs and I think little dashes of bacon. All infused with delectable sardine.' She glanced at the fire as it flickered with the rush of cold air from the door opening. She returned to her pie, barely registering that the general hubbub seemed to have died away somewhat. 'Tuck in, Clifford. When in Rome, you've always said.'

He eyed the other dish with suspicion. 'That doesn't apply in Cornwall, my lady. Not to butlers, anyway.'

'Oh for goodness' sake, anyone would think it poison.'

'And how right they'd be!' a strong Cornish voice said.

'Inspector!' Eleanor didn't bother to disguise her puzzlement. She held the stout policeman's penetrating gaze as he ambled over to their table, noticing his greying moustache twitch. Gladstone eyed him suspiciously as if he thought him a contender for any pie scraps. 'Surely it's not the done thing even for the police to cast aspersions publicly on the merits or otherwise of the local hostelries' fayre?'

Trevilick hooked his thumbs into the top buttonholes of his snow-spattered black overcoat, looking up at the soggy brim of his brown trilby. 'Not that I'm aware of, Lady Swift.'

Clifford rose. 'Then perhaps her ladyship might be allowed to continue her Cornish comestibles odyssey uninterrupted, Inspector?'

'I'm not here to stop her, Mr Clifford.' Trevilick shrugged. 'If that's what you were hinting at?'

'There was no hint.'

'What are you here for, Inspector?' Eleanor said placatingly.

'You,' came the blunt reply.

'Me? Then I shall take your "poison" joke in good spirit and eat while you explain because I'm in a hurry. I'm sure you won't mind?'

'About you eating, of course not. But about anyone thinking murder is a joke, I mind very much.'

She glanced at Clifford, who arched a brow.

'Murder?' she whispered. 'You mean?'

'I do. The coroner's post-mortem report is very clear. Mr St Clair was poisoned.'

'Gracious!' She floundered for anything else to say, having expected the report to cite only the impact with some particularly hard rock as being the cause of death. She'd only suggested one be done to cover Trevilick's back, after all.

Clifford caught her eye.

She clicked her fingers. 'That's why it didn't add up. Of course!'

Trevilick's brows rose. 'What didn't, Lady Swift?'

'Trigonometry, Inspector,' Clifford said matter-of-factly.

Eleanor pointed to another chair. 'I think you'd better shift my greedy tomcat to one side and bring up a seat.'

Not needing to be asked twice, Trevilick not only joined them but eagerly accepted the second pie dish, which Clifford inched over to him.

'I'm not depriving you, am I?'

Clifford shuddered. 'Really, Inspector, the pleasure is all mine.'

Sliding out his pocketbook, he opened his page of calculations from the spot where St Clair had been found and explained his method. Trevilick sat back when he'd finished and looked him over.

'Smart thinking you used there.'

Eleanor nodded. 'As always.'

Clifford tapped his diagram again. 'It is still a little... odd. But your explanation that he was already dead when he was, I

assume, thrown off the cliff, does seem to explain the matter.'
He waited until the inspector had swallowed a mouthful of pie.
'What was the poison used, if I might ask?'

'You may. Cyanide. Added to Mr St Clair's drink, likely as
not, the coroner thought.'

'Well, Inspector.' Eleanor pushed her empty dish away.
'Who is at the top of your suspect list?'

'Probably the same person who is at the top of yours.'

She gave a nonchalant toss of her red curls. 'I don't have a
list.'

Trevilick's eyes narrowed. 'Perhaps not on paper, Lady
Swift. But' – he tapped his nose – 'I have the measure of you.
And your Mr Cunliffe. He is as slippery as a bucket of eels and
you know it. He imagined Mr St Clair was trying to kill him, so
got in there first and did away with him instead.'

'Or,' Clifford added pointedly, 'someone else killed Mr St
Clair, mistaking him for Mr Cunliffe. As indeed, Mr Cunliffe
believes.'

'Possibly. But I usually find the most obvious solution is the
right one.' He stood up and retrieved his hat. 'I shall leave you to
decide on pudding. Good day.'

Clifford waited until the door closed behind him. 'A coincidence he found you here, my lady?'

She shook her head. 'Indubitably not, to borrow your
phrase.' She sighed. 'Are you thinking what I am? That if we
continue we may just be gathering evidence for the inspector?'

'Against Mr Cunliffe? Yes, I am. Principally because the
inspector did not once warn you off investigating, despite
knowing that is precisely what you are doing.'

'I know.' She shook her head slowly. 'So everything we do
from this point will just be laying out more rope for the
inspector to hang the man we're supposed to be helping!'

18

'But that's my problem,' Eleanor whispered, turning her collar up against the increasing snowflakes. 'Hugh is *too* charming. And *too* handsome. And everything else besides. How will I ever pull off a convincing pretence that I've never met him before? He's my fiancé, after all!'

'How indeed,' Clifford whispered back, before raising his voice as a couple passed them.

'Taking the train to Penscombe and back is a less arduous way to view the local scenery than driving in these adverse conditions, my lady. The station is through this gate.'

The couple gone, Eleanor bit her lip. 'Might you have one helpful suggestion up your butlering sleeves? Or do I just have to hope my face won't give me away?'

'Which it invariably does...' He shifted Tomkins' kitty kit bag further up his shoulder to better stroke an imaginary beard. 'However, perhaps one might emulate the traditional Christmas game of charades?'

She nodded. Catching the sound of animated chatter not far behind, she marched through the gate, Gladstone's lead looped around her wrist. 'Follow the plume of steam, do we?'

'Indeed, my lady. The line, built in 1873, runs from Lostenev to Penscombe. Designed to haul granite from the local works, shortly after its completion, a larger, more profitable works was established fifteen miles away. Three years later, it was sold off for a mere nine guineas. It now operates mostly to carry mail and goods between the two places.'

She looked the carriages over. 'So are you imagining I'll enjoy riding among the mail sacks or the fish crates most?'

'Neither.' He pointed along the platform. 'There are several passenger carriages at the other end.'

'Well, let's get good seats. The terrible two will enjoy looking out of the window as well.' She started towards the tiny booking office. 'Come on, Clifford. You can ogle the locomotive once we've got our tickets.'

As she crossed the threshold, however, she spied the dashingly broad-shouldered vision of her fiancé at the ticket window. Even sporting an unfamiliar grey wool overcoat and a matching peaked cap over his chestnut curls instead of his customary bowler, there was no mistaking him as the man she'd fallen for. But before she could join the queue behind him, Gladstone slipped his lead from her hand and charged over.

Dash it, Ellie. We forgot Gladstone would give the game away! He adores Hugh.

Even Tomkins scrabbled a paw out of his padded window as Clifford strode over. 'I do apologise, sir. The bulldog has never quite learned the etiquette of meeting strangers,' he said, far more convincingly than she could have managed.

'So I see,' her fiancé said, equally plausibly as he hadn't turned around.

'Clifford,' she said firmly. 'I wish to see every inch of this delightful stretch along the coast. For my, umm...' She stared down at the sketchbook and pencil roll he slipped into her hand. 'Artistic studies.'

'Commendable dedication, my lady.' With a firm grip on

the whining Gladstone's lead, Clifford stepped over to the counter, tipping his hat to the ticket master. Eleanor followed, spinning around halfway to address the supposed stranger. 'I'm not jumping the queue, I hope?'

'Not a bit, madam. I have my tickets.' Her fiancé turned with a polite nod, hat in hand. 'Good afternoon, incidentally.'

'Can one have an incidental afternoon?' she mused. 'Perhaps one can. Mr...?'

'Wellener. Miles Wellener.'

She played dumb that his chosen pseudonym struck her as hilarious. 'Lady Swift.' She offered him her hand, which he released far too quickly for her skipping heart. That he was also oblivious to the admiring glances from the group of women shuffling in behind made her smile as well.

Clifford appeared between them, raising a finger at the sound of the engine's piercing whistle. 'The train is leaving shortly, my lady. This way.'

A few minutes later, she found herself ensconced in a quaintly appointed four-seater compartment, diagonally opposite the fictitious Mr Wellener, deep in a perfectly natural exchange for two strangers. Save for the eager licking her bulldog was straining to give him.

'Good afternoon, ladies,' Clifford said smoothly to the gaggle of women as they crowded into the doorway, all eager to grab the other seats. 'Allow me to assist with your bags.' He herded them onwards. 'The larger compartment along there will accommodate us all far more comfortably.'

'Ooh, we're spoilt for fine gentlemen today, girls!' one of them tittered loudly.

'My butler is indeed totally incorrigible with the fairer sex,' she said loud enough for him to hear.

'All aboard!' cried the station master.

As Clifford left with the women, Eleanor pulled her coat

around her and smiled at her companion. 'Do feel free to slide the door shut, Mr Wellener. It's decidedly chilly.'

Having done so, Seldon glanced up and down the corridor, discreetly running an affectionate hand over her bulldog and tomcat behind his back. He folded his athletic frame back into his seat.

'Hello, Eleanor,' he said quietly, without looking at her. 'You look radiantly beautiful, as ever. Even with a cherry-red nose.'

She busied herself with her sketchbook. 'Hello, Hugh. You look too delicious for words in your new coat and hat.'

His deep rich chuckle echoed against the glass. 'Actually, I was aiming for a convincing estate agent, so I can ask around about your Mr Cunliffe's Gwel an Mor.'

'Albeit a rather tired one who needs a week's worth of my cook's fine meals.'

'Good. Because I'm here on doctor's orders.' He shook his head at her gasp. 'I mean Miles Wellener is.'

This time she couldn't help but laugh. 'Of all the names you could have picked!'

He produced a newspaper from inside his coat and pretended to wrestle with the pages. 'What's wrong with it?'

'Because, if we got married, I would be Mrs Eleanor Wellener. It's such a mouthful!'

He risked dropping the newspaper an inch. 'Darling, I rather thought I'd marry you as Hugh Seldon.'

Her shoulders rose. 'Oh good. I like him enormously.'

'Even though he's just a policeman?'

'I'm totally in awe of what you do, silly, as you well know. And I'm sorry to call you down to help. But at least I'll get to see you for some of Christmas. And, it's actually rather fun playing strangers, wouldn't you say?'

'No.' He stared at her hands. 'It's complete torture. All I want to do is scoop you into my arms and hold you until New Year. After asking, of course.'

She felt her cheeks flush. 'We're engaged, Hugh. You don't need to ask.'

He sighed. 'I meant ask how it is that I let you out of my sight for two minutes and you are knee deep in dead bodies? Again!'

'It's only one. Which is one too many, I concede.'

Clifford came to her rescue, appearing in the corridor. She waved him inside. He closed the door and sat down with a shudder.

'A timely escape on my part, my lady.'

She laughed. 'It's your own fault for turning on your inimitable charm.'

Seldon smiled. 'Blast it! I wish I had nothing better to do but ride around and listen to you two squabble. It's very entertaining. But you'd better bring me up to speed quickly or we'll be back in Lostenev before we know it.'

With Clifford filling in where needed, she recounted events while Seldon's pen flew across the pages of his notebook behind the newspaper. She kept quiet about the roller incident, however, to save him from worrying any more than she knew he would already.

Once she'd finished, he tapped the last entry.

'Poison? So it's definitely murder now!' He looked at Eleanor with deep concern and sighed. 'Right. Let's run through the suspects you've got so far. Starting with Cunliffe's maid as she is the only one with an alibi for the time of St Clair's death that the police have been able to verify.' He checked his notes. 'It seems she was visiting her sick mother?'

Eleanor nodded. 'Correct. Which is why Clifford is standing in as my maid.'

Seldon's lips twitched. 'Sincere sympathies, Clifford. Now. Dewi Odgers and Tristan Brae, under-gardeners, alibi only verified by each other. Motive: that Mr St Clair was "disturbing the garden's spirits". Really?'

'We are in Cornwall, Chief Inspector,' Clifford said. 'Super-stition and folklore are taken *very* seriously.'

'Very well. They still seem the least likely to my mind if we are working on the assumption that St Clair was killed in a case of mistaken identity?'

'Agreed,' Eleanor said as Clifford rose to help Gladstone up beside Tomkins so they could enjoy the passing view, paws together on the window.

'There is another possible motive, Hugh,' Eleanor said. 'I got the distinct impression that St Clair's arrival upset some-thing they had going on. Something illegal.'

'I see. Any idea so far what?' She shook her head. 'Okay, something to investigate further, maybe, although it might be completely unrelated. Next, Mr Cunliffe's nephew, Edwin Marsh. No substantiated alibi. Now the sisters...' He glanced at his notes. 'Flora and Clara Cunliffe claimed they saw Marsh creeping through the garden.'

'Yes. But he claims it was actually one of the under-gardeners and his aunts are as blind as bats. Isn't that right, Clifford?'

'Regrettably not. It's a popular misconception about bats.'

'Clifford!'

Seldon hid a smile. 'So Marsh appears to have no motive for killing St Clair. Unless, that is, he mistook him for his uncle and was trying to get rid of Cunliffe so he could... inherit the house, perhaps?'

Eleanor frowned. 'Good call. The inheritance passes to the male heir, I found out.' She frowned. 'Maybe Cunliffe was lying when he told me he hadn't the heart to throw Marsh out, though?'

Seldon looked up from making a note. 'Can you find out?' She nodded. 'Good. Then on to the aunts themselves, Clara and Flora.' He frowned. 'You said they're properly elderly, Eleanor?'

'And nuttier than Christmas cake.' She shook her head at Clifford's sniff. 'Which is true and works as an analogy. But Marsh said he was watching them snooping at their window, so if he isn't lying, that's their alibi substantiated.'

'And,' Seldon said, 'if they killed St Clair by mistake for Cunliffe in an effort to get the house, they'd have to kill Marsh as well. And I can't imagine they would have found it particularly easy to push a man off a cliff at their age, even if he was incapacitated after being poisoned.' He tapped his notebook. 'We need to concretely ascertain the beneficiaries of Cunliffe's will. In the meantime, when finding out if Mr Cunliffe has actually asked, or threatened, for Marsh to leave, can you also find out the same for Flora and Clara?'

'We can try.'

'Remaining staff, then. The Liddicoats.'

Eleanor wrinkled her nose. 'She seems alright, but he's a surly sort.'

He nodded. 'And their only alibi seems to be each other.'

'But Mr Liddicoat likely has a motive for murdering St Clair, according to the under-gardeners.'

He jerked straighter. 'Which is?'

'St Clair was trying to entice Mrs Liddicoat between his sheets.'

Seldon's cheeks coloured. 'Really?'

She nodded. 'I'll investigate further. Decorously and discreetly,' she added huffily at Clifford and Seldon's joint look.

'Ah!' Seldon buried his head back in his newspaper. 'Moving on. Any trouble between Mr Cunliffe and the Liddicoats you're aware of?'

'Yes! He disapproves heartily of married staff. But they were there when he inherited the house.'

Clifford cleared his throat. 'Perhaps Mr Cunliffe is keen for everyone to leave so that he might sell the house?'

Eleanor nodded. 'And move back to London. Brilliant, Clifford! He told me the restoration had cost a fortune, like the gardens will. And that he wished he'd never moved down here.'

Seldon looked up from his notebook. 'Excellent, well done, both! But there's much more you need to find out.'

'No problem, Hugh. Although... hang on. If Mr Cunliffe is trying to sell the house, Marsh, the aunts and the Liddicoats will all be in the same boat. Maybe they've joined forces and are all trying to kill him, together?'

'And whoever was appointed assassin, as it were, mistook St Clair for him?' Seldon see-sawed his head. 'I have come across something similar in a few cases over the years. Very few, though.'

Clifford whipped out his pocket watch. 'Four minutes until we arrive back at Lostenev, Chief Inspector.'

'Quick then. Mr Cunliffe himself,' Seldon said. 'He has no alibi. He found the body. And not only believed St Clair was plotting to seize his gardens over some sort of devil worship, but that he was attempting to kill him as well.' He held his hands up. 'I'm sorry, but it sounds like he's covering his actions. Deadly ones at that.'

Eleanor sighed. 'I know. But why would he send a letter to Clifford? Why would he want him, or me, down here if he intended to kill...?' She winced at Seldon's look. 'Of course. To cover himself.'

Seldon nodded. 'The timing is suspicious, too. Having told him roughly when you'd arrive—'

'He kills St Clair just before.' She shook her head. 'That might be correct, but something very odd was definitely going on with St Clair in the last few weeks.'

Seldon listened intently as she detailed the notebook and burnt remains of the landscape plan for the gardens they had unearthed.

'And I thought I was supposed to be the detective,' he said appreciatively.

Clifford's eyes twinkled. 'Actually, Master Gladstone's unruliness was responsible for the latter discovery.'

Seldon laughed and whispered to her bulldog, 'Well done, old friend!' He turned back to Eleanor and Clifford. 'Actually though, that maybe tallies with the only snippet I've found out so far. From the landlady of the inn. I was asking casually if any people outside of the village frequent it. Helpfully, she immediately mentioned Gwel an Mor.'

Eleanor nodded eagerly.

'None of the family ever visit her establishment,' Seldon continued. 'Not even the nephew, Marsh, which you might imagine he would. Younger chap, unmarried. Spending every day with his elders, like that. But St Clair, he was a regular. And, she just happened to mention he'd started out as the cheery newcomer. "More chat than a whole shoal of sprats," as she put it. But in recent weeks, he'd taken more and more to sitting alone, away from the bar, staring into his pint or poring over a notebook.'

'But that's got to be related, Hugh!'

'Possibly, Eleanor. Men can be affected by lots of things.'

'Yes, but they don't normally show it!'

Seldon fiddled with his tie. 'Look. Maybe we are wrong and Mr Cunliffe has told you the truth. If St Clair *was* acting out of character recently, he might have had some sort of breakdown. Possibly due to occult practices. Possibly not. Maybe he burned his plan to make sure Cunliffe couldn't use his design after he was gone. And then poisoned himself.'

'And then threw himself off the cliff?' she said sceptically.

He grimaced. 'A ritual suicide. Those, I have definitely come across before. Two methods of death are often employed. The second as a backup. Hence why it sprang to mind. If St Clair had jumped but just broken a fair few bones, the poison would have made sure he was still killed. Or the other way around.'

She shivered. 'As if one wasn't a grisly enough way to go!'

'Lostenev is approaching, Chief Inspector.'

Seldon rose.

'Quick then,' Eleanor said. 'Clifford and I will grill the family and staff and Mr Cunliffe to see if anything supports our theory of there being a power struggle for the house.'

'Very carefully,' Seldon said firmly. 'And I'll contact my office and have checks made on St Clair, particularly in regards to links with any known occult groups. I'll also get them to check everyone else at Gwel an Mor. Plus, I'll find out what I can in the village about St Clair and the under-gardeners.'

'Wait, Hugh. Are you actually staying at the Kerensa Come Quick?' At his nod, she laughed. '"Kerensa" means "love" in Cornish. So watch the landlady, Hugh. She was all over Clifford like a rash.'

The train lurched to a stop.

'Look after Eleanor for me,' Seldon hissed as Clifford opened the door to the platform and stepped out.

Seldon pretended to fold his newspaper so he could squeeze her hand underneath. 'Please be careful, my *kerensa*,' he whispered, and was gone.

19

'You can open your eyes now, Clifford,' Eleanor said, only partly in jest. They'd left the train station in Lostenev and gone straight back to the Rolls where they'd parked it just outside the village. She tried to peer beyond the flurry of snowflakes defeating the windscreen wipers. 'Just that one last tricky bend to navigate and I'll have got us back to Gwel an Mor's front door. Assuming,' she muttered, 'we can find it at the rate this snow is covering everything.'

'Bravo, my lady.' Clifford's voice held an uncharacteristic hint of relief. 'I anticipated conditions might deteriorate dramatically, but not that Mr Liddicoat would not have troubled himself to clear even part of the driveway.'

'We would still have gone to secretly meet Hugh on that scenic train ride, whatever the weather threw at us.' The joy of having seen her fiancé faded as quickly as it came. 'Dash it, though, he's right. It's torture having to stay apart like this.'

'Heartening news, my lady.'

She risked glancing away from the road ahead to see if he was teasing her.

He shook his head, his tone softening. 'Because it means the gentleman truly is the one to have mended the hole in your heart.'

Before she could reply, she braked hard. Fortunately, the Rolls slid to a stately halt inches from the bonnets of two police cars. She let out a sigh of relief.

'Missed them! Inspector Trevilick's men must still be here. I'd better hurry and check on Mr Cunliffe.' She groaned. 'And I thought he was hard work before.'

Slinking past the echo of police boots and voices further down the main hallway, she tried a series of doors before finding her host pacing the library. Instead of floor-to-ceiling bookcases packed with well-thumbed leather tomes like her uncle's library, the sparse reading material here was locked in lead-latticed, glass-fronted cabinets. The only chairs were of the stiff-backed, armless variety, certainly not inviting one to curl up for a cosy afternoon's reading. Even the four sprigs of holly gracing the two windowsills had the air of being the Christmas decorations found at the bottom of the box.

'This house is full of surprises,' she said brightly, stepping in and pointing at the incongruously gold-painted plaster roses of the inset ceiling.

Cunliffe turned to eye her ruefully over his wire-rimmed spectacles. 'Yet none of them pleasant ones, Lady Swift.'

Given the vehemence of his tone, she had the feeling her presence might be among the ones he was referring to. She pressed on regardless. She had a murder to solve. 'I see you've other unexpected visitors. How are you faring?'

His lips set in a thin line. '*Intruders*, not visitors. I do not appreciate them marauding about my house. As I have told them repeatedly, to no avail. But as to your question, I am faring perfectly well, naturally. A gentleman always does. Particularly one blessed with intelligence and an unwavering grasp on his faculties. Unlike that fool of an inspector!'

'Ah. So Trevilick is here too.'

'Yes! And poking his unwelcome nose into any corner of my home he sees fit to sully with his preposterous assertion.' He struck the top of the desk with the flat of his palm. 'This would never be considered acceptable in London!'

Clifford glided in carrying a small silver tray.

'Assertion,' Cunliffe continued, 'which is beyond ridiculous!' He glanced coldly at her butler. 'What is it, man?'

'A warming beverage for her ladyship, sir. And a digestive tonic which I took the liberty of preparing for yourself, given that your afternoon constitution has likely been interrupted?'

'Well, of course it has,' Cunliffe grumbled, having the manners to wait for Eleanor to take hers before scooping up his glass and sniffing it pointedly. 'Where's Mrs Liddicoat, then?'

'Rather occupied with the police, sir.'

'Ridiculous!'

Eleanor caught her butler's mouthed, 'Fortitude, my lady.' Thinking this was going to require every last screed she could muster, and she might still be found wanting, she took a glug of her drink.

'What is Inspector's Trevilick's "assertion"? Aside from being ridiculous, to your mind, Mr Cunliffe?'

'It is nothing to do with my mind, Lady Swift,' he snapped. 'The inspector's is clearly addled. He is determined that St Clair was poisoned.'

'Gracious!' she said innocently. 'But surely that must be a modicum of comfort for you?'

She gritted her teeth at his condescending look while somehow keeping her smile in place.

'How can it be a comfort for me? The man I engaged to fulfil my plans is no longer able to do so. And my reputation is being besmirched by the presence of uniformed buffoons blundering about my house!'

'Upsetting, of course. But your original concern that St Clair was trying to kill you has been removed, since he is, well, dead. As has the possibility that he was murdered after being mistaken for you.'

'I fail to see how the latter applies,' he barked.

She held his gaze. 'Simple. It seems most unlikely St Clair was mistakenly poisoned *and* mistakenly pushed off a cliff instead of you, Mr Cunliffe. It doesn't make sense.'

He rolled his eyes. 'No. It doesn't. Which is my point entirely. St Clair was *not* poisoned. Either the inspector is even more of a fool than I suspected from the outset, or he is lying. Which, having thought it over, I am now convinced he is.'

Goodness, he's positively raving now, Ellie.

'Well, I just hope this awful matter won't ruin your long-term plans. I mean, anyone in your position might think of leaving and—'

Cunliffe glared at her over the rim of his glass. 'What if I have thought of it? A man's decisions are his own business.'

'Absolutely. Sometimes one just has to make a hard choice, no matter the result. Your aunts and nephew would miss you terribly though, I'm sure. And the Liddicoats.'

He snorted loudly in reply, his back to her as he stared out of the window at the falling snow.

'Only your company, I meant,' she said hurriedly. 'Since they were coping fine before you inherited Gwel an Mor and moved down here. Unless, of course, you were to sell the house?'

Cunliffe spun around, his features livid. 'An excellent suggestion, Lady Swift. If that other buffoon I was lumbered with hadn't made a mess of that as well!'

Her brow creased. 'Who are you referring to, Mr Cunliffe?'

'A... a former relative of mine. In his infinite wisdom, he had the deeds altered to include a clause which stipulates' – he held up a shaky finger – 'that the family have the right to reside here in perpetuum! Thus, it cannot be sold if there is even one relative living on the premises. Let alone three!'

He jumped at the sharp rap on the door.

'Come!'

Inspector Trevilick walked in.

'Ah! Mr Cunliffe, I came to tell you—'

'More nonsense, no doubt,' he snapped.

Trevilick raised an eyebrow but kept his tone level. 'That various items have been removed by my men on my orders. From Mr St Clair's office, and his bedroom. Along with others from the kitchens, here in the house itself.'

'My house!' Cunliffe spluttered.

'So I understand it to be, sir, yes. Now, did Mr St Clair take any meals in the house?'

Cunliffe eyed him coldly. 'Naturally. At least, for a while.'

'So what happened "after a while"?'

'He stopped, obviously. Of his own accord,' Cunliffe added hastily. 'A few weeks ago, actually. In fact, he stopped coming into the house at all unless I summoned him.'

'Thank you, that will be all for now. Before I leave, however, I would like a moment with Lady Swift.'

Cunliffe gripped his temples and grumbled from the room. Clifford closed the door and then busied himself with flicking a gloved finger along the leaded glass panes as if inspecting for dust.

'Hello again, Inspector,' Eleanor said. 'Twice in one afternoon is twice as unexpected, you know.'

Trevilick's lips pursed. 'What were you and Mr Cunliffe talking about before I came in, please?'

'Things. Mostly.'

He put his hands behind his back. 'Lady Swift, you can tell me here, or in the police station. Your choice.'

Not appreciating his bullish manner, she smiled sweetly. 'Actually, Inspector, as it was a private conversation, I can choose not to tell you wherever I am. However, I appreciate you are merely doing your job. So, we were talking about the fact that St Clair was poisoned. Not that Mr Cunliffe considers that a fact at all.'

Trevilick snorted. 'Then I'll spare you having to tell me exactly how he described my methods and ask you something else instead. If I may?' he added with a slight smile.

She nodded. 'Of course.'

'The wheel track on the cliff path which ended where Mr St Clair went over...'

'What wheel track?'

She looked questioningly at Clifford, who shrugged almost imperceptibly in reply.

'I was unaware of any imprint on the path along the cliff, my lady, wheeled or otherwise.'

Trevilick tapped his nose. 'As I expected. It wasn't very pronounced. And the light was fading fast when you "happened" to be there, pretending you weren't investigating.'

She let that go. 'Credit for being so observant, Inspector. But you said "wheel track" in the singular. That could only have been made by a bicycle or... yes!' She clicked her fingers. 'A wheelbarrow! From the gardens here. That's it, isn't it?'

He nodded approvingly. 'I've never been able to see a woman's mind actually working before. But that was like sitting inside, watching the cogs.'

Clifford cleared his throat. 'Not always an advisable or comfortable seat to choose.'

'Thank you for the warning, Mr Clifford.'

Eleanor raised a finger. 'Now, I have a question for you, Inspector. Why didn't you mention this before? Or point it out at the time?'

'Because I didn't think anything of it at the time, Lady Swift. It struck me that the gardeners would probably sometimes dump their prunings and what-have-yous outside of the gardens to save the bother of burning them. But driving back up here—'

'You were ruminating on the coroner's verdict and realised St Clair's body could have been moved fairly easily in a wheelbarrow! Which explains the conundrum in Clifford's trigonometry calculations. St Clair didn't fall or jump. He was tipped over the cliff!'

20

With Inspector Trevilick having finally rounded up his men, Eleanor watched discreetly through the library window until the two police cars had crawled out of sight down the snow-covered driveway.

'Right!'

She set off down the confusion of corridors towards the main hallway, where she met her butler.

'Ready, Clifford?'

He nodded. 'Masters Gladstone and Tomkins are safely ensconced in their quilted kingdom in your sitting room, my lady, snoozing off their generous portions of Christmas Eve treats.'

'Cooked lovingly by Mrs Trotman, and which you had the uncanny foresight to bring along, I see. That's wonderful. It means we're free to find the wheelbarrow that might have been the vehicle for St Clair's last ignominious journey.'

'Indeed. An unexpected turn in an already perplexing conundrum. Though I cannot imagine that the police will not have checked them all.'

'Yes. The ones they found, which might not be all of them

because I now remember seeing one tucked away somewhere. Or at least two handles that looked like they belonged to one. But where, dash it?' She tapped her forehead, trying to picture it more clearly. 'It was just after our brush with the roller.'

'In the ornamental thicket, perhaps then?'

'That's it! When we tried to search for whoever set that garden roller charging down the slope at me. I just glimpsed two handles in that thicket. But wooden ones, not metal like on the barrows the under-gardeners were using.'

'Yet we cannot be certain the fatal one wasn't found. The police were very thorough. Or maybe we can?' he added at her knowing look.

'Maybe. Trevilick's men certainly didn't load one into either police car before leaving. Unlike the two crates of glass jars filled with what I assume were samples to be tested for poison. So I intend to check every barrow we can find thoroughly. Now come on, we—'

She put her finger to her lips at the sound of trilling voices.

'And those that were good shall be happy, Flora, they'll sit in a golden chair...'

'They'll splash at a ten-league canvas, Clara, with brushes of comet's hair.'

Eleanor glanced around the alcove to see Mr Cunliffe's aunts huddled together along the corridor, both peering through lorgnette spectacles at a large portrait of an artist at work. She motioned for Clifford to follow her lead. Stepping out, she pointed at the framed landscape in oils on the opposite wall.

'I should like to commission something just like this, Clifford. But of Henley Hall, obviously. It's rather reminiscent of— Oh, good afternoon, ladies.' She smiled as if surprised to see the matching indigo taffeta-clad sisters who had paused at the next painting. 'You're enjoying this remarkable collection, too?'

'It's nephews all over,' Clara said earnestly. 'But we've made the best of it, you see?'

Fearing she might not even after the pair had explained, she tried to word her reply to cover all possibilities.

'Do you mean Mr Cunliffe? Or Mr Marsh, your great-nephew?'

'Pfoof! Beans in pods,' Flora huffed. She polished the glass of her spectacles on the silk fringing of her sister's matching scarf, then turned back to the seascape. Eleanor waited. And then waited some more.

'You were saying, ladies? About nephews?'

Clara clapped her hands. 'In which it seemed always afternoon. All round the coast the languid air did swoon.'

'Really, dear!' her sister chided. 'That's cheating.'

They both stared expectantly at Eleanor.

'Do you think it is?' Clara said sharply.

Clifford's amused arch of a brow in reply to Eleanor's pleading glance for help was no help at all.

'Umm, I'm not entirely sure I've grasped the rules?' She smiled hopefully. 'Does it have to do with nephews at all?'

They shook their heads, making their long, beaded necklaces rattle.

Now completely lost, Eleanor decided she had nothing to lose. 'Do forgive me, by the way. I should have said at the start that I hope you weren't too shaken by the police being here again?'

'Horrible man!' they shrilled together.

'And he brought more boots!' Flora cried.

'Boots, boots, boots! And voices like hungry drains,' Clara said vehemently. 'Neither one came to check on us, of course. Yet again.'

'Nephews, finally, perchance?' Clifford murmured to Eleanor.

'Maybe Mr Cunliffe and Mr Marsh were both too busy with the police?' she said hurriedly.

Tutting, the sisters stepped past her to a painting a little further along.

Momentarily closing her eyes and taking a deep breath, she followed them. *No more time for pleasantries, Ellie. You need to get their attention.*

'Ladies, the police did have a good reason to search the house. Mr St Clair was... *poisoned!*'

'Obviously,' Flora said airily, without taking her eyes off the painting.

'Obviously?' Eleanor stuttered.

This is hopeless, Ellie. You can't rely on a single word they've uttered since you met them. She stiffened. *Or can you?*

'Ladies. When did you learn Mr St Clair had been poisoned? Did the police tell you?'

Clara shook her head. 'We knew it before that horrible man and his boots came stomping around again.'

'And we know who is responsible,' Flora said.

Eleanor's mouth dropped. 'For poisoning Mr St Clair?'

'Yes, dear,' Flora said pityingly, as if to a dim child. 'Mrs Liddicoat did, didn't she, Clara?'

Her sister nodded. 'Naturally, Flora. They bit the babies in the cradles...'

'And licked the soup from the cooks' own ladles!' Flora chimed in.

Eleanor looked between them. 'You sound very sure.'

Clara gave her a pitying glance. 'Well, naturally. She's poisoning us all.'

'Me and Clara, Godfrey and Edwin,' Flora said slowly, as if talking to a dim-witted child again. 'To keep the house, don't you see?'

'With that awful man, Mr Liddicoat.'

Eleanor caught Clifford's encouraging look. 'Ladies. Are you saying the Liddicoats believe they will inherit Gwel an Mor if they poison you all? Because, surely—'

'Not the house, dear. The cottage.' Flora beckoned her along the passageway. With Clara's arm linked in hers, she stopped at a nondescript framed oil depicting a tumbledown stone house set in a dark wood. 'There is a house with ivied walls, and mullioned windows, worn and old. And the long dwellers in those halls...' The sisters turned expectantly again to Eleanor, who could only stare back blankly.

'Have souls that know but sordid calls,' Clifford intoned.

Eleanor threw him a grateful look, still none the wiser. 'Are you saying, ladies, that the Liddicoats are poisoning you so they can stay in their cottage? Because if you were...'

Flora smiled. 'All dead, dear, yes?'

This is one of the most bizarre conversations you've ever had, Ellie.

'Then the new owners would surely just evict the Liddicoats? Unless, I suppose, they wanted them to stay on as staff.'

Clara shook her head even more firmly than her sister had. 'Nobody would want them. The two of them despise work. So, when we are all gone, they'll have none to do. Forever free, free, they'll be. Secure in a cottage, lazy as can be.'

Flora tittered at Eleanor's increasingly confused expression. 'It's very simple, dear. It's written in the deeds to Gwel an Mor that the Liddicoats and their descendants—'

'Awful descendants!'

'Yes, Clara, awful descendants, can live in their cottage forever just as we can in the main house.'

Eleanor stared between the sisters, her mind reeling. 'So where does Mr St Clair, and him being poisoned, fit into any of this?'

'Fortune didn't favour his constitution, dear,' Flora said. 'Not like the family's.'

Clara nodded knowingly. 'We've eaten here so long, you see. Poison comes as our daily three. Breakfast, lunch and even tea. But not so Mr St Clair.'

Before Eleanor could reply, Clara grabbed her sister's arm and spun her around. 'I've thought of just the one, Flora. Sunset and evening star. And one clear call for me!'

'And may there be no moaning of the bar when I put out to sea.'

They giggled while walking away down the corridor.

'So delightful you're staying for dinner, dear,' Clara called as they disappeared around the corner.

With them gone, Eleanor threw her head back and let out a long breath. 'I fear, Clifford, that I might spend my entire Christmas here playing cuckoo games with those sisters!'

He gave her an admonishing look. 'Character assassinations of one's elders—'

'They're as batty as a couple of fruitcakes, as I think I said before.'

'As I remarked earlier, their word game means we were treated to Rudyard Kipling, Lord Alfred Tennyson, Robert Browning, I believe, plus Thomas Hardy. And Aunt Clara,' he ended wryly. 'Quite impressive for a "couple of elderly fruitcakes".'

Her brows knitted. 'Mmm. Being able to pull out memorised lines like that, and make them up on the moment, suggests they may be rather sounder of mind than we originally thought?'

'Ahem, my lady. If I might be excused from being included in such defamation? However, as you are asking my opinion, then, yes. It is my belief the ladies are quite sane. Well, largely sane.'

'Sane enough for murder?'

'Perhaps, my lady.'

'But what about their insistence that the whole family is being poisoned?'

He cocked his head. 'Well, Mr Cunliffe is likewise convinced that he was being poisoned. And it seems Mr St

Clair *was* poisoned, although after he stopped coming to meals, which perhaps contradicts the ladies' statement?' He pursed his lips.

She regarded him quizzically. 'Clifford, you're looking decidedly uncomfortable. Which means you're thinking as I am. About those clauses added to the will, assuming that's true. And given Mr Cunliffe's own admission that the family has the right to stay in the main house...' She waved a coaxing hand.

'It is possible the Liddicoats are indeed afforded the same privilege regarding the cottage. Unless all of them were removed, as it were, this house and grounds could not be sold. And Mr Cunliffe let slip he heartily desires returning to London.'

She nodded. 'So, I'll say it for both of us. If there is a mass poisoner loose in Gwel an Mor, it is most likely Mr Cunliffe himself!'

21

'I have checked, my lady.' Clifford removed his bowler hat and brushed the fresh snow from it. 'Mr Cunliffe's car is no longer parked in the garage.'

Eleanor stamped her feet against the cold. 'Well, he must have gone for something fearfully important to venture out in this increasingly icy weather. Especially on Christmas Eve.' She stared along the muddle of tyre marks snaking away down the drive, watching them fill with the thickly falling white flakes. 'But at least he's out of the way for the moment. Now, we know St Clair was definitely murdered. And poisoned at that. So, I suggest we search his office again. But first of all, let's scour that thicket for the barrow.'

'Agreed. And perhaps keep a watch out for wayward rollers?'

She glanced at his injured arm and grimaced. 'Absolutely!'

As they passed the Liddicoats' cottage, she paused. 'I wonder?'

'Wonder what, my lady?'

She tutted. 'Have a moment of patience, Clifford. It's usually your most favourite thing in the world.'

She took his sniff as being assent and continued scanning the windows. As she did, she felt a respectful tap on her wrist.

'Might one enquire what we are waiting for?'

'Not what, Clifford, who. We're checking if Mr Liddicoat is home or not.'

'Not. He is chopping logs for the Christmas Day luncheon as per Mr Cunliffe's orders. Albeit with little enthusiasm. Listen.'

It was only then she caught the dull repetitive thud of an axe striking wood in the distance.

'Well, if you'd said so before...' She shrugged. 'Yes, I know, if I'd asked before. Anyway, I thought it might be a good time to try and speak to Mrs Liddicoat again, without her brute of a husband bullying her into silence. I know what I said before, but it's worth a go. With her, anyway.'

She headed for the cottage door and knocked smartly. A moment later, the housekeeper opened the door a crack. Wary eyes looked back at her.

'Yes, m'lady?'

'I'm looking for Mr Cunliffe.'

The housekeeper's eyes widened. 'He's not here. Never once stepped in here, he hasn't!'

'That's very surprising. After all, you've lived here for how long?'

'From the start.'

'Really? Since you were employed here, do you mean? But how long is that? Just out of curiosity?'

The housekeeper fiddled with the lace frill of her dark conservative dress. 'I meant, the tide came in for my mother in this house. Just as it did for her mother.'

'So...? Oh, I see. I think. Your family were here in service as housekeepers two generations before. How marvellous.'

'Perhaps, m'lady.'

'No, definitely. It's as marvellous as Mr Cunliffe being so

broad-minded. I must say it seems surprising he's happy to keep a married couple on his staff.'

Mrs Liddicoat stiffened.

'He moved here ten years ago, didn't he?' Eleanor pressed. 'You must have got to know him well by now. Would you say he was, well, an easy-going employer?'

The housekeeper eyed her suspiciously. 'Mr Cunliffe, he's a... he's one for wantin' things done just as he's used to.'

'Which isn't much like delightfully sleepy Cornwall, I bet! London simply couldn't be more opposite. It must have been hard for him to adjust. Or maybe he never did? Perhaps he's mentioned returning there? Or of selling Gwel an Mor?'

'It's not my business to encourage chitterin' from him, nor any other, m'lady.' Mrs Liddicoat's red knuckles tightened as she gripped the door, her tone icier than the weather. 'Now, seein' I'm more behind than all the cows' tails, and Mr Liddicoat'll be needin' me soon.'

The door slammed shut. Eleanor ignored the snort of outrage from her butler at the woman's rudeness towards her and raised her fist to knock. But then she lowered it.

You've more important things to do first, Ellie.

She shrugged at Clifford and continued towards St Clair's office. A moment later, however, she ducked into the shadows of a large weeping willow.

'A worthy diversion to our plan, I have no doubt,' he murmured stiffly, following her. 'However, given that "indecorous" and "compromising" appear to be inherent elements, might one ask what we are doing, my lady?'

'Man on the opposite path,' she murmured. 'Creeping towards the cottage. Fifty yards.'

Risking a quick peep between the branches, she caught the man rake a thick forelock of hair from his face. 'It's Marsh!'

They watched Cunliffe's nephew slinking along the

shadows to the side of the cottage. His knock was swiftly answered, and he slid inside.

'I would have never imagined a man like him would hobnob with the staff, Clifford,' she whispered.

'Quite.'

Silently, the two of them stole out from the canopy and, keeping in the shadows, returned to the Liddicoats' cottage. Crouching down behind a rain butt, they both strained an ear towards the open window.

'Nothing changes, I tell you,' Marsh's clipped voice sounded tense. 'We continue with the shipments as planned.'

'And I say it's too risky!' a rough voice said.

'Mr Liddicoat!' Eleanor mouthed to Clifford, who nodded.

'Nonsense!' Marsh replied cooly. 'Just hold your nerve, man.'

'Easy for you to say,' Liddicoat said gruffly. 'But that nosy sow and her stuffed shirt been hangin' around here botherin' my missus.'

'Let them. Couldn't care less.'

'But they was askin' questions. It's too risky, I said!'

Marsh's childish laugh made Eleanor's skin prickle. 'It's not risky, Liddicoat. They are a blessing. Don't you see?'

'What I see is that they'll find—'

'Nothing except what we want them to. I've been trying to think of a way to get rid of dear old Uncle since I got here.'

Mr Liddicoat laughed sardonically. 'You'll never shift old Cunliffe.'

'Precisely! But that nosy sow and her stuffed shirt just might! If they root around enough, maybe they'll find "evidence" that Uncle Cunliffe killed St Clair. Evidence we might even have a hand in ourselves. And then I'll be rid of him.'

Eleanor's hand flew to her mouth.

'I still don't like it,' Liddicoat replied sulkily.

'Remember, we're in this together,' Marsh snapped. 'If one of us goes down, we all go down.'

A moment later, Marsh slid out of the back door and set off in the direction he'd come. Eleanor waited until he'd faded from sight and waved for Clifford to silently follow her away from the cottage.

Once they were a safe distance, she turned to him.

'So it seems the under-gardeners are not the only ones running their own little racket up here. I wonder what those "shipments" they referred to are.'

'Possibly smuggled goods coming in? I doubt if Cornwall has entirely turned its back on its murky heritage.'

'Mmm. But that wasn't what worried me, Clifford.'

'Indeed not, my lady,' he said sombrely. 'It was, perhaps, the reference to you and I unwittingly, or at least unwillingly, being instruments of Mr Cunliffe's... er, undoing.'

She shook her head unhappily. 'Well, what can we do?'

'What we always do, my lady. Find out the truth, and let justice take its course.'

She sighed. 'True. Now, let's leave any more discussion until we speak with Hugh. We've a barrow to find...'

A few minutes later, she glanced around the last row of topiary chess pieces. The light spilling from the rear windows of the main house seemed brighter, its yellow fingers reaching further than she remembered.

'Reflecting on the snow, my lady,' Clifford said, as if having read her mind. 'Extra caution therefore needed.'

'Yes. But I've got a hunch something else might see us, anyway. At least I hope so.'

'Some *thing*?'

'The peacock that frightened the life out of me when we were in that thicket last. Might he roost in the same tree each night?'

'Possibly.'

'Good. Because I've remembered that I only saw the barrow handles at all because I spun around in fright when it screeched above my head.'

Clifford handed her a torch of her own. 'Then fingers crossed for a bird of regular night-time habits.'

They crept along the unlit edge of the lawn and darted up the slope.

'Ten yards or so to the right is where we entered, I believe,' Clifford whispered, leading the way.

As a third branch of dislodged snow fell onto Eleanor's shoulders, she scoured along the sweep of her torch beam, wishing trees weren't so dashedly similar.

'I'm sure we didn't go much further before...'

Even though she had been hoping for it, the peacock's screech still made her clutch her chest. Clifford picked up her fallen torch.

'Handles ahoy! Bravo, my lady.'

She waved him back, pointing at his sling, and pulled the barrow from the deepest of the thicket. He then knelt and examined its hard-pitted rubber wheel. 'Hmm. Small sandstone fragments embedded. I haven't noticed any in the garden itself, only along the cliff path.'

She straightened up from examining the wooden sides and base. 'So, it's been out of the garden, but no unusual marks or anything to show it recently transported a body. As expected, really. Poor St Clair would just have been a dead weight... literally, having been poisoned, not a bleeding weight, I mean.'

She wheeled it out towards the flat grassed area which ran around the thicket.

'Jump in.'

'My lady, really!'

'Stop whining, Clifford. I only need to push you a few yards to see if it wheels with a person's weight in.'

He took a determined step backwards. 'If I might respectfully decline on this occasion, my lady. Riding in a murdered man's final carriage falls short of appeal. And dignity.'

'You're right, Clifford.' She held her hands up. 'But I haven't got any other ideas how we can check if the aunts could have wheeled St Clair together. Even though you're half a foot taller than him, you're as trim as a greyhound. And I'm probably as strong on my own as the two of them combined. And with your injured arm, we can't do it the other way around. But never mind, let's go with whatever you've thought up instead?'

With a resigned sigh, he brushed his gloved hand over the inside of the barrow, before whipping his jacket tails up and stepping in.

She lifted the handles without too much trouble, but the minute she tried to push forward, the wheel sank into the spongy grass.

'That's no good at all. Hop out and I'll wheel it to the path over there. It's in darkness.'

With great reluctance, Clifford did as he was asked, but it made no difference.

'I could just about make it a hundred yards,' she puffed. 'If I had half an hour. But there's certainly no chance of making it to the cliff. And certainly not then tipping you neatly out over it.'

He sprang back out with the nimbleness of a cat. 'Heartening news, my lady.'

She nodded. 'It is for aunts Flora and Clara. That definitely wipes them off the suspect list for St Clair's murder!'

22

Before, St Clair's office had seemed bare. But now it also seemed forlorn. And it wasn't just the oil lamp throwing flickering shadows onto the bare walls. The police had been through with a heavy hand. And foot.

'I can't think there's any point spending much time looking again, Clifford,' she called quietly up the ladder. 'Trevilick's men were obviously very thorough this afternoon. They've cleared absolutely everything off the desk and shelves. The cups and wooden plant labels that were here before are gone. Even St Clair's drawing pencils and pens have been rifled.'

Clifford slid back down the ladder, arching a brow as she obscured the middle shelf by holding her coat sides out.

'It's best you don't see his precious drafting tools tipped out of their case and left in a heap. You'll never sleep again.'

'Greatly appreciated, my lady.' He straightened the perfectly aligned seams of his gloves. 'Mr St Clair's living quarters have also been comprehensively turned over. Quite literally with regard to the bed and washstand. Every item of clothing has also been pulled inside out. And' – he winced – 'left so.' He stepped to the door and glanced out. 'What next? Remembering time is far from on our side. Given the moonlight is but snatches between thickening clouds, I fear the snow will return soon. And thicker than ever.'

She raised a finger. 'Don't worry, I've just remembered somewhere that the police may not have searched as thoroughly as here. Something my own wonderful gardener, Joseph, taught me.'

He scanned her face before nodding in understanding. 'The greenhouses. Because Mr St Clair's crowning glories in every landscaping project would be the *flora exotica*, grown by his own hand and tailored for each individual design.'

'Exactly.'

They crunched across the snow-covered quadrangle to the rows of greenhouses.

'We'd better split up for speed, Clifford,' she said, watching her words freeze in front of her in a frosty plume.

He checked her torch was the brighter of the two. 'Then, if I might respectfully request that you start here while I tackle the far ones?'

She shrugged, thinking it made no difference which of them started where. The moment she entered the first one, however, she realised his rationale. Unlike the bitter air outside, the temperature inside felt positively cosy.

Ever thoughtful, Clifford's given you the hothouses to search, Ellie.

She closed the door, resolving to be as quick as possible. That way, they might both soon be back in the house with a rewarding warm toddy.

And perhaps a clue as to who killed St Clair, Ellie.

Looking down the long run of sloping glass, she could see in her torch beam the hothouse was divided into three sections, each separated from the other by a door.

Setting off along the ornate grillework which served as a walkway, she stepped around a half-sized potting spade and fork near the entrance. Looking down, her torch beam revealed the fine mist of steam pervading the room was coming from a series of ancient pipes running below the grillework. On either side, plants were contained in raised beds formed with low brick walls.

The plants in the first bed bore spiny leaves and a budding velveteen fruit of a captivatingly vivid crimson. It was like nothing she'd seen before, even on her travels. But the overarching smell was vaguely familiar. She took several deep sniffs to place the aroma, regretting it immediately as she coughed violently.

She moved onto the next set of plants, rubbing at her throat distractedly. They had unusual, furry-edged leaves. So furry they seemed out of focus, as if she had borrowed someone else's strong spectacles. She leaned closer, blinking hard, her eyes stinging enough to draw tears.

Gracious, whatever these plants are, they need a warning sign, Ellie.

After another fit of coughing, she hurried towards the last section of the hothouse, now wheezing badly. Disturbingly, however, it didn't seem to get any nearer. Finally, she reached the interconnecting door, only to find it locked.

The hiss from the underfloor pipe roared in her ears.

It's the steam, Ellie. Get out!

She stumbled back around, making for the door she'd come in from, the echo of her footsteps sounding strangely booming and hollow as they resonated through the grillework.

Progress seemed agonisingly slow, the far end of the hothouse swimming towards her and then away as her blurred vision worsened. Finally reaching it, she tripped over the spade and fork, grabbed at the door handle and pulled.

Locked, Ellie! How?

She spun around unsteadily, lurching along the grillework like a drunken sailor, clutching at the walls of the raised beds.

Her only chance was to break the glass. If only her arms would do what she wanted, instead of feeling like lead weights.

The spade, Ellie.

She lunged for it and missed. The door crashed open. A hand grabbed her and propelled her up the steps.

'My lady, roll in the snow!' Clifford's concerned face came into focus as he pressed her down firmly. 'Whatever that gas is, we need to remove what we can from your clothing immediately.'

She did as he said, rubbing handfuls of the icy snow over her face at the same time to lessen the stinging in her eyes.

After a few minutes, she sat up, feeling far less woozy. Clifford pressed his hip flask into her hand. 'For rinsing only. Do not swallow a single drop.'

He turned his back as she swished and spat the brandy out.

'Shocking waste, Clifford,' she said, trying to ease his obvious worry. Her immediate fit of coughing and dry retching, however, rather ruined the desired effect. 'And thank goodness you smelt the gas.'

'I didn't. Fortuitously, I just caught sight of you floundering towards the door and realised it was a trap. In fact, given that I detected no odour, there can be only one conclusion. Cyanide!'

23

'*Cyanide?*' She felt her head spin at what might have been had Clifford not been so quick thinking.

They were back in her sitting room, Eleanor having quickly bathed and changed. Her throat was still sore, and she had a pounding headache, but she felt she was doing a reasonable job of hiding it from him.

'Of course. Bitter almonds! That's the smell I was too foggy to place. I remember now, though, you can't smell cyanide at all, can you, Clifford?'

'Quite, my lady. It is, indeed, fairly uncommon to have the ability. And no.'

'No, what?'

'No, you are not convincing me that you have recovered sufficiently to carry on where we left off.' He held up a hand. 'You are still slurring some of your words slightly.'

'I know,' she said earnestly. 'But the person responsible may very well have fled when you intervened and rescued me from the hothouse. But he might recover his, or her, composure at any time and return to remove any evidence that might lead back to him. Or her.'

He hesitated, then glanced at his pocket watch. 'By now any gas will have escaped or be very diluted as I left the door open. So, we will wait another half-hour *at least* to make sure you are fully recovered, then return. That is, if you do not enter the hothouse again under any circumstances. Assuming that is good with you, of course, my lady?'

She nodded meekly. 'Of course, Clifford. You're the boss...'

Clifford's uncanny understanding of all things engineering had never failed to amaze her, just as it didn't now. They'd returned to the garden, but not to the hothouse. Instead, he'd led her around the back of the walled quadrangle to a low door set in another wall. He held a finger to his lips as he cautiously led the way down a steep flight of steps.

'All clear,' he whispered at the bottom.

'How could you know to come here?' she marvelled as her torch picked out an ancient boiler with all manner of pipework attached, occupying the centre of the large cellar they had emerged into.

'The chimneys run along the eastern wall, my lady, those being the "stacks." The trapdoor in the ceiling over there allows coal sacks to be emptied, while the old iron ladder bolted to the wall directly underneath would have been used by the coal boy.' They stepped over to the boiler. 'Omitting the immaterial components of the steam system for expediency, this large-bore pipe is the flue. This second one feeds the heat into this expansion chamber which regulates the pressure of the steam released into this manifold. From which, this series of five pipes lead off into each of the hothouses, I would warrant. And then on to join the coupling with the perforated pipes underneath the vented floor.'

'Where I saw the steam rising from?' At his nod, she

frowned. 'But it would surely take a lot of cyanide to fill all the hothouses?'

'Indeed. However, the shut-off levers on each of the five pipes are set in line after' – he followed the pipes along – 'this reservoir.' He pointed to a cast-iron box, but signalled for her to stay back. 'As I thought,' he said a moment later. 'The reservoir's top cover has been unbolted to allow...' He shone his torch into the chamber. 'Yes! Crushed laurel leaves to be added, as I suspected.'

As she moved to peer closer, he threw an arm across her path. 'You have been exposed to too much already, my lady. We need to leave.'

She nodded, regretting it as her head swam, and followed him back towards the steps. 'Laurel leaves?'

'Likely soaked in alcohol first. All parts of the plant are poisonous to some extent. Along with the stems, the leaves contain hydrogen cyanide, which is released when crushed or burnt. Laurel's history as a poison has been traced, perhaps most notably, to Emperor Nero. He used it to contaminate the drinking wells of his enemies. Later, Europeans employed it to kill butterflies when building exotic collections.'

'Poor little things. And poor St Clair. Maybe that's how he was poisoned with the cyanide the coroner found in his system?' Something about Clifford's explanation of the boiler's workings struck her. 'Those shut-off levers you pointed out. They were all off except one?'

'Yes. Which I guarantee is the pipe leading to the hothouse you were in, my lady.'

Her breath caught. 'But that means whoever it was, was watching!'

'And waiting to see which you entered. And if I hadn't suggested you searched the hothouses, the trap would never have worked.'

She tugged his sleeve, regretting it at his wince. 'Oops!

Sorry, I forgot about your elbow. Anyway, I shan't accept you feeling bad, Clifford. The incident was obviously intended only to scare me. The hothouse is made of fairly easy to break glass, after all.'

'Not if you had been overcome first, my lady. Whoever was responsible cannot have known of your exceptional constitution.'

'Well, whoever it was must have left some footprints. It only eased up snowing a short while ago.'

'An excellent observation. However, I thought to check on our way to the boiler room and saw none.'

'Then how... oh, the coal boy's ladder! That's how they nipped down and then back out of the cellar after releasing the gas.'

'Bravo, my lady,' Clifford murmured a moment later, pointing at the ground around the trapdoor. 'Fresh boot marks. But with what looks like one heel worn down. See how the tread on all the left prints disappears in the last inch and a half.' He rubbed his chin. 'I believe a visit to Mr Brae and Mr Odgers' boot room is justified.'

After a few minutes trudging, they arrived at the under-gardeners' small hut. Just inside, two pairs of work boots stood neatly. Clifford turned the first pair over, examining the heel, then the second.

'We are in luck, my lady!'

Eleanor leaned forward. 'Excellent! Whose are they?'

He examined the name inside of the boots. 'Mr Brae's.'

'Mmm?' She frowned, trying to hide the fact that her head still hurt from the gas. 'There are two sets of boots, so both Brae and Odgers changed their work boots for different footwear when they set off home. So it could be Brae or—'

'Or his colleague, Mr Odgers, who put them on to try and draw suspicion onto Mr Brae, as I notice both pairs of boots are the same size.'

'Yes. Or someone else could have slipped them on to mislead us. The real culprit. Maybe Marsh.' She glanced at Clifford and shrugged. 'I know, or Cunliffe. His feet would fit with room to spare, they're petite like the rest of him.' She shook her head. 'Dash it! It doesn't tell us anything.'

'Actually, it does.'

She looked up in confusion. 'It does?'

'Yes, my lady. It tells me, despite your best efforts to hide it, that you are still feeling the effects of your exposure to the gas. We should return to the house. It is—'

She held up a hand. 'For once, I agree with you, Clifford. It's too dark and the culprit would have made their escape ages ago anyway. Let's call it a night.'

Outside, she marvelled at the other-worldly silence that came with thick snow. And being Christmas Eve, it should have felt even more magical. But despite Clifford striding protectively beside her as they hurried along the main path, she found it eerily sinister. The wall of crisp flakes falling thickly again on every bush and tree they passed only served to smother the landscape in a ghostly shroud. She drew level with the folly with its unusual fish gutters, wishing it was Gwel an Mor itself, welcomingly lit and with her bathtub filling.

'Clifford?' She cocked her head as she slowed in confusion. 'Remember what Mrs Liddicoat said about hearing water dripping when there isn't any?'

'Yes. That it is a portent of death. But I fear your shock over the hothouse incident is beginning to unnerve you, my lady. It is but a superstition.'

'I know. But why then can I hear the drip, drip of water splashing onto something?'

He listened intently for a moment. 'I do not know, my lady, but your hearing is exceptionally acute. Perhaps it is melting snow dripping from the folly's roof?' He shone his torch on the nearest fish-shaped drain. 'Hmm, no water dripping here, however.'

She shone hers at the next one, then at the snow beneath. 'That's because it's not coming from that one, it's coming from this one. And it's not water. It's blood!'

24

Clifford overtook Eleanor as she raced up the stone steps to the folly's roof terrace. Face down in the rain gully on a patch of crimson snow was the motionless, contorted form of a man.

'Oh, gracious!' she gasped.

He crouched down, feeling for a pulse.

'Too late,' he muttered gravely.

Her head fell to her chest. 'It's Brae. Stabbed with a pair of hedging shears!'

Overcome with sorrow for a young life taken so cruelly, she turned her face up to the cascade of snowflakes and sent words heavenwards that he might rest in peace.

Clifford stood up slowly, and, gently turning her away from the sight, offered her his good elbow. 'My lady. We need to get you back to the house.'

'But—'

'Whoever did this will be long gone.'

She shivered. 'Or back in the house themselves. They've killed twice now, but we have no idea who it is.'

'Hence the need for extreme prudence.' He steered her respectfully towards the steps.

Before they could start down, she stopped. 'It's too awful, Clifford. To leave him so alone like that. In the snow.'

Without a word, he returned to the body and laid his coat over it. He rejoined her. 'My lady, there really is nothing more we can do for him.'

'Yes, there is,' her impassioned words flew out. 'We can make sure whoever did this faces justice!'

He nodded as they continued back. 'I suggest then that we call Chief Inspector Seldon to come and examine the scene first. Trevilick, by his own admission, is unused to this type of crime, whereas—'

She sighed. 'Hugh is all too used to it!'

With the utmost stealth, they returned to the house where Clifford quietly rang the inn while Eleanor kept watch. His hunch was right, and the landlady answered guardedly. Once she was convinced her butler wasn't the authorities trying to find out if she was operating rather lenient opening hours over the festive season, she fetched Seldon from his room. After the briefest of exchanges, Clifford put the phone down.

Then it was a case of waiting...

'I still can't see any sign of him,' Eleanor muttered, peering through the glass door of the summerhouse.

No one had replaced the pane broken by Marsh's golf ball, and an icy wind swirled around her shins.

'Patience, my lady,' Clifford whispered a second time. 'It has been less than twenty minutes since we rang.'

She spun around. 'But just look out there! The road up from the village must be treacherous now with all the snow that's fallen. Supposing Hugh's had trouble? You know how greasy, sorry, icy it will be. And how steep it is.' Her hand flew to her mouth. 'Suppose he skidded and went off the—'

He shook his head quickly. 'Most unlikely, my lady. Really.

Aside from the chief inspector being an expert driver, his Crossley motor vehicle is far lighter, shorter and more manoeuvrable than the Rolls. And, besides,' he said gently, 'your heart would have told you if something had happened to him.'

Before she could reply, he held up a hand. A torch flashed on and off out in the dark. 'Three. Four. Two. Henley Hall's telephone number. It's the signal.'

Stealing out, they skirted around the house, keeping in the shadows, the wind whipping the dancing flakes into swirling eddies helping them hide. But no matter how hard she tried to be silent, the crunch of snow beneath her boots seemed to echo off the walls. The bitter air scratched at her cyanide-irritated throat as if she was swallowing ground glass, forcing her to fight the cough that threatened. Panting heavily, she followed Clifford as he scrambled over the stone wall to drop down onto the patchily repaired cobblestoned track.

'Here!' a deep voice whispered. 'Eleanor, it's me.' Seldon's arms reached out from the shadows and pulled her into a close embrace.

'Oh, Hugh. Thank goodness you're safe.'

He ran his thumbs gently down her cheeks. 'No. Thank goodness you are safe! Clifford only told me to come immediately. I've been imagining all sorts of horrors.'

'Sincere apologies, Chief Inspector,' Clifford said. 'Brevity was essential.'

Seldon pulled her tighter against his chest. 'Eleanor, before my heart gives out, tell me everything that's happened.'

She shook her head. 'No time, Hugh. The bottom line is, I'm fine. But poor Tristan Brae is far from fine.' She shuddered. 'And never will be again.'

'I see,' he muttered grimly. Linking fingers with Eleanor, he gestured for Clifford to lead the way.

Having slid back over the wall, Clifford paused until Eleanor and Seldon had joined him. 'Chief Inspector, aside from my checking for a pulse, neither her ladyship nor I touched anything in the hope any material evidence would be preserved for your experienced eye.'

'Good work, both. Blast it, though! In this snow, I'm going to add a third set of footprints, which will raise suspicion and skew things for Inspector Trevilick's men. And speaking of which, I suggest you come clean with him on any information we learn, as we're all on the same side. Only nothing about me being involved. I'm way out of my jurisdiction!'

'Agreed.'

Eleanor's gaze darted to his boots and then to Clifford's. 'I've got it! I go first and walk in my original prints. Hugh, you walk in Clifford's first set and then he comes behind you and leaves his over yours, which will then magically disappear.'

The two men gave her an appreciative look. 'Bravo, my lady,' Clifford whispered, gesturing for her to lead the way.

The sight that greeted them at the top of the folly's steps felt no less horrific a second time. If anything, the now frozen stain of claret-red blood seemed to defile the otherwise pristine, glittering snow.

'Barbarous does not cover whoever did that,' Seldon muttered as he pressed his hands gently over her eyes. 'You shouldn't be here, Eleanor.'

'Well, I am. And, in truth, it's nothing worse than I saw as a nurse in the war. Less, if I'm honest. Now, go and do your best for poor Brae.'

With a deep breath, he stepped forward, with Clifford following in his wake a few steps behind. Having carefully removed Clifford's coat from Brae, he handed it to him. Deep in thought, he scrutinised the body, then lifted the sides of his coat and crouched down.

'Brae didn't come up here to meet someone,' he said slowly. 'He was chased, I'd say. The snow has covered any footprints to the folly, but here,' he pointed to the dead man's feet, 'the compacted snow on the base of his boots indicates he was running. A heavier strike of the foot presses deeper into the snow and collects more of it.' He stood up and pointed. 'Also, there was a struggle starting around three feet from where the body is lying, I'd say, given the snow is most disturbed there. But it didn't last long. Brae staggered only a short distance before he fell.'

'So might it have been a quick end for him?' she said hopefully.

'Yes,' he said gently. Pulling off one of his gloves, he stepped up to the dead man's coat collar to slip one hand inside. He withdrew it with a puzzled expression on his face. 'Soaked?'

She frowned. 'Why does him being soaked strike you as odd? He's been lying out in the snow since it happened.'

'Yes. Though it hasn't all melted. Far from it, as you can see for yourself. And he's wet through on his back. Almost as if he'd been outside for the last hour working. But this late? What could he have been doing? How long ago did you find him, Clifford?'

He peered at his pocket watch by a veiled torch beam. 'About twenty-five minutes, Chief Inspector.'

'Hmm.' He turned to Eleanor. 'And you said it was the sound of the dripping from out of that drain which alerted you?'

'Yes. It was the colour that made us run up here.' She swallowed hard.

He rubbed his chin. 'Well, an accurate time of death is going to be tricky because it's freezing tonight. A body cools to the temperature of the surrounding environment, but he is also lying in snow so that will be more pronounced.'

Clifford nodded. 'But if he had run here, Chief Inspector, as you surmised, would that not have increased his body temperature?'

'Absolutely. And he's wearing a jumper and a coat over wool undergarments, so more heat would have been trapped.

However, the dripping you heard, Eleanor, may help us establish a more accurate timing. The dripping only occurred because the heat from his body initially melted enough of the surrounding snow to create a trickle of blood that reached the drain. It's already re-frozen, as you can see. So it seems likely that he was killed not that long before you found him.'

They all ducked down as the moon emerged from the clouds, throwing a luminescent shaft of light on them like a celestial spotlight.

'Wait!' Seldon said. 'What's that?' He carefully pulled an object from the snow.

She peered at it. 'Another plant label, Hugh. I found one before—'

'I imagine there's plenty of them around.' Without moving his feet, he leaned over and handed it to her.

She took it and glanced at the wording written on it. She could just make out "L.L.", but it meant nothing to her. 'Actually—'

'Headlights, Chief Inspector! Coming this way. And quickly.' Clifford checked again. 'Two sets, I believe.'

'The police!' Seldon said, leaning around to see for himself. 'It has to be. Who else would be coming up here in two cars at this time of night?'

Eleanor shook her head in puzzlement. 'But we haven't called them.'

He groaned. 'Either way, I absolutely cannot be found here. My superior would have me for breakfast.'

'Then go, Hugh. We'll ring you at the inn as soon as we can.'

Hastily retracing their footprints as far as the stone wall, Seldon spun around, brushed his lips with hers and slid over.

Hurrying up the drive, Eleanor was just in time as two police cars slewed to a halt.

'Inspector Trevilick?' she called as he stepped out of the car. He looked dishevelled, with dark rings around his eyes and the bottom of his trousers. 'What are you doing here?' It wasn't very inventive, but she needed to keep him talking until Seldon was far enough away.

Trevilick's moustache twitched suspiciously as he waved at his men to wait. 'I might ask you the same question, Lady Swift? Seeing as it's as good as the middle of the night. Peculiar time to decide on a stroll around the gardens?'

'Not exactly a stroll, Inspector,' she panted. 'But you didn't answer me. What are you doing here?'

'My job,' he said firmly, waving his men on.

Before they could climb the steps, however, the front door flew open.

'What is the meaning of this!' Cunliffe thundered, his slender, dressing-gown-clad frame shaking. 'How dare you descend upon my house at this hour. Get out! All of you.'

'Oh, we will, Mr Cunliffe,' Trevilick said smoothly. 'But you might wish to collect your coat first because you're coming with us. You are wanted for questioning concerning the murder of Mr St Clair.'

Eleanor's heart sank.

At least all this is giving Hugh a chance to get away, Ellie.

'Preposterous! I shall do no such—'

Trevilick clicked his fingers at the two nearest policemen who stepped up to Cunliffe.

'Are you going to come quietly, sir?'

For a moment, she thought he'd refuse again. Instead, without a word, he disappeared inside, only to emerge in a wool overcoat and scarf. As he drew level with Trevilick, he hissed, 'I will have your badge for this!'

As Cunliffe stiffly climbed into the police car, she hurried up to Trevilick. Seldon should have had plenty of time to escape and there was no more to waste.

'Inspector, I wasn't taking a stroll. There is another body.

Brae, one of the under-gardeners, is dead on the roof of a folly behind me. Murdered.'

Trevilick jerked his gaze to Clifford, who nodded. 'Regrettably it is true, sir.'

The inspector hesitated, then spun around. 'Symons, stay with Mr Cunliffe in the first car. The rest of you follow me.'

Remembering Seldon's words, by the time she and Clifford had led Trevilick to the base of the folly, she had explained everything that had happened since their last conversation.

'Cyanide gas, Lady Swift?' He shook his head. 'That's likely how St Clair was poisoned then. You got your dose in the greenhouse, you say?'

She nodded. 'Because Clifford insisted I return to the main house that's why we noticed the blood dripping just there, do you see? Then we ran up to the roof and saw... Brae.'

He looked at her quizzically. 'And when exactly was it you were up here, queering over the body?'

Eleanor caught Clifford's cautioning cough. 'We were here just as your cars came along the road. I saw your headlights, so we rushed back to meet you.'

Trevilick stroked his moustache. 'Hmm. Lucky thing we were here to collect your Mr Cunliffe just at that moment then? I'll also be questioning him now over a second murder.' He held her gaze. 'Amateur detecting is a dangerous game. I hope you realise that now, Lady Swift? Because, if your butler hadn't rescued you from that greenhouse, I'd be taking Mr Cunliffe into custody to interrogate him about your murder as well!'

25

Eleanor slapped her arms against her sides to stop her bones from freezing in their sockets. As if Cornwall's snowiest winter for eighty years wasn't arctic enough, the police interview room Trevilick had left her alone in felt icier still. Built from granite blocks, the interior walls had been left as nature had hewn them; punishing, unforgiving and gravestone grey.

In the corridor, Clifford caught her eye. 'Yes, my lady. I would hazard it is actually warmer outside.'

She jumped as Inspector Trevilick's moustache twitched behind her butler's shoulder.

'I'm sorry, Lady Swift, but I've no men free to waste on boiling a pot of tea to warm up. They're too busy bringing in the other under-gardener, Dewi Odgers, for questioning.'

She nodded. 'It's quite alright, Inspector, I understand. However, what I don't, is on what evidence you are holding Mr Cunliffe?'

Trevilick hooked his thumbs through his coat's top button-holes. 'A very pertinent detail he omitted from his statement, Lady Swift. That he had arranged a meeting with Mr St Clair for the very afternoon he was murdered.'

Eleanor groaned. 'Really? How did you find out?'

'A reliable tip-off. But no, I won't be saying who, so please don't ask.'

No need, Ellie. Judging by the conversation you overheard outside the Liddicoats' cottage, it was Marsh.

Trevilick's brow darkened. 'I therefore brought Mr Cunliffe in and have since detained him to see if he might "remember" other significant details he failed to tell me!'

'Sir?' A frostbitten constable appeared in the corridor. 'It's Odgers, sir. His landlady swears she's not seen hide nor hair of him all evenin'. We've scoured and woken half the village, but it's the same answer everywhere.'

Trevilick let out a long breath. 'Then keep searching, Sergeant!'

'Right away, sir. But one result.' He passed Trevilick a bag. 'You were right. It's definitely nicked. Reported stolen from a house in Dartington last month.'

Trevilick's face lit up. 'Good work! We've got him. Well, we will have once you actually find him.' He glanced up. 'Your Mr Cunliffe might just have had a stroke of luck, Lady Swift. Stay put. I'll be back shortly.'

Before he could, however, two policemen strode into view, each with one wrist handcuffed to a rattled-looking Odgers stumbling between them.

'Weren't easy, sir,' the stoutest one said. 'Just caught the beggar steamin' up the drainpipe of his lodgin's like his boots was on fire.'

'Good job, Constable.' Trevilick jerked his thumb in the direction of the interview room, then eyed Eleanor pensively. 'Lady Swift, I'm a fair man.' He ran his hand over his moustache. 'And you've helped in this investigation. And not only in discovering Brae's body. So, I'd like you to sit in on this.' He gestured for her to join him as he marched inside.

Clifford arched an amused brow at her apologetic look as

she followed Trevilick. 'Do not worry, my lady,' he whispered loudly. 'I imagine I will hear a fair amount of the proceedings from here.'

In the interview room, Odgers was hunched like an exhausted animal on a chair, his wrists now cuffed to the seat's wooden backstays. Trevilick faced him in a courtroom pose, legs apart, hands behind his back, eyeing him with a steely gaze. The leaner of the two officers waved Eleanor into the remaining chair against the opposite wall.

'Why did you do it, Odgers?' Trevilick snapped.

Odgers jerked his head up. 'I didn't do anythin', I tell yer!'

Trevilick snorted. 'So if you didn't do it, who killed Tristan Brae then?'

Odgers swallowed hard. 'Tristan is... dead?'

'Very. But you knew that already.'

Odgers shook his head, lips flapping. Trevilick leaned menacingly into his face.

'You're sweating like a poultice. But it's cold enough to freeze hell over in here.'

'I was runnin'!' Odgers stammered. ''Cos I heard boots. That's all. How was I to know who was chasin' me?'

'How indeed?' Trevilick said darkly. 'Though you should have known it was only a matter of time before the police caught you. See, it's not just murderers, but thieves get my nose twitching, too.'

Odgers' startled look would have been comical in less serious circumstances. She watched with bated breath as Trevilick swiped the sackcloth bag his constable had given him earlier from the table and held it open under Odgers' nose. 'Recognise this necklace and earrings?'

Odgers tried to stand, only to be pinned back into the chair by both officers. 'Where... where did you get that?' He looked around wildly. 'This is a set-up! I didn't kill Tristan. He... he was dead when I found him, I swear!'

Trevilick's face lit up in triumph. 'So you *did* know he was dead! Now you're a doomed man, Odgers. Once you've lied, how can I believe anything you say?' He waved the bag at him. 'We found this at the murder scene.'

'Lies again, I tell you,' Odgers stuttered.

Eleanor frowned. They'd checked the area carefully, including Hugh. How did they miss that?

Trevilick dropped the bag on the table. 'It's no use denying it. It was found in Brae's pocket.'

'That's why we didn't find it,' Eleanor murmured to herself. Trevilick and his men arriving unexpectedly had interrupted Hugh turning the body over and searching it. She snapped back to the present as Odgers spoke again.

'Why would I want to kill Tristan? We did everything together. Always have, since we was kids.'

Trevilick laughed mirthlessly. 'Including being party to a stolen goods racket? Stop wasting my time and tell the truth.'

Odgers hung his head with a sob. 'Alright. A bloke Tristan knows nicks things from the towns yonder of Penscombe. He'd bring them to us of a night-time and we'd hide them in them tumbledown sheds what no one goes into. He'd then tell us when everything had gone hush after each set of stealin' so as we'd drag the stuff out and boot it down to our contact in the village. I don't know after that. We just got paid. But then St Clair started clearin' the garden and I wanted to stop. But Tristan badgered me into carryin' on.'

That explains, Ellie, why Brae and Odgers went on about St Clair having no respect for the 'spirits of the garden' and tearing things down. They were just worried he'd find their stashes of stolen goods.

Odgers hesitated. 'We were moving stuff from the old shed to take down to the village, but Tristan disappeared. That's why I went lookin' for him. Only I found him.' He swallowed hard. 'Dead. On that folly's roof. That's when I ran. Ran blummin' scareder than my insides have ever knotted, 'cos I knew it would look like I did it. So I legged it back to the village to me lodgin's to look as if I'd been there all night.'

Trevilick scoffed. 'Odgers, you haven't enough days left to learn how to lie better. I'll tell you what happened. You thought Brae was taking his time coming back, and you had a sneaking suspicion why. So you went looking and found him rifling through the stolen stuff and pocketing a few choicer pieces. Same as you had a feeling he'd been doing all along, only you'd never caught him at it until then. There was an almighty row, and he tried to treat you like a fool one time too many. No one likes to be taken as a fool, Odgers. You'd been his lackey boy forever. You saw red and killed him. But now, you're trying to treat me like a fool because you don't want to hang for it.'

'Hang?' Odgers croaked. 'I'm not. I didn't. I—'

'Change the tune,' Trevilick snapped. 'You should have given up your thieving game when St Clair got the job at Gwel an Mor so you didn't have to take double for his murder.'

Odgers' jaw trembled. 'I don't follow.'

'You will. St Clair probably caught you moving some of your stolen goods, didn't he? Maybe into those disused sheds, maybe out of them. It doesn't matter. Thing is, you couldn't let him tell Cunliffe, could you? Then all that extra money coming your way would stop. And your jobs as well. I think you and Brae might have killed St Clair together, but now your work-mate's gone, there's only your word. And your neck for the noose.'

Odgers fought with his handcuffs. 'I didn't kill anyone! This is a set-up, I tell you!'

'Lock him up.' Trevilick waved for the two policemen to uncuff Odgers from the chair.

As he was being led out, he twisted around, staring at Eleanor, his eyes wild. 'You saw me and Tristan workin', m'lady.

When we were teachin' yer about the plants. We was like brothers, weren't it? Tell 'im.'

She shook her head sadly. 'I really couldn't say, Mr Odgers. But I do have a question for you. If that's alright, Inspector?'

Trevilick paused in the doorway. After a moment, he replied, looking less than enamoured. 'It's been a long night, Lady Swift. But let's hear it.'

She nodded and turned back to Odgers. 'Was it true about St Clair getting fresh with Mrs Liddicoat?'

He hung his head. 'No, m'lady. I was just bluffin' so as you'd leave us be because we was on the way to check the stuff. Tristan ripped me down a riot after 'cos he thought it might have got you on to our backs more, not less. He... he always were smarter than me.'

'Well, thank you for being honest.' She hesitated. 'Actually, one last question. Why did you and Mr Brae take the plant labels from St Clair's office?'

Odgers looked confused. 'What labels? Weren't me. Haven't been in there since it all kicked off after St Clair going over the cliff. Can't think Tristan did neither.'

She shrugged. 'Forget it then.'

Trevilick looked at her oddly, then clucked his tongue. 'Lady Swift, two men are dead. I don't think we need to worry about some pilfered wooden plant labels.'

'Of course. Silly me, Inspector.'

He pursed his lips, then turned to one of the policemen holding Odgers. 'Did you see plant labels, or sticks, recorded on the items taken from Gwel an Mor when it was searched?'

The policeman shook his head. 'No, sir. Nothing like that.'

'Thank you for asking,' she said.

He nodded and signalled for the prisoner to be led away. Once alone, he addressed her again. 'Well, there it is. Christmas is yours to enjoy once again. It will take me a short while to make the arrangements for Mr Cunliffe to be released. Despite his lying to us, it's obvious he's not the guilty party. He'll be back at Gwel an Mor in good time for the festive luncheon. And, on my part, I wish you, your butler, and your fiancé a safe return journey to Henley Hall.'

She nodded. 'Thank you, Inspector, I...' Her brow furrowed. '*Fiancé?*'

A smile played around Trevilick's lips. 'As a matter of course, Lady Swift, once I knew St Clair's death was murder, I had my men check on any strangers seen in the area. One such, a Mr Miles Wellener, was staying at the Kerensa Come Quick inn.'

Her frown deepened.

If Trevilick had looked into Hugh's identity and story, Ellie, they'd have checked out. He's too professional for them not to.

Trevilick nodded, as if he'd read her mind. 'Mr Wellener's details were confirmed as being correct. However, my nose told me otherwise.' At her startled look, he shook his head. 'You turn up here, Lady Swift, at the behest of a man who tells you his gardener is trying to kill him on the very day that gardener is himself found dead. No, murdered! And not twenty-four hours later, a stranger turns up in the village asking questions. Coincidence? Maybe. Maybe not. So—'

She groaned. 'You rang Chipstone?'

Trevilick nodded smugly. 'And spoke to your Sergeant Brice again. Asked him if Lady Swift ever had any other help on the cases she'd solved other than her loyal butler? And guess what? One name came up. Chief Inspector Seldon. And the remarkable thing is, not only is he your fiancé, but his description fits our Mr Wellener to a tee.'

Eleanor opened her mouth, but then closed it. After a moment, she shrugged. 'I'm sorry, Inspector. I can't say any more.'

Trevilick held his hand out. 'Lady Swift, I would have

preferred to be told straight, but in the end, you helped bring a double killer to justice. Now, you are guests in my village so forget all about it and enjoy a real Cornish Christmas before you return home. Then,' he said, rolling his eyes, 'maybe I might get back to enjoying life without bodies everywhere!'

26

A sneaky gust of sea air whipped Eleanor's green velvet hat from her head and away over Lostenev Harbour.

'Oh, botheration!' she cried, realising it must be a hopeless cause as her butler hadn't even attempted to rescue it.

'I believe that is what hat pins were invented for, my lady,' he said impassively. 'The clue being in the name.'

'And how is that helpful, Clifford, after I've lost my most favourite hat?'

He arched an ambiguous brow in reply.

'Lady Swift? What a coincidence,' a rich deep voice said.

She spun around, immediately thinking her fiancé really was the most dashingly handsome and divinely built man she'd ever seen. With his wind-tousled chestnut curls and cutting such a broad-shouldered figure in that flattering charcoal-grey coat, he looked too delicious for words. He stopped a courteous stranger's distance from her, hands behind his back. 'Miles Wellener, from the train. Perhaps you remember me?'

She darted forward and planted a long kiss on the corner of his lips. Stepping back, she nodded. 'I do now. Merry Christmas!'

Cheeks burning, he produced her hat from behind his back with a confused mumble. 'I believe this belongs to you, Lady Swift?'

'Perfect! That deserves another kiss.'

Clifford cleared his throat. 'I sincerely apologise, sir. Her ladyship appears to have been indecorously overcome by Christmas morning euphoria. Or a lack of breakfast, perhaps?'

She shook her head. 'Neither, for once. It's seeing Hugh.'

Seldon's brown eyes flickered with exasperation as he muttered, 'I know you think it's silly, but it's too late to change my assumed name now, Eleanor. For the duration in Cornwall, I'm Miles Wellener.'

She cocked her head thoughtfully. 'Nice fellow. I was just starting to find all manner of things quite tantalising about him.'

'Help a man out on the done thing, won't you?' he said awkwardly to Clifford. 'Is this kind of aberration still your domain as her ladyship's butler, or is it for me to wade in now we're engaged?'

'Suffice to say I hope you packed your sturdiest of wellington boots, sir.'

Eleanor buried her quiet chuckle in her gloves. Even Clifford's eyes gave away his amusement.

'Blast it, you two! What's going on?' Seldon smiled, clearly caught up in the festive mood.

She laughed. 'Oh, I'm sorry, Hugh. That was rather unfair of me. To answer your question, a lot has gone on. One good bit of news is that we've been discovered.'

He stiffened. 'You mean people know who we really are?'

'Who *you* are, more to the point. Not due to any lack of excellent acting on your part, though. It seems Inspector Trevilick had an enlightening telephone call with our Sergeant Brice, back at Chipstone Police Station.'

His eyes widened. 'Brice? Not again! You'd better not tell

me any more. Except, how is that good news? We're knee-deep in a double murder investigation—'

'Not any more, Chief Inspector,' Clifford said with uncharacteristic relief.

'So it would seem.' She shrugged, feeling her mood dip. 'Trevilick has charged Dewi Odgers, the second undergardener, with both murders.' She recounted the details.

'Odgers, eh?' Seldon said. 'Well, hats off to Trevilick, then. All the more so, as I'd imagine murders in this area are usually few and far between.'

Clifford eyed Eleanor sideways. 'The inspector confirmed such, sir, and remarked upon her ladyship's evident propensity for attracting, ahem, deceased persons.'

'Traitor!' she muttered. 'But yes, alright, he did say that. Just as you have, Hugh.'

'Many times, Eleanor. Because it's worryingly true.' Seldon scanned her face anxiously. 'Rather like your sudden change of mood is. I don't understand why Odgers' arrest wasn't your good news? If he's the murderer, it means Mr Cunliffe will be cleared of all charges and have his mind put to rest as to who was actually trying to kill him. Mission achieved. We can head straight home to celebrate Christmas, or stay here, whichever you want. As long as we're together, it doesn't matter to me where we are.'

'That's lovely of you, Hugh. Thank you,' she said flatly. 'It is a case of "if" though, isn't it?'

Seldon scrutinised her face. 'Eleanor, what's wrong?'

She bit her lip. 'I... I have a doubt.'

'That Trevilick has the right man?'

'Y-e-s.' She cleaved a line in the snow capping the harbour wall with her gloved finger. 'Look. I realise Trevilick believes Odgers has the opportunity, means and motive. And I confess, I even saw him using what looked like the very shears which killed poor Brae.'

Seldon pulled her to his chest. 'You should never have seen such a thing, Eleanor. Clifford, you and I are both unforgivably to blame there.'

'Unquestionably, sir,' Clifford said remorsefully. 'Your doubt though, my lady?'

She bit her lip. 'I know what you're going to say, Hugh. But Odgers just doesn't seem like a killer. He is far too... gentle. And timid. Now, if Brae had killed Odgers, I could believe that. And there's another thing I... I can't put my finger on it, dash it!' She scrubbed at her forehead with her gloves. 'It's like a tiny mute mouse nibbling away at the back of my brain. No, at my conscience. Something I've seen or heard, perhaps?' A seagull flew over their heads with a mournful cry. 'Chaps,' she said earnestly. 'Suppose there's even a whisker of a chance it wasn't Odgers? I wouldn't be able to live with myself if I thought an innocent man...' She shuddered.

Seldon ran his hand around the back of his neck with a sigh while Clifford pinched his nose. After a moment of silence, the two men shared a resigned look. Seldon cupped Eleanor's chin.

'The thing is, from everything you've said so far, we'll only prove that Trevilick is right by continuing to investigate. The evidence points that way. But, yes, if it will settle your thoughts, we'll continue. Discreetly though! I don't want Trevilick to think his judgement is being questioned. That would be wholly unprofessional of me.'

She sighed in relief. 'Discreetly it is. And the minute we're convinced he has the right man, we stop investigating and return home. Agreed, Mr Wellener?'

He leaned forward and planted a long kiss on the corner of her lips. 'Agreed.'

27

A vigorous five-minute stomp saw them tucked away around the steep-sided cove, beyond sight of the harbour. Clifford produced two thick newspapers from inside his coat and spread them out on a salt-pitted bench set in a natural alcove of the cliff.

In a blink, she found herself cosied up beside Seldon, both of them furnished with a steaming cup of Thermos coffee. Clifford slid an anchor-print napkin parcel onto her lap with an apologetic look, offering another to Seldon.

'Hog's pudding and pressed egg toasted sandwiches. Unorthodox, but kindly prepared in lieu of a sit-down breakfast by the landlady of Kerensa Come Quick.'

'Your number one fan. I shan't ask what you offered in return.' She smiled at his horrified look as she unwrapped the napkin.

Seldon took a bite from each. 'Unorthodox maybe, but they taste delicious.' He pulled out his notebook. 'I suggest we come back to the information I've found out later and concentrate first on Tristan Brae's murder for a moment. Which we're coming at from the assumed notion that Dewi Odgers is not responsible despite any evidence to the contrary, yes?'

Eleanor spread her hands. 'Look, to be clear, it's not that I think Odgers *is* innocent, it's just that I must be sure he *is* guilty.'

Seldon nodded. 'I understand. Now, it seems clear to me that unless there was an intruder, the only person who could have been responsible for Brae's death was someone in Gwel an Mor house itself. And since Trevilick will have men sweeping the grounds, we certainly can't risk looking for any signs of an intruder ourselves.'

She winced. 'I think this time he might actually slap us all in jail if he found out we were still investigating. So, of those in the house, I doubt anyone has a verifiable alibi given it was so late and everyone would have been in their separate beds. Including the Liddicoats, who are bound to confirm each other's alibi, anyway. Mrs Liddicoat certainly wouldn't dare do otherwise.'

Seldon frowned. 'Mmm. And any one of them could have made it out to the garden, killed Brae and slunk back into bed by the time the police arrived. They don't use fingerprinting down here yet, and even if they did, I'm pretty sure Trevilick will find gloves were worn.'

'I have noticed the tool store is not locked at night,' Clifford said matter-of-factly. 'And there are plenty of gardening gloves there as well as shears.'

Eleanor waved her second sandwich. 'So any one of them could have got hold of the murder weapon.'

'Alright.' Seldon tapped his page. 'We'll go through the list of suspects. Dewi Odgers we're discounting for this run-through. The two aunts?'

'Definitely insufficient strength to despatch a vigorous young man with shears in such a regrettable manner,' Clifford said. 'Even working together.'

'Mrs Liddicoat next, then. Strong enough, is she?'

'Perhaps if she was enraged,' Eleanor said.

'Though the lady is of compromised strength and agility given her rheumatism, my lady, which is worse in cold, damp conditions such as these.'

'I didn't realise that, Clifford. And anyway, she has no motive that I know of. In truth, neither has her husband. *He's* definitely strong enough, though. But when we were eavesdropping on him and Marsh, their beef was with Mr Cunliffe alone.'

'Moving on again, then.' Seldon tapped the next entry in his notebook. 'Cunliffe?'

Clifford's hand strayed to his tie.

'He's positively petite,' Eleanor said quickly.

'But he's probably still strong enough to have killed Brae,' Seldon said quietly. 'Particularly if he caught Brae by surprise. But a motive? St Clair was already dead, so...' He shrugged.

'So for some peculiar reasoning of his own, he could have decided it was Brae, not St Clair, who had been trying to kill him all along?' Eleanor said falteringly.

'Or he could have caught Mr Brae in flagrante, as it were?'

'Clifford!'

'My lady! I was referring to him catching Mr Brae red-handed, re his trade in stolen goods, not... ahem.'

She laughed. 'I know, but it's Christmas, and the mood needed lightening.' Her tone grew serious again, however. 'Although, I have to own up, if you rule Odgers out of the equation, the finger of guilt does still point squarely at Mr Cunliffe.' She sighed. 'Why is there no good outcome whichever way we go?'

'Because no good ever comes of murder,' Seldon said grimly.

Clifford busied himself shaking the picnic crumbs out to the squawking gulls on the path. 'Perhaps a timely moment to switch to hearing your new information, Chief Inspector?'

'Okay. Word from my office suggests Mr Cunliffe is as

respectable as he seems. Likewise the aunts. The nephew, Edwin Marsh, though, he has something of a record but no actual details yet. Christmas is slowing everything down. Even at headquarters.'

'Anything on the Liddicoats?'

'Nothing. And it's the same for St Clair in regard to any connection with known occultists or satanic worship groups. But I had better luck in the village. The estate agent's assistant was my source for this. I used Clifford's inimitable trick of loosening his tongue.'

Eleanor gasped. 'You gave him a thrashing, Hugh?'

'Ahem,' Clifford said hurriedly. 'I believe the chief inspector was referring to the loosening effect of *alcohol.*'

Seldon nodded. 'Yes, I was. Thrashing, Clifford?' He rubbed his temples. 'I hope I never find out everything you two have really got up to on previous investigations. Anyway, I loosened the estate agent's tongue with a few drinks at the bar and he let slip Cunliffe approached his boss for a valuation on Gwel an Mor. In strict privacy, mind.'

She bit her lip. 'There's also an old clause, added to the deeds of Gwel an Mor, that states any of the family wishing to live there have the right to do so. Cunliffe reluctantly told me that himself.'

'Likewise the Liddicoats, in relation to their cottage, Chief Inspector,' Clifford said. 'Her ladyship was entertainingly informed of such by the aunts.'

'Interesting,' Seldon said. 'All of which adds up to a definite power struggle over the house. Cunliffe wants to sell, but no one wants to leave, so he can't.'

'Though no one else is supposedly aware of the gentleman's desire to do so?'

'You've seen how they all are with him, Clifford!' She shook her head. 'It's hardly sweet and light when any of them meet him around the house.'

Seldon scratched the back of his neck. 'So, you think they've guessed he wants to sell, Eleanor?'

'Maybe. Or he's told them. Which gives them a possible motive for wanting to get rid of him. Clifford?'

Her butler nodded. 'I concur, my lady.'

Seldon held his hands up. 'On that theory then, ironically, it would mean Mr Cunliffe was right all along, and St Clair was mistakenly killed in his place.' He glanced from one to the other with a frown. 'Though neither of you seems elated by that possibility?'

Clifford's impassive expression flinched. 'Because there is an unsavoury complication, sir. Quite literally.'

Eleanor nodded. 'Hugh, we can't be certain it's not the other way around and *Mr Cunliffe* is the one poisoning the family. Which, incidentally, the aunts insist they are all being. And by Mrs Liddicoat. But it's much more likely it's Cunliffe, given what we know.'

'You're right.' Seldon unfurled his long legs stiffly. 'But why then would he have killed St Clair? It wouldn't have helped him sell Gwel an Mor after all.'

Eleanor shook her head. 'Unfortunately, I can think of one reason immediately. If St Clair had caught Cunliffe crushing, or even just collecting, laurel leaves, as an experienced gardener he might have guessed their intended purpose. Or at least been highly suspicious. Enough to get him killed, certainly.'

Clifford nodded. 'A shrewd point, my lady. And one which might explain Mr Brae's death, perhaps. The poisonous effects of laurel are well known even among the lower ranks of gardeners.'

Seldon looked between them. 'Then, if Odgers isn't the murderer, the picture is blackest for Cunliffe again.'

Eleanor buried her face in her gloves. 'Maybe I should have left well alone!'

Clifford cleared his throat. 'My lady? Chief Inspector?

Might I be so bold as to suggest any further investigation is paused until tomorrow, that the magic of Christmas itself might not be entirely lost?'

'Hear, hear,' Seldon said without hesitation. 'With Odgers behind bars for both murders, no one would have any reason to strike again even if by any remote chance the real killer was still free.'

Eleanor nodded slowly. *Let's hope Hugh's right, Ellie. If not, the festive season could turn very deadly indeed!*

28

The luxurious feel of Eleanor's new emerald velvet gown was reconciling her to having to leave Seldon to play the good guest at the Christmas Day luncheon at Gwel an Mor. And Clifford's thoughtfulness in leaving her a little tissue-wrapped box of chocolates outside her door was also helping. So, feeling in greatly restored festive spirits, she joined her butler waiting at the bottom of the stairs. Holding her arms held out, she twirled her wrists to show off the pearlescent beads adorning the cuffs of her fluted sleeves.

He stared at her. 'Elegant, ladylike and decorous?' He glanced up the stairs. 'Where is my mistress, I wonder?'

'Here, you toad! Only do me a favour and button me up down the back, would you? I simply couldn't reach.' She laughed as he ran a horrified finger around his collar. 'Just joking. As were you, I'm sure.'

His eyes twinkled. 'Of course, my lady. And speaking of mischief, the terrible two are eager to accompany you.' He clapped his hands like a maître d' summoning a waiter. 'Masters Gladstone! Tomkins!'

As her bulldog and ginger tom skidded gleefully around the

corner, she doubled over with laughter. 'Matching Christmas bow ties and miniature felt reindeer's antlers!' She cupped each of their chins, noting the daintily tied ribbons holding their headwear in place. 'You both look very dapper. And wonderfully ridiculous.'

'Courtesy of your housekeeper's sewing ingenuity.'

'But none of us expected we'd still be here on Christmas Day!'

'And packed by your butler, courtesy of sober experience. Shall we?' He turned towards the dining room.

She groaned. 'Will you walk ahead and wave a white flag for me?'

'If you so desire, my lady, but it is unnecessary. It appears Christmas has worked its magic and wrested an unspoken truce from the family.'

'Really?'

A moment later, as she stepped into the dining room, she had to agree. Over by the festive, wreath-decorated windows, in a blackberry velvet jacket with a boutonnière of whorled claret petals, Cunliffe was admiring the snowy view with Clara. Only a few feet away, Marsh was helping Flora hang orange and clove pomanders on the second Christmas tree. Both ladies were dressed in identical cornflower taffeta gowns, while even the usually apathetic Marsh had troubled himself to don a juniper-green jacket. 'Deck the Halls' tinkled from the gramophone, a row of festive stockings swung above the crackling fire and the scent of cinnamon and pine suffused the air.

'Ah, Lady Swift!' The first hint of a smile she'd seen since she'd arrived crossed Cunliffe's face. 'A somewhat belated Happy Christmas to you.'

'And to you, Mr Cunliffe.'

Tomkins bounded past her, antlers bobbing, followed by Gladstone, the silver bell in his bow tie jingling as he added his season's greetings by barking excitedly.

'Oh, and your companions too, I see,' Cunliffe said less enthusiastically.

Clara tittered. 'Flora, just look at the furry darlings. They've come in fancy dress as little cows!'

Marsh rolled his eyes. 'Reindeers! Forgotten your spectacles again?'

Eleanor joined them by the tree. 'Merry Christmas, Edwin, Clara and Flora! It's such a treat to be here, thank you. And everything looks so pretty.'

'As do Flora and I, dear,' Clara said, both sisters flapping their identical long lace neck ruffles.

Eleanor smiled. 'They were going to be my very next words.'

Clifford glided to a stop with a silver tray of fluted glasses.

'Bubbles, Uncle?' Marsh watched his great-aunts ooh-ing and ah-ing over which glass to choose. 'Careful! Anyone might think it's Christmas.'

Before Cunliffe could reply, the dong of a small gong made everyone spin around. Clifford bowed.

'Luncheon is served.'

'Isn't your man a treat,' Clara said wistfully. 'Verily, he sounds the herald's trumpet of ladies entertaining.'

Eleanor hid a smile. 'Actually, he plays the trumpet very well. Do you have one to hand?'

'Thankfully not!' Cunliffe hurriedly waved her into the dining room.

Decorated in sweeping folds of ivory linen, the table was a feast for the eyes. The centrepiece ran the entire length, garlands of intricately woven silvery spruce, gold ribbon, rich red holly berries and soft white Christmas roses were peppered with Lilliputian gingerbread stars. Each place on the table was set with a filigree porcelain plate in the shape of an exquisite snowflake. Accompanying it was a silken napkin folded meticulously to form magnificent wings on the glass angel who held a cracker out to each diner. Individual gold-rimmed fairy lamps threw out dancing patterns from the flickering candle inside. The cutlery shone as smartly as the wind-up tin nutcracker soldiers marching around each place card. And suspended above it all was a shimmering paper-chain snow scene of Father Christmas riding the sky in his sleigh, filled with presents. She mouthed a heartfelt 'thank you' to Clifford, detecting his hand in arranging and creatively adding to what must have been Gwel an Mor's decorations handed down through the generations.

Over a sherry and dish of roasted chestnuts, everyone pulled crackers, which Gladstone and Tomkins thought endless fun as they ran off with the discarded wrappings. Gladstone's enthusiastic woofing was only matched by the delighted squeals from Clara and Flora as they each pinned their prize of a dainty paste brooch to the other's lace ruffle. Mr Cunliffe's slender spectacle-mending kit seemed to please him as well, as he slipped it straight into his pocket.

While the trinkets from the remaining crackers were shared around, Clifford returned with the first course; crab chowder with onion croutons, served in holly-patterned bowls.

Eleanor took a long sniff. 'Goodness, that smells sublime.'

Flora nudged her sister with a pout. 'No consommé!'

Keen to keep the mood upbeat, Eleanor jumped in. 'I confess I know very little about Cornwall. Does it have many festive traditions of its own?'

'"Guise" dancing is one,' Cunliffe said with a shudder.

Leaning over to serve her, Clifford murmured, 'Locals disguise themselves during the festive season, my lady, and go from door to door dancing and singing, among other things.'

Cunliffe grunted. 'Fortunately, Gwel an Mor is too far from the village for the masked horseplay they get up to!'

Clara shook her head. 'Bah! Humbug isn't tradition, Godfrey.'

Flora nodded. 'Unlike carolling gay, and the mummers' plays...'

'Treats, treats, for twelve whole days,' Clara chirped.

'Gin and cake are also given out by the shopkeepers,' Marsh said languidly. 'And murder, I suppose.'

Clifford caught her eye as he served smoked mackerel mousse cups and liver pâté toasts garnished with a peculiar-looking parsley. She turned to Marsh. 'I shan't add that to my list of Cornish memories. As it's hardly festive. Nor a tradition, I'm sure.'

Cunliffe snorted. 'Do try your best to be agreeable for once, Edwin. Or indeed, try your best to do anything other than lie around the house!'

'Boots!' Flora trilled. 'Too many boots.'

Clara gasped. 'Will they be back?'

Cunliffe tutted. 'Compose yourselves. The police have found all they wanted. They have no need to return.'

Clara waved a chiding finger. 'Godfrey, keeping secrets is as dreadful as whispering. Terribly bad manners of you.'

'Shocking show, Uncle!' Marsh said gleefully.

Cunliffe shuffled in his seat. 'I've no need to keep anything secret. Why should I? If you must know, that preposterous buffoon, Inspector Trevilick, told me one of the bottles they took from St Clair's office contained traces of cyanide. The same poison as was found in the post-mortem.' He nodded knowingly. 'It's so obvious now. Brae and Odgers were in the perfect position to have slipped it into St Clair's drink.'

'Which is which?' Flora peered around the table through her lorgnettes.

'Brae is the dead one,' Marsh said carelessly.

'And Odgers is the one behind bars,' Cunliffe said firmly. 'Where he belongs. I say they killed St Clair together. Then fell out and Odgers took his shears—'

'Well, that was nice of him, dear,' Clara said. 'Troubling to finish his work first.'

Marsh's childish giggle gave Eleanor goosebumps. Evidently her butler too, as he raised an eyebrow while setting down in front of her a ramekin bubbling with whiting and leek crumble topped with a devilled egg.

Oh, well, Ellie. As everyone else is talking about it...

She picked up her glass. 'Mr Cunliffe, I hope it doesn't seem insensitive if we toast our relief that you have come out of all this unscathed?'

His brows met. 'No. But why shouldn't I have?'

'Oh, only because you told me you believed St Clair might have been killed in mistake for you?'

Marsh smirked. 'Bad conscience, Uncle?'

Cunliffe scowled at him. 'That's quite enough! I see my error now. It wasn't St Clair that was trying to kill me. It was Brae and Odgers. However, St Clair was definitely an occultist. And practising his wicked black arts in my gardens, the mongrel! But fate made that his undoing.'

'How so?' Flora said, clearing her plate.

'Because it seems Brae and Odgers were running a stolen goods scam. On my property, no less! But even fools like them knew that a man with such a tight grasp on his faculties as I would soon realise their deception. Which is why they tried to kill me. Only they mistook St Clair instead.'

Marsh sniggered into his drink. Cunliffe shot him a filthy look.

Everyone ate in silence until Clifford cleared the dishes and served the next course; roast duck, pickled figs, chestnut stuffing, redcurrant cauliflower, honeyed gammon, and the greenest of herb-crusted potatoes.

Eleanor waved at the food. 'Gracious! How spoiled I feel!'

'Gratitude elsewhere wouldn't go amiss,' Cunliffe grunted

with another filthy glance at Marsh. 'However, *you* are welcome, Lady Swift.'

She felt uncomfortably aware that all eyes now seemed to be on her. 'Did Inspector Trevilick tell you your likely discovery of their scam was why Odgers and Brae wanted you out of the way?'

'He... he didn't disagree with me,' Cunliffe said stiffly. 'So, there it is.'

'Maybe. Just a thought, though...' Eleanor hesitated. 'Mightn't that reasoning suggest that St Clair was the original target because *he* was likely to find out about their scam, too? Maybe even before you, given it was all happening in the gardens?'

Cunliffe shook his head vigorously. 'Out of the question!'

He seems very sure, Ellie.

She changed tack. 'Flora? The man you saw in the garden the day St Clair was killed. Was he, perhaps... pushing anything?'

Clara clapped her hands. 'Silly gardener! Summer goes, and winter comes with pinching toes.'

'When in the garden bare and brown, Flora...' They both pointed expectantly at Clifford.

'You must lay your barrow down.' He intoned with an apologetic look to Cunliffe. 'Robert Louis Stevenson, sir.'

The ladies both applauded.

Clara peered at Eleanor. 'But no, dear. Of course we didn't see him with his wheelbarrow.'

She nodded. 'I see, I just wondered—'

Flora spun around. 'Because he would have wheeled St Clair's body along the shadowed edge of the lawn where the light doesn't reach, obviously.'

Clara laughed shrilly. 'Yes, yes. Edwin isn't that stupid. Are you, dear?'

'Me?' Marsh spluttered. 'It's nothing to do with me! I told

you it was one of those conniving under-gardeners.' He thumped the table. 'Neither of you old biddies can see further than the end of your noses!'

Flora polished her spectacles on Clara's lace ruff. 'Edwin, it's not nice to blame the servants, dear.'

Her sister smiled indulgently. 'And we know you would have been clever enough to cover the body with garden clippings.'

Marsh glared at her. 'I tell you, I—'

'Don't be upset, Edwin, dear.' Flora looped her finger around her long string of blue beads. 'It's Christmas, remember. And anyway, you would have been too busy.'

'Busy?' Cunliffe scoffed. 'How exactly does lying about all day constitute being busy?'

'Godfrey, let the boy be,' Clara scolded. 'You obviously haven't seen him and his friend carrying all those boxes and hiding them—'

Marsh sprang up, scraping his chair back. 'If you two weren't so ancient, I'd—'

'Sit!' Cunliffe thundered.

As Marsh slowly sat back down, Eleanor's brow furrowed.

Could Marsh's 'friend' be Mr Liddicoat, Ellie? And that's what they were arguing about at the cottage?

She looked up to see him staring at her. She waved her napkin.

'Dash of gravy on my chin, is there?'

'No,' he said casually, slinging one leg over the other. 'Just wondering if you're enjoying your stay? Cornwall's delights captivating you?'

'Yes, Lady Swift,' Cunliffe said hurriedly. 'You really must detour via some on your way home.'

She ignored the implication. 'Honestly, I haven't seen much of anything. I haven't even found a moment to explore the gardens here at Gwel an Mor.'

Marsh shot her a look. 'Shouldn't bother.'

'Of course you haven't, Lady Swift,' Cunliffe cut in. 'To the estate's shame, it is just a wilderness beyond the immediate lawn and kitchen garden. No one goes any further. That is why I was paying to have the whole lot landscaped. Dear, dear. We talked about that in my study.'

She nodded slowly. 'We did, yes. But Mr Marsh has made me think.'

Marsh spluttered in his drink. 'No, I haven't.'

She smiled sweetly. 'Yes. About gaining the most from being here.' She turned to Cunliffe. 'Would it be terribly rude if I excused myself after luncheon? Someone in the village invited me to experience a traditional Cornish Christmas. And I thought—'

'And so do I. Tremendous idea,' Cunliffe said, rather too readily to her mind.

Flora shook her head. 'Unlike the plum pudding, Godfrey.'

Her sister sighed dolefully. 'And the comfrey custard.'

'And the empty glass,' Marsh added, waving his pointedly.

Eleanor rose and, having wished everyone a happy Christmas again, darted to the pantry, empty save for Clifford who was placing the rest of the plates ready for Mrs Liddicoat to wash up.

'You need your boots.'

He frowned. 'Just to sit in the Rolls while you drive us back to the village to "bump into" a certain gentleman?'

'No, it's a horrible number of hours before we've arranged to meet Hugh. I thought after luncheon I'd have to struggle through endless rounds of drinks and games like charades first, but now I can escape.'

He frowned. 'My lady, guest etiquette—'

'Does not apply when one's host couldn't be more pleased to see the back of one.'

'Possibly. If I might enquire, however. Boots?'

'Yes. We're going to take a walk around the gardens. But don't ask me what I'm looking for. Nor what I expect to find. I just have a feeling we'll recognise it when we do.'

His brow flinched. 'Then let us hope, whatever it is, it doesn't recognise us first!'

29

Outside, Eleanor trudged across endless white-blanketed lawns and paths, her belief waning that she would know what she was looking for when she saw it as she scanned the snow-covered gardens.

'Gladstone's got the right idea, Clifford.' She pointed a mittened-hand at her bulldog who, nose furiously twitching, was charging through a clump of frosted bushes. 'He who seeks will find!'

'If you say so, my lady.' Clifford's tone was sceptical.

Scooping up Tomkins, she set off again. Her ginger tom, however, despite his usual aversion to cold weather, hopped out of her arms onto a low retaining wall and bounded after his friend.

She soon had to admit to herself, however, that Clifford's scepticism wasn't entirely unfounded. Dusted head to foot in snow, she halted in front of a soaring box hedge that looked as if it had never seen Brae or Odgers' shears. The chill nipping at her frost-red cheeks combined with the memory of the last time she'd seen a pair of shears sent a shiver down her spine. The enormity of the task she had impetuously set herself and Clifford sank in.

'The end of the maintained gardens, would you say?'

'Most assuredly, my lady. And surprisingly further out from the house than I had imagined.'

She shrugged. 'Surprising because?'

'Because the head gardener died two winters back and was not replaced. Mr Brae told us so.'

'So only he and Odgers had been caring for the gardens since then, you mean? Right up until St Clair was engaged only a few months ago, in fact.' She cocked her head. 'Somehow that sort of work ethic doesn't fit the image of two unsupervised rogues only interested in running their stolen goods scam?'

'Hmm, inconsistent indeed. Unless their dedicated labours were to ensure they were left to their own devices so that their roguery would not be discovered?'

'It could be. We overheard them saying just that when they were hedge trimming! What's still inconsistent though, is Mr Cunliffe's decision to save money by employing only the two of them all that time after he went to the expense of restoring the house so magnificently. It meant that when he finally did take on St Clair, it was a much bigger job than it might have been.'

Clifford eyed her sideways. 'Like ours.'

She held her hands up. 'I might have underestimated the difficulty of exploring the estate's extensive garden and woods. Mostly as it has been allowed to run wild for half a century or more. And it is covered in snow. And with a butler with one arm in a sling. But *listen...*'

At her unexpected earnestness, he half-bowed. 'Do proceed, my lady.'

'Thank you.' She gathered her thoughts. 'We've been fixating on Gwel an Mor and its...'

'Somewhat "eccentric" inhabitants?'

'Exactly, Clifford. But everybody, and everything, has been connected to one thing.'

For a moment, he said nothing, then he nodded slowly. 'I assume you are referring to the *gardens* of Gwel an Mor, my lady, not the house?'

'Yes. We're only here because Mr Cunliffe believed St Clair was out to kill him. And St Clair was only here because he was employed to completely renovate those gardens. The very gardens Mr Cunliffe accused St Clair of wanting to get hold of for his supposed black arts practices, whatever they were. And the same gardens Mr Brae, an under-gardener, was found murdered in.'

He nodded grimly. 'And in which two attempts were made on your life.'

'And in which Brae and Odgers were hiding their illegal goods. And in which we think Marsh and the Liddicoats were equally up to no good in, it seems.'

'In fact, my lady, the only person, or persons, without a link to the gardens are—'

'Clara and Flora, the only two people we have discounted as suspects.' Her eyes widened. 'Clifford. Do you remember what that... er, unsettling woman said the first time we went down to Lostenev?'

'Addled Aida?'

'Yes, her. I told her we were from Gwel an Mor and she said something about "what's buried in the past"?'

'I believe the lady said, "Let what's buried in the past, stay in the past."'

'Well, suppose she wasn't just... you know, eccentric. And suppose she wasn't speaking metaphorically? Suppose St Clair stumbled on something that got him killed. Something actually, physically buried here in the gardens at Gwel an Mor. We know smuggling was rife around these parts not fifty years ago.'

Clifford rubbed his chin, deep in thought. 'And looting the

cargo of ships that had foundered on the rocks was a common practice. If that was the case, however, then it is almost certain it would have been discovered by now. Unless...'

'Unless it was buried in the overgrown part of the estate grounds that haven't been touched in over half a century!'

He pursed his lips. 'If I might recommend that you never search for a needle in a haystack, my lady. Especially a needle whose presence is dubious to begin with.'

She waggled a finger at him. 'Hardly the spirit, Clifford. It's not like you to forget to pack hope and fortitude in your travelling case.'

He sniffed, gesturing at the ribbon-thin opening in the hedge Gladstone, and now Tomkins, had disappeared through. 'I was merely lamenting not having Mr St Clair's landscaping plan at our disposal. I assume he would have explored the gardens thoroughly first in order to compile it. At least, in so far as time allowed before his regrettable demise. We might have used it for orienting ourselves at least.'

She nodded. 'I agree, but he burnt it. Which still seems peculiar for a man so passionate about his work. No worry, you can use the details in his notebook as a guide and sketch us a new one as we go. Onwards!'

With a resigned look, he followed her as she pushed her way through the gap in the hedge. Emerging drenched in snow, the biting wind nipping at her cheeks, she waited for him to appear beside her, equally snow laden. In front of them, three long, interconnecting pools were flanked by a regiment of crumbling fluted columns. The water was covered in congealed algae and slushy snow. Clumps of dead brown rushes and half-concealed rusting pipes that were obviously once dancing fountains stood out against the blanket of white all around. Gladstone lumbered to the water's edge, but to her relief, before she could call out, he wrinkled his nose and turned away.

'Clifford. Look! The pools are rectangular. Why is that striking a chord?'

'Because they are recorded here in Mr St Clair's notebook, my lady. But again, without any particular symbols or measurements. So, I assume, again, he did not think them of particular consequence.'

She scrabbled in her pocket and flicked through the pages. Together they turned in a circle, repeatedly peering down and back up.

'Dash it! No urns or whatever that other thing was you said, Clifford.'

'Amphora, my lady.'

Wafts of rotting vegetation rose around her as she led the way along the water to a ruined folly at the far end.

A forsaken tribute to Italianate romance, a particularly insidious dark ivy had threaded itself into every inch of the temple's walls, adding even more dankness to the musty air. The intricate black and white tiled floor was scattered with crumbled pillar posts and arch cappings she could imagine Romeo chasing a laughing Juliet in and out of.

A wash of sadness passed over her. 'It must have been beautiful in its day. I wish we could offer Mr Cunliffe Joseph's services to help restore this part back to its former glory. It's like love has been lost forever here.'

Clifford cleared his throat. 'Love can never be destroyed, my lady.'

Her long-burning curiosity over whether his heart had ever been made whole by a special girl flared brighter at the tinge of wistfulness in his tone. But he was far too private a man to even think of asking.

'Well, unfortunately a murderer destroys whomever their evil hand sees fit to.' She gave up trying to pull some of the ivy away, much to Tomkins' meow of disappointment. 'But why they saw fit to do so at Gwel an Mor evidently isn't going to leap out and reveal itself. So all I can think to do is keep exploring this wonderland.'

His lips quirked. 'Then, Alice, let us continue down the rabbit hole...'

30

The path leading out of the opposite end of the Italianate folly led to a patch of dense greenery. It clawed at her cloak and snagged her laces until she was stopped short by a vast impenetrable expanse of interwoven woody vines, each thicker than her arm. Then she saw it.

'Here, Clifford! Someone's sliced their way through. And fairly recently, by the look of these cuts.'

He stepped up and examined them. 'Indeed. I believe we may be blundering inelegantly in Mr St Clair's footsteps.'

She rolled her eyes. 'Yet, remarkably, you aren't making a fuss about it!'

He made some more additions to his own notebook and then brushed the snow pointedly from his coat sleeves and hat brim.

After an uneven tussle, she wrenched herself clear on the other side of the vines only to flinch at the eerie rustling now filling her ears.

'What an incredible bamboo forest! Even on my travels, I didn't see such a wide variety of colours and stems that thick.'

'Indeed. Most impressive.' Clifford coaxed Gladstone

through a larger gap in the vine wall than the one the bulldog was adamant he could follow Tomkins through. 'To the extent one might have been transported to the tropics and subtropics all at once.'

She slipped off her mittens to run her hands down the striated joints of a sturdy black stem. 'But we're in Cornwall. In freezing December.'

'Testament to the hardiness of the bamboo family. It is found in many climes. If memory serves—'

She nudged his good arm gently. 'Before it serves you any more, Mr Walking Encyclopaedia, I say we keep moving forwards before we freeze standing here. We're trying to find out what it was that St Clair might have stumbled upon that might have got him killed, remember.' She frowned. 'Although the only path through seems to be over there.'

He followed the direction of her finger. 'Because it is a natural seam of granite, I would suggest. And the first sign nature might not be entirely opposed to our endeavours. Shall we?'

With virtually no snow having penetrated the bamboo's canopy, progress was easier underfoot. However, it was less so in other ways, as they fought their way around the thick stems, the ground littered with fallen stalks ready to trip unwary feet.

'No, Master Gladstone!' Clifford called firmly as the bulldog lumbered forward gleefully to pick one up. 'The fine hairs will cause irritation to your throat.'

'Gracious, I never knew that.' She ruffled her disgruntled dog's ears. 'Don't worry, old chum, treats a plenty will be yours. When we finally get out of here,' she muttered. 'And you, Tomk—' She broke off, realising her cat was not also pawing her enthusiastically at the mention of treats. Instead, he was sitting a yard ahead, back turned, batting at something with his paw.

'What have you got, you monster?'

Clifford stepped forward. 'If I might spare you the sight of whatever your ginger menace has caught and chewed half of?'

She grimaced. 'Willingly. But I thought he was too indulged and fed to actually hunt anything faster than a worm?'

Standing over the cat, who was staring up at him innocently, Clifford nodded. 'How right you are, my lady. If I may relieve you of that, Master Tomkins?'

Eleanor hurried over as her butler straightened up, palm outstretched.

'Clifford! It's one of St Clair's drafting pens like we saw in his office. He must have dropped it, ducking around all this bamboo. So we really are on his heels.'

'Yet nothing in that notebook even vaguely represents bamboo or a forest.' He held up a finger. 'If whatever Mr St Clair discovered in the garden was the reason he was murdered, however—'

'Yes, I shall personally hold hands with Prudence the rest of the way. Tomkins, double treats for you!'

After a lot more gymnastics to stay on the path, the bamboo forest finally seemed to thin.

'It's very dark ahead, though,' Eleanor murmured. 'Dash it, it might be a dead-end wall of rock.'

Clifford, torch in hand, pulled aside a section of the tangled curtain of juniper-green creeper. She gasped.

'Oh my! It's a head carved into the rock. With enormous protruding eyes and flared nostrils. It's even got giant fiendish teeth like a proper monster. But St Clair hadn't noted that down in his notebook either. Have we suddenly lost his trail?'

'Or maybe this is as far as he got before...' He poked his top half and torch through the gap in the central teeth. 'Fortunately, my lady, it seems to be the entrance to a short tunnel and, thus, hopefully, our exit.'

A moment later, she emerged from the other side, rubbing her eyes as they shuffled out into the daylight.

In front of them was a semicircular stone wall, a giant earthenware pot set on top. Strangely, it had a slit on one side. Peering in, she could just see an old lantern. Just below the slit were the letters 'S.R.' Walking around to the back of the pot, she was drawn up short.

'It's a flower bed, hedged by very overgrown box.'

'Quite. Presided over by a weeping fig, I think I am correct in saying.' He frowned.

'Weeping fig? Oh, the maiden's hair!' she cried. 'That's how St Clair must have noted it to himself. And the lantern pot is the urn with the rectangular cut-out!'

Clifford skimmed through the notebook. 'Ah, here! It is, indeed. The box hedging is depicted by this frame. And the curve of the wall behind the flowerbed, by this ellipse curve below the urn. Bravo, my lady.'

'But I've no idea what it means,' she groaned.

'Likely neither did Mr St Clair, but it struck a man of his extensive experience in garden design as odd enough to note.'

'Then there must be more to this.'

'There is, my lady. A variety of shrubs has proliferated in each bed in every section of the garden we have seen so far, the key being the mixture of the plants. Notably for providing a wide palette of colours in season, or shape, or scents. Here, however, there is only one.'

She peered at the waist-high, soft needle-leaves, unable to put her finger on what seemed odd about them until she ran one of the silvery green swathes through her palm, releasing a familiar aroma. 'It's rosemary, Clifford. Have we come full circle and are nearly back at the house then?'

He studied his incomplete plan. 'Partially, I think, my lady. But we are still a distance from there.'

'Then why grow an entire bed of one herb so far from the main house? No one is ever going to enjoy it on their roast potatoes.'

His eyes twinkled mischievously. 'Perhaps because not everyone is such a devotee of food as yourself?'

'Very droll. Seriously though, you remember I said I wouldn't know what I was looking for until I found it? Well, emerging from that tunnel, I think I might have found it. Or at least part of it. Although, what "it" is, I still have no idea.'

Clifford tutted. 'Master Gladstone, no digging!'

She waved him down. 'No wait. Why is he digging? He hasn't done that once all the way here.' She held her bulldog aside and parted the woody stems of the rosemary. 'You silly thing, that's not something we can throw for you. It's an engraved metal plant label.' She looked closer, wiping away the soil only to find a patina of iron red corrosion. '*Salvia Ros... Rosmarinus*, maybe? Latin for rosemary, Clifford?'

'Almost certainly.'

Slowly, she straightened up, a frown on her face. Hurrying back to the urn, she pulled the two wooden plant sticks out from her pocket. As she glanced between them and the urn, her eyes widened.

'Clifford! I thought so! There's two letters engraved in this urn just below the slit. And they match the letters on the plant stick I found near St Clair's body!'

31

As they continued in St Clair's footsteps, Eleanor and Clifford discussed their latest discovery. Neither of them, however, could work out its significance by the time they were halted by a wall of giant umbrella leaves.

'Clifford? Is that... no, I must be dreaming. Is that an enormous wheel in a bed of gargantuan rhubarb? Those plants are surely eight or nine feet high.'

Clifford eyed them. 'Close on both counts, my lady. And I believe the "wheel" is the remnants of an oriental-style viewing bridge in the middle of a small lake or pond. Those plants are growing in or around water.'

'Gladstone, no!' Her hands flew to her mouth at the sight of her bulldog's stumpy tail disappearing excitedly under the giant leaves.

Clifford seemed unmoved. 'Master Gladstone is usually cautious enough around water, my lady.'

'I know, but imagine how enormous any fish in there will be after all this time! If he ventured in, they'd probably think lunch had finally come after years of waiting.'

Her butler's eyes shone with amusement as he busied

himself adding to his drawing of the garden so far. 'I have never tried bulldog as bait when fishing, my lady. A top tip for reeling in a prize behemoth, perhaps.'

'Clifford!'

'Did you hear an ungainly splash?' he said calmly. 'Neither did I.'

She ducked down to her haunches and peered under the fan of overlapping leaves. 'Gladstone! Dry and safe. Oh! And stepping stones. Come on!'

She scooped Tomkins into her arms and placed a boot gingerly on the first stone. 'It's perfectly firm. Not that you'd struggle anyway, Clifford, even with one arm. You're part mountain goat, I swear.'

Stepping across the unexpectedly clear water under the vast canopy felt even more otherworldly than anything so far. Bathed in weak, green light, it felt like a miniature world of its own. Even more so, now she could see it was also home to extensive clumps of bulrushes, reeds and water lilies.

'Clifford. Don't you feel like Alice again? You know? Having drunk from the bottle labelled "Drink Me", you've now shrunk?'

He shook his head. 'No, my lady. I feel like a beleaguered butler. Though on an equally preposterous journey.'

The stepping stones deposited them on the other side of the lake, helpfully dry, but now facing a seemingly impenetrable jungle of rhododendrons and ferns.

'Dash it! How are we supposed to follow St Clair's footsteps now? I can't see any sign of anyone having cut or forced their way through that lot.'

Clifford seemed too deep in thought to be listening. 'There must be a way through,' he murmured. He looked up. 'And close by since, as you mentioned, none of the undergrowth has been cut.'

He strode up to a large boulder and peered over the top. She joined him, a hand flying to her mouth.

'How did you know there was a grotto? I bet even Mr Cunliffe doesn't realise it's here. I can't imagine he's ever come out this far. Unless he is our murderer.'

'Let us sincerely hope not,' Clifford muttered. 'And to answer your question, I did not know, I guessed. No self-respecting garden of this size would be complete without such.'

Steps wound down until they were inside a small cave, the walls covered in pearlescent shells. As she went, she examined every inch, but nothing struck her.

Which, as you're still not sure what you're looking for, Ellie, isn't surprising.

Over in the furthest corner, Clifford waved his torch, then pointed it at the floor.

She darted over.

'The floor is covered in frescoes made from pebbles, Clifford. They look like those Roman gods in that ancient book you once showed me one wet afternoon.'

He tutted. 'Most unmemorably, it appears, since they were *Greek* gods.' His brow flinched as he swept the torch further along. 'And these first few tell the tale of Hercules, or *Heracles*, as he is also known.'

'But that's just mythology. Hardly significant to a double murder investigation in Cornwall.'

'If you say so, my lady. However, Hercules met his end by *poison.*'

Her eyes widened. 'Like St Clair?' He nodded. 'Coincidence, do you think?'

He shrugged. 'It is recorded here in Mr St Clair's notebook, but quite plainly. So it seems he did not see it as unusual, unlike the lantern flower bed.'

She shivered and tapped her leg for her bulldog and cat to

stay close. 'How about we check the rest but get out of here as soon as possible?'

They hastened along the grotto's passageway, which quickly emerged into the garden again. Having tottered obediently alongside, Gladstone collapsed next to an ancient metal seat, Tomkins curling up with him. Clifford spread out a pristine handkerchief on a nearby fallen tree trunk and waved for her to sit down.

'Perhaps a warming snifter from my emergency hip flask with a baked apple ring chaser and a mint humbug for afters?'

'Well, since you remissly forgot to pack your pockets with roast pheasant and all the trimmings, they'll more than do.' She smiled affectionately as she accepted his flask. 'I wonder who last sat on this? And what they were thinking?'

'Not about murder, one would hope,' Clifford muttered.

She interspersed feeding Tomkins and Gladstone baked liver treats while watching his pen float across the page. She marvelled at how much of the garden's detail he had included on such a limited canvas. As she finished the last of her humbug, he held it out to her. She studied it for a moment.

'It's beautiful, but have we learned anything obviously related to the murders?'

'Mmm. Perhaps not that I can see at this juncture.'

'Then, once you have had several sips of brandy for your elbow, which I know must be painful – don't argue – we'll continue.'

Once Clifford had fortified himself and the brandy was safely stowed away, they set off again with Gladstone and Tomkins in equally restored form. A shingle path led them down a short flight of precariously sunken stone steps to a long walkway that snaked between overgrown herbaceous bushes and eroded classical statues.

'More Greek gods and the like, are they, Clifford?'

'No, my lady. Merely maidens riding dolphins or carrying plentiful baskets. Of herring or mackerel, I think.'

'They're supposed to ride swans or unicorns, aren't they?'

'This is Cornwall.'

'I know. But even in Cornwall, some rules still apply, surely? In gardening terms at least. You said so yourself.'

'I did?'

'Yes. You said a grand house like this would be ashamed not to have a grotto, an Italianate sanctuary, a walled kitchen garden, and so on. And surely a maze?'

'Or a labyrinth as this is. A maze has a multitude of paths, only one of which usually leads to the centre. A labyrinth, on the other hand, has a single path which always leads to the centre... ah! I believe we have indeed arrived.'

She glanced around. 'It's just a sundial on a plinth.'

'Indeed it is. However, it is an unusually large plinth that allows one to look over the labyrinth and view the majority of the garden, it seems.' He frowned. 'And it is recorded here in Mr St Clair's notebook in some detail. As is the sundial...'

As he studied the notebook, she looked around from the plinth's raised vantage point. Her gaze was caught by an object only a short distance away.

'Clifford! That's that giant earthenware urn with the old lantern in, isn't it?'

He grunted without looking up. 'From the layout I have been able to draw so far, possibly yes, my lady. As I mentioned, we have been walking in a circle and it isn't actually that far as the crow flies.' He glanced from the notebook to the sundial and back. 'A disgraceful amateur mistake, however.'

'What is?'

'It seems Mr St Clair has recorded here in his notebook a peculiarity of the sundial I have just noted myself. See the gnomon here on the dial's face?' He looked up and ran his gloved finger along the top of the solid triangular protrusion attached at the middle point of the dial. 'When the sun hits this tapered metal edge, it creates a shadow which points to an engraved number.'

She nodded. 'Which tells you the correct time. I know.'

His brow flinched. 'Only, it doesn't.' He clicked open his pocket compass. 'This is orientated incorrectly.'

'So it will tell the wrong time?'

'Precisely.' He glanced between his compass and the dial, muttering to himself. Finally, he looked up. 'At midday, this will read three o'clock in the afternoon.'

She waved a beckoning hand. 'Odd. But I'll show you something even odder.'

She led him back to the vantage point where she'd been able to see the earthenware pot and lantern, then pointed off to the left.

'Clifford, do you see! It's another giant pot.' They hastened over, Gladstone and Tomkins picking up on the excitement. 'Look! This one has the same long slit as the previous one. And another old lantern inside. And there are letters below the slit again!' She pulled the two plant sticks from her pocket again. Her face fell. '"V.T."? That doesn't match the letters on either plant stick.'

He peered at the plants in the bed behind through his pince-nez.

'And there is but one plant again. I am minded to identify it as sea lavender, but that is a far from confident claim. And presiding over it is a weeping mulberry tree. Mmm. Similar to the weeping fig in the last one, in fact.'

'Represented by maiden's hair again in the notebook?' She scrabbled in the earth, nudging an exuberant Gladstone out of the way. 'And there's a metal name marker, too.' She pulled it out and wiped it clean. "*Limo... nium Lati... latifolium*", I think.'

She handed it to Clifford, who studied it closely, then shook his head.

'I'm afraid I cannot decipher with any more certainty... my lady.'

She waved him to join her, then pointed as she slowly turned in a circle.

'What do you see, Clifford?'

'More urns, my lady!'

'Exactly. And what's the betting that one of them matches the other plant label I've got in my pocket? And that the others match the plant labels that were taken from St Clair's office?'

He nodded gravely. 'I think, my lady, we may have partially uncovered one of the secrets of Gwel an Mor.'

She nodded gravely. 'Yes. We have. But has the killer?'

32

A tall, athletically built form emerged from the blanket of pearl-grey fog swaddling Lostenev's harbour. Eleanor's heart skipped.

'You should have waited inside. It's bitterly cold out here.'

'Is it?' Seldon's handsome features broke into a smile. 'I had something far too important on my mind to notice.' He cleared the distance in two long-legged strides to wrap her in his soft wool coat. 'You.' He buried his face in her fiery red curls.

'Suddenly I wish we were back at Henley Hall,' she breathed, stirred with even fiercer yearning by the delicate scents of cedar, citrus and fresh soap lingering on his neck. 'You were right, Hugh. This is torture.'

He pulled away and ran his thumbs gently over her rosy cheeks. 'No, this is Cornwall. And we're still here because you care too much about bringing the guilty to justice.'

'And making sure the innocent don't suffer for the guilty's sins,' she muttered. 'Thank you.' She fiddled with her sage-green kid gloves. 'I know we said we would leave the whole matter alone for Christmas Day but—'

'But.' He shrugged sheepishly. 'Maybe I haven't actually managed to leave it either.'

She laughed in relief. 'Good.'

He turned her towards the inn. 'Now, if we are going to discuss it, at least let's do so in the warm and dry, please.'

She nodded, having had no intention of mentioning their discoveries that afternoon, quite yet. Clifford had agreed with her. Seldon's long-experienced policeman's brain worked best on solid facts and hard evidence. Until they had either, or both, she wouldn't clog it up with what might just turn out to be fanciful notions in the end.

As they neared Kerensa Come Quick, Seldon peered over his shoulder. 'Where's Clifford?'

'Staying out of the way so we could at least say hello properly, I imagine.' The side door into the inn's snug bar opened. 'There you are.' She tutted teasingly. 'It's hardly playing chaperone, skulking off inside the warm here with Tomkins and Gladstone like that. Tsk!'

The homely-proportioned landlady shuffled past with a tray of empty glasses, cackling. 'That's not what I'd call what me and Mr Clifford's been playin'!'

A round of tipsy laughter rang around the room, which Eleanor now noticed was awash with Sunday best jackets and dresses and lots of wonkily worn newspaper hats. Clifford rolled his eyes, but said nothing as they hurried in and closed the door behind them to keep the chill out.

'Over there, my lady. A Cornish Christmas awaits.'

He gestured towards a cosy table near the fire, already set with two drinks. Beside it, on a wool blanket, her bulldog and cat were sharing a bowl of something evidently delicious. Extra sprays of holly looped along the mantelpiece and bar, while candle lights strung between the multitude of model ships twinkled. A modest Christmas tree also added a seasonal feel, infusing the room with the welcoming smell of fresh pine. Strings of baked red and green apple slices wound around the branches like tinsel, adding extra hints of cinnamon. She peeped through the open door on the other side of the bar into the main saloon, delighting in the riotous merrymaking going on in the pub proper. She hadn't expected to spot Inspector Trevilick in there, but she returned his genial wave and call of 'Happy Christmas!'

She slid into the seat Clifford held out, appreciating Seldon waiting for her to be settled before taking his.

'Assorted nibbles are on their way,' Clifford said. 'If you will forgive the presumption.'

She nodded vigorously. 'Always where food is involved. Only you'll need a drink and a plate too. It's a matter of business first, Hugh and I decided. If you can bear it?'

He nodded guardedly. 'Unquestionably, in regard to business, my lady. However, flouting the rules any further and sitting in the presence of one's mistress...'

'Oh, here, man!' Seldon dragged a chair up. 'It's a bit late for pretending anything is even remotely as it should be around here, isn't it?'

Clifford perched stiffly on the edge of the seat. 'If you say so, Chief Inspector.'

'That means no, by the way, Hugh,' Eleanor whispered loudly behind her hand. 'I'm just longing for the day it breaks out of my quietly implacable butler and he actually voices his mind for once. Although, he'll most likely start by spluttering out that he's been aching to boil my head from the moment I arrived at Henley Hall.'

Seldon laughed as Clifford pretended to think that over. 'He probably would if he could squeeze a word in.'

The two men shared an amused look.

She folded her arms in a mock huff. 'Rotters, the pair of you, as I've said before! Now, let's get this unpleasantness over with before the food arrives, if we can.' She pointed over her shoulder as an accordion wheezed into life in the main salon, inciting many of the others in the snug to burst into spontaneous song. 'Helpfully, no one's going to overhear us with that jolly racket going on. But you can't have much to tell, Hugh?'

'Actually, you'd be surprised. I'll start with what my office discovered about Edwin Marsh.'

'But hang on. You said before that getting any information from there would be as good as impossible over Christmas.'

'I did. And it should have been. But there's a new man, a bright young chap, who's looking to get on in the force and he excelled himself.'

'So what did he unearth about Marsh?'

'That he used to live in London. On an allowance. But lived way beyond his means.'

'Gambling debts?' Clifford said. 'Owed to unsavoury types, perchance?'

'Very unsavoury types. And debts which he couldn't pay. He was also in trouble with the police for running a series of small betting scams. So, lo and behold, he flees to the relative safety of Cornwall.'

'And bolts to Gwel an Mor,' Eleanor said. 'Or is it "retiring", Clifford, that gentlemen like to say in difficult circumstances?'

'Yes, my lady.' He sniffed. 'But "bolting" serves admirably in Mr Marsh's case.'

Seldon nodded. 'Marsh is clearly here to hide from those who want their money. Or retribution. Possibly both.'

Eleanor savoured a sip of her sherry. 'So if Marsh inherited Gwel an Mor, he could sell it and pay off his debts. And then go back to his old disreputable life in London. He must be screaming with boredom down here in sleepy Cornwall.'

Seldon frowned, distractedly tickling Tomkins who now purring against his broad chest. 'I think his sort would be more likely to start up again somewhere else, without paying anything off. Either way, he would need Cunliffe disposed of first.'

'And his great-aunts,' Clifford said. 'A third share of the

estate would not go far enough for a person with such expensive habits.'

Eleanor hid a smile as her butler flinched at the landlady bustling into his chair on the pretext of setting a tankard of porter down in front of him. 'One on the house. For all your keensome help.' She winked and trotted off, laughing.

Eleanor eyed him teasingly. 'I will nag out of you what shenanigans you and our comely hostess have been up to later.'

'Shenanigans, as if!' Clifford muttered into his drink.

She hid a smile. 'Go on, Hugh. Oh, no wait. Remember I touched on the fact that my disgraceful butler dragged me into eavesdropping on Marsh and that man Liddicoat?'

He nodded. 'Not that I believed for a second it wasn't the other way around, but yes.'

'Well, at the time I overheard them, I thought they were just discussing the hope that Trevilick, or me and Clifford, would find evidence Mr Cunliffe killed St Clair. Possibly, evidence they'd planted. But now I realise they were also arguing about something else they are involved in together. In fact, Aunt Clara mentioned at the Christmas luncheon that she and Flora had spotted Marsh and his "friend" basically up to no good in the gardens.'

He threw his hands out. 'Is anyone in this part of the world not running something illegal?'

'It is a simple matter of being acquainted with Cornish history, Chief Inspector,' Clifford said.

'Which I am not.' Seldon sat back, cradling Tomkins, and took a sip of his ale. 'But I'm sure you are. Like everything else. So explain away.'

'Even as recently as fifty years ago, much of the population was still involved in activities deemed unlawful in certain quarters.'

'Quarters like the law,' Seldon said pointedly.

'Quite. But a different view was held strongly in this region.

Smuggling was considered a legitimate business. One merely bypassing the onerous, and grossly unfair, import taxes of the time. Often two hundred per cent or more. And with its remote clifftop position, Gwel an Mor would have been a perfect base of operations for hiding smuggled merchandise.'

Eleanor rapped the table. 'And not just in the past. Right now.'

Seldon stroked his chin. 'Hmm. Well, it sounds like Marsh and the Liddicoats both have reasons to want Cunliffe out of the way. And if their so called "business interests" clashed with those of the under-gardeners, then they had a motive for killing Brae as well.' He frowned. 'It's odd, though, Trevilick not uncovering anything about their illegal dealings.'

'Mightn't he have been too caught up in trying to solve St Clair's murder?' Eleanor said. 'And there was no evidence it was murder to begin with.'

Seldon tapped the table thoughtfully. 'True. And even when it was confirmed, Brae's death occurred only a short while later, so Trevilick actually had very little time to investigate anything.'

Eleanor bit her lip. 'Maybe that's why I have a doubt he's got the right man?'

Seldon sighed. 'Maybe. However, I have some more information. On another likely candidate for both murders.'

'Mr Cunliffe?' she said tentatively.

'Yes. Sorry, Eleanor. In short, he overstretched himself some years back with investments. He borrowed money to buy stocks which, apparently, even the financial gurus in the city thought a safe bet. Unfortunately, they weren't. Cunliffe's stocks were among those which crashed dramatically, leaving him in a vulnerable position.'

Eleanor winced. 'Let me guess, that was around the time he moved out of London to Gwel an Mor?'

'Good guess. Yes, it was. After he sold his London property.'

'Sold?'

'You thought he still owned his house there?'

She nodded along with Clifford. 'But why would he then have gone to the expense of doing up Gwel an Mor if he was strapped for money?'

'Social standing, my lady,' Clifford said. 'To a gentleman like Mr Cunliffe, that is everything. Restoring Gwel an Mor's grandeur would have been the only way to quell rumours he was leaving London for pecuniary reasons.'

'Poor fellow! That reminds me of what Lord Wickhamshaw said at the wrestling match. About a gentleman's duty being to his estate for future prosperity. I thought that's why Mr Cunliffe had restored the house.'

Seldon grimaced. 'Definitely not. In fact, he borrowed more money to pay for the house restoration.'

She frowned. 'But he seemed genuine about wanting to move back to London. Mind you, not surprisingly, as it seems he never wanted to leave, but was forced to. Unless he has a hidden pot of gold, though, that's obviously out of the question.'

Seldon winced. 'I haven't told you the last, and worst, part yet.'

'Another stock market crash?' Clifford said sagely.

'Correct. Which wiped out the remainder of Cunliffe's capital.'

Eleanor's eyes widened. 'You mean he can't even pay back what he borrowed for the restoration works?'

'No. Which is why I had Christmas Day lunch with the chap I mentioned before, the estate agent's assistant. Fortunately for me, he was feeling sorry for himself, still being single at the end of another year.'

'So you got him drunk again! Poor fellow will wake up on Boxing Day *still single* and with a thumping headache. But good skulduggery, Hugh.' She glanced at Clifford. 'I can't imagine where he learned such a dastardly trick, though.'

'Shocking indeed, my lady.'

'Very funny, you two,' Seldon said, with a chuckle. 'But returning to my story. After a few, admittedly stiff, drinks, he lost the last of his rather tenuous discretion. Then he let slip that his boss told Cunliffe he would never sell Gwel an Mor with the grounds as they were. Apparently, most of it is quite overgrown? I've only glimpsed the section up to the fatal folly.'

'You could say that. It's more a case of scrambling—'

'Ahem,' Clifford coughed quietly.

'So what you're saying, Hugh,' she hurried on, 'is that Mr Cunliffe was damned if he kept St Clair on because he'd have to pay him. But damned if he didn't, because he'd never sell the house without the grounds at least restored.'

Clifford's brow rose. 'Worse, I imagine, my lady. A project of such size would mean Mr St Clair committing himself for a year or more. In such cases, normally a pay-out clause would be included in favour of the contractor should the works be cancelled.'

Seldon pointed at him. 'Exactly! So he needed to sack St Clair without honouring any penalty.'

Eleanor clicked her fingers. 'What about this scenario? Mr Cunliffe sacks him and tells him he won't honour the severance clause, citing some fanciful reason. St Clair, enraged, burns his design for the garden plans so Mr Cunliffe cannot pass them on to anyone he subsequently hires. Then he meets Mr Cunliffe again to try and get his money one last time before he leaves.'

Clifford tutted. 'But unwisely, Mr St Clair had already burned his only advantage. His design plan. Which Mr Cunliffe would have immediately demanded he hand over.'

She grimaced. 'Exactly! So he is forced to admit he burned it, but still wants paying. There's an argument and...'

Seldon looked between them. 'And Cunliffe pushes him over the cliff. Brilliant. Except he was poisoned *before* he was pushed. Which suggests, rather, that he threatened to sue Cunliffe for his money...'

Eleanor groaned. 'And Mr Cunliffe didn't have the money and couldn't countenance the public shame of the matter going to court.'

Seldon nodded. 'So Cunliffe poisoned him and *then* threw him over the cliff to make it look like an accident or suicide.' He shrugged apologetically. 'It's only a theory, Eleanor, but it's a pretty conclusive one. The only more likely theory is that Trevilick does have the right man in Odgers. In which case, Cunliffe is in the clear.'

She stared at her glass. 'I agree, but... but something is still nibbling at the back of my mind. And...' She hesitated, glancing at Clifford. He nodded. 'Look, Hugh. I wasn't going to mention it, but ... I don't think either murder was committed to avoid paying St Clair. Or to gain control of the house. Or necessarily over what area of the garden anyone runs their small-time scams in.'

Seldon held her gaze. 'Then what on earth have two men died for?'

33

As Eleanor finished her account of their potential discoveries in Gwel an Mor's garden, the singing in Kerensa Come Quick's main bar swelled with more rough, salty male voices. And a clearly unrehearsed but exuberant cast of instruments which set Gladstone off howling, his stumpy tail wagging furiously.

Seldon cocked an ear towards the noise. 'Fiddles, accordions and... is it just me, or is that a Scottish instrument?'

'Actually, the Cornish bagpipes.' Clifford winced. 'And the bombarde, a type of reedy horn-pipe of fearful intensity. All accompanied by a host of tin whistles now, I fear.'

Eleanor realised her foot was tapping of its own accord. 'It's irresistibly cheery and festive, though.'

'Unlike our conversation so far,' Seldon muttered with a sigh. 'It's too much, Eleanor. Stuck talking murder with you yet again. And on Christmas Day, blast it!'

Clifford glided away.

'I know, Hugh,' she said gently. 'So let's stop. And instead, I shall furnish my two favourite rotters with just a few small emergency presents until we can celebrate properly back at Henley Hall.'

'Her ladyship's favourite rotters, you and I!' Seldon called to Clifford as he returned carrying a small leather holdall. 'Are we going to take that lying down?'

'Actually, a most acceptable accolade, Chief Inspector. Since "favourite" implies permission not only to continue with, but to heighten, any future acts of collusion on our part, perhaps?'

As the two of them rubbed their hands with gusto, she laughed and pulled out their gifts from the holdall. As her hands closed around them though, she had a sudden pang of worry she might be putting Seldon on the spot. But as she looked up, he slid a beautiful small wooden box wrapped in sage-green velvet ribbons in front of her.

At the same time, Clifford produced two small meticulously tissue-wrapped packages.

'You really shouldn't have in my case, Clifford,' Seldon said, taking his in surprise. He pulled a long slim packet from his inside pocket. 'I've a proper thank you waiting back at home for our planned festivities, but I couldn't resist this extra one for you.'

'A thank you, sir? Whatever for?'

'For keeping Eleanor safe throughout all the dangerous matters she impetuously blunders headlong into almost every other week!'

'There is no "almost" about that. But too gracious, sir.'

Eleanor thought her heart might burst with affection for the two of them and busied herself carefully unwrapping her present from Seldon first. Inside was a slip of paper;

To the most unorthodox and unladylike lady of the manor who makes my heart leap but my arms ache more than I can bear when she isn't wrapped in them.

'Too beautiful for words, Hugh,' she breathed, lifting out a bracelet of gemstones running from a captivating olive-green through to mesmerising turquoise.

He ran his hand around the back of his neck, before reaching across to close the delicate clasp against her wrist. 'I saw them and could think of nothing but you. But apologies, they're also an emergency present. They're not the proper valuable sort and—'

'Yes, they are! They mean the world, Hugh, because you chose them. I shall treasure this always. Now, remembering it's only your temporary present until we get back to Henley Hall, it's your turn.'

He nodded and opened her present to him.

'Cufflinks! Perfect, Eleanor, thank you. Somehow I've ended up with only one pair which I waste minutes I haven't got trying to find every morning. But these will live beside my bed every night.' He looked at them again, frowning. 'Each one has a clock face. And they both show a different time?'

She pointed to his lean cheeks. 'It's my subtle reminder for you to eat at least twice in a day! And I don't mean a piece of plain toast or a hastily gulped down goodness-knows-what!'

He smiled ruefully. 'I'll try to improve, but I don't promise. Now, your turn again.'

She picked up her present from Clifford and carefully unwrapped it. A small wrinkle appeared on her forehead.

'A notebook? It's beautiful. And covered with silk, but what...?' She opened the cover, her fingers tracing the meticulously inked map of the world on one side dotted with his impeccable copperplate handwriting in tiny cursive script. Her breath caught as she turned to the first page. 'A journal of Uncle Byron's adventures with you!'

'More a timeline of places and dates, my lady. That, ahem, discretion permitting, one might fill in the details later during the inevitable evenings into the small hours when the mistress cannot sleep. With your permission of course, sir,' Clifford added to Seldon.

He smiled as she pressed it to her chest, eyes shining. 'Of course. There's nothing between the two of you that will ever need my permission. Even after Eleanor and I are finally married. And rest assured, I shall never ask what you've imparted about what you and Eleanor's uncle really got up to.' He laughed. 'Though it eats me up with curiosity!'

Clifford bowed from the shoulders.

'Go on,' she coaxed, pushing her butler's present closer. 'Unless you'd rather wait?'

In silent reply, he reached for it.

'A genuine specimen!' he murmured, as he folded back the wrapping paper. 'My lady, I don't know what to say. It's too special for words.'

Seldon peered over at the large plate-sized item. 'It's clearly very exciting, but what is it?'

She shrugged. 'A piece of history, I was reliably informed.'

'The *ultimate* history,' Clifford said animatedly, carefully lifting up with both hands what looked like a large polished amber and silver rock spiralled like a giant snail's shell. 'This is a goniatite. A form of ammonite, if you will. A fossil of unimagin-able fascination since this would have been alive over two hundred and fifty million years ago.' He turned to her, eyes bright. 'His lordship would have loved to hold this.'

She nodded, a lump in her throat.

Clifford cleared his. 'Maybe it would be an opportune time for you to open my present to you, sir?'

Seldon peeled open the tissue, eyes instantly shining with amusement. 'Now I cannot wait to read how that turned out!' He picked up the small book and turned it so Eleanor could read the title aloud.

'*When Logic and the Lady Collided.*'

She laughed. 'If logic wins in that, I'm going to hunt down the author and set him straight.'

'Your turn, Clifford.' Seldon said, avoiding her eye. 'Although, mine to you is perhaps a selfish one.'

Clifford removed the wrapping paper to reveal a small box. A moment later, she jumped as he lifted the lid and roared with laughter.

'Oh, that I could, sir!'

'Oh, come on!' She pleaded. 'Share the joke?'

He slid the box towards her. She peered inside, and then sat back, arms folded, hiding a smile.

'Antique wooden handcuffs, chaps? For keeping me out of trouble, I assume?'

Seldon nodded. 'Mostly. But also to let Clifford have a moment of peace on occasion.'

She shook her head in amusement. 'Very funny! But he'd better watch out. I might decide to use them myself!'

34

'Food's a-comin' folks,' the landlady hollered over from the bar.

Quickly, they cleared the table. A sprightly old man leaned over.

'The treat's just blown in as the wind turned as well. Penrose is pulling out his horse's leg!'

'How marvellous,' Eleanor said. 'It'll be a novel experience. I've eaten horse abroad, but never a leg.'

Clifford's eyes twinkled. 'For her ladyship's sake, I hope the gentleman has brought his entire animal to cater for her inordinately robust appetite.'

The man laughed wheezily and clapped Clifford on the back before jostling his way through the merrymakers to the bar.

Seldon frowned. 'Is it really a delicacy here?'

Clifford shook his head and gestured at a middle-aged fisherman in long black boots and a thick cream jumper slotting his musical instrument together at the bar. 'No, Chief Inspector. I believe a "horse's leg" is a Cornish term for a type of bassoon.'

'You absolute terror!' Eleanor gasped. 'Now everyone here thinks—'

'The truth.' Seldon grinned. 'I'm usually in awe of how much you put away with a knife and fork anyway.'

'Well, it is Christmas!' she huffed good-naturedly. 'So I intend to eat, drink and party heartily!' Gladstone gave a loud woof of agreement over Tomkins' enthusiastic meow.

'Too right!' a squiffy man chortled as he gripped the back of her chair to steady himself. 'The one day a little extra whisky is fine. And it's lucky to fall up the stairs,' he added as he swayed off.

'Not if you break your leg falling through the door first!' Seldon called after him.

'Here it comes!' Eleanor's nose twitched as much as her bulldog's at the delectable scents wafting towards them. The landlady arrived with the fisherman who had evidently abandoned his bassoon and volunteered to negotiate the loaded food tray through the crowd while she managed the smaller one of drinks.

'Thank you, kind, sir.' Eleanor smiled at the fisherman, then the landlady. 'And our sincere compliments to the chef.'

She nodded and nudged her helper. 'I poured yer a pint to thaw out before yer play.' She indicated one of the glasses she'd set down and left with the trays.

As the ruddy-cheeked fisherman took a sip of his drink, Eleanor leaned forward.

'Mr Penrose? Surely, you haven't been out fishing in that fog?'

'Bah! That wouldn't have stopped my kind of fisher folk. But a change of work is as good as a rest. I've been deliverin' instead.' His voice sounded raw, as if he'd spent years smoking strong tobacco and shouting over the sea wind.

She jumped at the rousing burst of merry voices.

'"The Carnal and the Crane",' Penrose said. 'We always sing it at this time of year. It's a kind of Cornish carol. A "carnal" is a crow to you.'

There was something in his bright cheery eyes and the laughter lines etched around them that made her instantly warm to him.

'Where have you been delivering to then? And on Christmas Day, of all days?'

'Out to the lighthouse. Only go there once a moon. Keeper don't like no company except his own.'

Her skin prickled. Clifford's almost imperceptible twitch suggested he, too, was intrigued to know more.

'Would you care to join us?' she said hopefully. Seldon shot her a questioning look, but she shot him a discreet 'be patient' look back. She pointed at the array of plates. 'My butler has remissly ordered far too much food, Mr Penrose.'

He guffawed. 'Not from what I heard up at the bar. But, that's kind, thank ye.' He yanked off his black woollen skull cap, revealing a thick head of salt-crisped brown hair, and sank into the chair Clifford magicked up. It didn't escape her that he placed it so Seldon had to shuffle up closer to her. Nor that Penrose's cream jumper was identical to the cast-offs uphol-stering the seats. Gladstone threw his top half into the fisher-man's lap, receiving a scratching of his wrinkled jowls in return.

Clifford stepped around the table, setting out the anchor-print napkins, plates and oddments of cutlery that had come with the food. When he'd finished, she pointedly added the same for him. He tutted quietly, but said nothing.

She leaned forward eagerly again. 'What delicious festive Cornish delights do we have, then?'

Clifford turned to the fisherman. 'Aside from the roasted hazelnuts and assorted local cheeses, if I might defer to you, Mr Penrose?'

'Introduce the food?' Penrose scratched his head. 'Strange notion, but why not?' He waved a rope-weathered hand across the selection. 'These is splits. Them's boiled limpets. This here's aval and onion pie. Those is finger oggies. And these beauties is buttered crab. Which I caught yester eve. Oh, and figgy dowdie for clearing the plates. How'd I do?'

She jerked a thumb at her butler. 'Suffice to say, if you ever fancy swapping fishing for butlering, Clifford's got a strong contender.'

Everyone tucked in to the food, including Gladstone and Tomkins as Clifford discreetly tipped his portion of limpets into their bowl. Eleanor ignored his treachery and smacked her lips.

'These splits are divine. Bread rolls, made like cake with butter and milk, I think. And these oggies are sublime little meat and potato pasties.'

'And the "aval" in the onion pie is apple.' Seldon loaded another forkful. 'It shouldn't work, but it's moreishly good.'

As they continued eating, she nodded towards the main bar. 'You've missed the start of the music-making, Mr Penrose.'

'It must be quite a trek out to the lighthouse?' Seldon said.

'Single and her daughter.'

Seldon shook his head. 'I meant how far is it, Mr Penrose?'

'I just said. One and a third nautical miles. Folk often gets three daughters to one son around these parts.'

Eleanor nodded. 'That's about what I reckoned.'

'Ah, a sea-faring maid!' Penrose said appreciatively.

'If living mostly aboard my parents' sailing boat until I was nine qualifies me as such, then, yes.'

He gave her a stiff salute. 'It does alright, Captain!'

'Is the lighthouse the one that can be glimpsed from Gwel an Mor?' Clifford passed Seldon the bowl of limpets a second time with a circumspect look.

'Yep! Only one on this part of the coast. Yer stayin' up at Gwel an Mor, I heard? A lot of bad goings-on up there of late, for sure.'

Not wishing to get sidetracked, she simply nodded. 'Mr Cunliffe is an old friend of the family.'

'Then you'll know about the connection.'

He raised his pint of ale to Eleanor before taking a long sup. She waited patiently until he'd finished.

'Connection? Between the lighthouse and Gwel an Mor, do you mean?'

'Do tell, Mr Penrose?' Clifford said encouragingly. 'Her ladyship is studying the local history.'

'I thought it was sketching,' Seldon whispered teasingly. 'Or is it eating?'

'I'm a busy girl, don't you know?' she murmured back. 'What is the connection, Mr Penrose?'

He set down his fork. 'Well, never used to be that many ships up and down this part of the coast, but then near on hundred year back trade started to pick up. But the extra trade meant more ships needin' to navigate these waters. And beyond treacherous at night, they be. 'Specially in poor weather.'

'Oh dear, none were lost, I hope?'

'Too many. And then, one fearful storm blew up December 1871. A ship foundered on the rocks off Lostenev. The crew drowned. Every man of them.'

'Oh gracious!'

She bowed her head and offered silent words for the lost souls. When she looked up, Penrose gave her an appreciative nod before continuing. 'The captain was a local lad. The son of the old man who owned Gwel an Mor at the time.'

Eleanor's brow furrowed. 'Wait, 1871?' She quickly counted on her fingers. 'That makes him—'

'That's right. He was Cunliffe's father. And it was Cunliffe's older brother as perished.' He shook his head. 'Anyway, the old man swore no more lives would be lost at sea around this coast. So, he petitioned to have a lighthouse built. He hawked his petition from pillar to post, finally endin' up on the steps in London, appealin' to government theirselves. But he came back empty. Told it was too troublesome and costly.'

'But how could money matter when more lives might be lost?' she demanded angrily.

Penrose shook his head. 'Bah! What was one more nameless sailor buried in Davy Jones' locker to them fancy folk in London?'

'Yet Mr Cunliffe's father, the "old man" as you call him, must have succeeded somehow,' Seldon said, 'because the lighthouse exists. You've just sailed back from there.'

'Yes, he did. Finally. First, he started a campaign to have it built by public subscription. Folks were keen enough to support, naturally, the sea's been everyone's livelihood here since forever.' He coughed. 'In one form or another.'

'Mostly the other, I've heard,' Seldon muttered.

'Did he raise sufficient funds, Mr Penrose?' Clifford said smoothly.

He shook his head. 'Folks were scratchin' for farthin's at the time, as always. They did what they could, but it weren't enough. So, the old man put up the difference himself. Which was the goodlier portion by a long rope, to all accounts.'

Eleanor let out a relieved sigh. 'Then it did all end happily?'

Penrose grimaced. 'Seein' as it's Christmas Day, I won't tell yer otherwise. Now, thank yer for yer hospitality, but I'd best get to blowin' my horse's leg.'

As he left to collect his bassoon, Seldon turned to her. 'What was all that about? Is it somehow related to why two men were murdered and what you told me about the gardens?'

She bit her lip. 'Honestly, I don't know, Hugh. I need to talk to Mr Cunliffe in the morning.'

'Well, tonight it's Christmas,' he said firmly. 'And it's party time now, Eleanor.'

Clifford nodded. 'Indeed, my lady. The night is but young and the singing has only just started in earnest.'

She took her drink distractedly. 'Yes, of course. But what do you suppose Penrose meant by it not ending happily?'

Seldon shrugged and raised his tankard. 'I've no idea. But I intend for *your* evening, Eleanor, to end very, very happily indeed!'

35

The following morning, as Eleanor surveyed the dining room, she decided last night's spirit of Cornish Christmas cheer from Kerensa Come Quick must have reached even Gwel an Mor. The family's mood at the Boxing Day breakfast table seemed positively relaxed. Maybe the bright sun sending soft orange fingers across the table had infused everyone's spirits with belated festive cheer. Accentuated, perhaps, by the fresh garland swinging between the lights in which she detected her butler's hand. Flora and Clara were chatting away to each other like a pair of twittering birds, while Cunliffe meticulously marmaladed his toast from edge to edge. Even Marsh was humming happily as he chose a hard-boiled egg from the basket. Although she did notice his eyes slide to Cunliffe at the moment he decapitated it with his spoon.

She took a long sip of her coffee to soothe her croaky throat, which was still sore from the lusty singing she'd joined in with the night before. Putting her cup down, she beamed around the room. 'My apologies to you all again for disappearing last evening, but it seemed a shame to miss the experience of a traditional Cornish Christmas.'

Cunliffe looked up from his plate. 'No matter, Lady Swift. I take it you had a pleasant time?'

'Yes. Very. Everyone was in good spirits. Singing fascinating shanties among the carols, dancing, laughing, swapping tales. It was a privilege to be welcomed into such a close-knit community. And Clifford got a rousing ovation for his solo on the fiddle.' She threw her butler an impish look, since she'd been the one responsible for him being dragged up to perform.

Clara beamed at her butler through her lorgnettes. 'Oh, your man took to the stage!'

'Under duress,' Clifford mouthed to Eleanor. But the shine in his eyes gave away how much he'd secretly enjoyed the whole evening. It had ended with the two of them quietly carrying on into the small hours in her private sitting room over a few glasses of port and Clifford's travelling chessboard.

She turned to Marsh. 'Did I miss you all singing around the piano? Or playing charades, or something equally festive?'

He pushed the remains of his egg to the side of his plate. 'No. Why would we? Christmas is just a lot of old pretending.'

'Not to my mind,' she said firmly.

Flora clucked her tongue. 'Take no notice, Lady Swift. Father Christmas didn't think Edwin had been a good enough boy to fill his stocking this year, so he's sulking.'

Clara glanced at him. 'Isn't that so, dear?'

Marsh glared at her.

Oh, dear, Ellie.

Mr Cunliffe stirred his tea as he peered over his wire-rimmed spectacles. 'Well, you might try being a little more... seasonal, Edwin. We do have a guest with us. Still.' He nodded pointedly at Eleanor. 'I haven't really seen a trace—'

'Oh!' Clara clapped her hands. 'If, through it all, you've nothing done that you can trace...'

'That brought the sunshine to one face, Flora!'

Her sister's shoulders rose with glee. 'No act most small,

that helped some soul and nothing cost...' They turned expectantly to Clifford.

'Then count that day as worse than lost,' he intoned.

The sisters applauded, their tinkling laugh ringing around the room.

He topped up Cunliffe's tea. 'George Eliot, sir.'

Marsh pushed back his chair. 'I've some... business to attend to.'

Flora exchanged a look with Clara and followed him out without a word.

Eleanor frowned briefly, but swiftly turned back to her host. She had questions that needed answers. As she discreetly studied him eating his toast, she felt a mix of emotions. He had hardly welcomed her with open arms. In fact, she'd found him aloof, and rigidly old-fashioned in his view of women. To her mind anyway. His undisguised disapproval of Clifford also bristled her. Especially, as he knew her butler had performed innumerable tasks around Gwel an Mor unbidden and without a hint of acknowledgement. But she'd learned from Seldon only yesterday that Cunliffe was in straitened circumstances. And the family certainly wasn't the easiest to live with.

Her thoughts were interrupted by Cunliffe laying his napkin across his plate and scraping his chair back.

Quick, Ellie.

'It's a wonderful treat to have you to myself for a moment.' She cringed the minute the words came out of her mouth.

'Really?' he said tautly.

'I mean, Uncle Byron clearly enjoyed your company immensely. I was hoping to do the same.'

A sad look crossed his face. 'Yes, well, perhaps you haven't met me at my best, Lady Swift. For which a gentleman should apologise.' He sank slowly back into his seat. 'It's all been rather distracting, you understand?'

'Having a visitor stay? Or the trouble with the police?'

'Both.'

'Then let's talk of something else,' she said brightly as she rose and nonchalantly stepped over to the nearest window. 'It's lovely outside. Can you see the lighthouse from here?'

'No.' Cunliffe hesitated for a moment, then stood and beckoned her to the furthest window. 'On a clear day like today, you can just spot it in the near distance from this one.'

She joined him. 'Oh, yes. I can see it now. You must feel so proud.'

He stiffened. 'Why should I be proud? It's just a... a lighthouse?'

She turned to face him. 'But one your family built! If I had a link like that to my father I would gaze upon it in delight every day. I did idly wonder last evening why you hadn't mentioned it was your father's doing.'

He shrugged. 'It was nothing of note for me to mention to you. You heard in the village, I suppose?'

'Yes. But surely his achievement must be held in high regard by your family? Like it is with the local people?'

Cunliffe scoffed. 'Lady Swift, my father went cap in hand to the local populace, begging for public subscriptions. Then, to compound the ignominy, he put the family's money into his foolish scheme to make up the funds he failed to raise! He is the very reason Gwel an Mor and her gardens fell into such a parlous state. He neglected his duty as a gentleman. And to his family!'

'But he acted in such a good cause.'

'Lady Swift, my father's ridiculous obsession led to him being marched to... to a debtors' prison!'

'Ah!' She winced. 'I'm sorry. I didn't know.'

He slapped his handkerchief over his mouth, eyes closed. 'I cannot bear to think of the shame.'

She mentally shook her head. *He might soon live out that*

same shame himself if he can't pay back the money he borrowed, Ellie.

She risked patting his arm but received only a flinch in response. 'I am sorry, Mr Cunliffe. It can't have been easy for you growing up in such conditions.'

His eyes snapped open. 'No pity is required, thank you, Lady Swift. I did not sit and succumb to the results of his discreditable actions. The moment I turned fourteen, I left to make my own way and never saw him again. And a successful life I made for myself too.' His tone rose. 'My only desires were to be financially secure and uphold my place in society. And most importantly, not to repeat the same mistakes my father made!'

Biting her tongue not to blurt out that it was probably a little late for that, she stepped to the serving table and returned with a glass of water. He begrudgingly accepted it with a trembling hand.

'I apologise for having raised old wounds, Mr Cunliffe. I just thought you would understand your father's actions. I mean, one of the sailors who lost his life due to the lack of a lighthouse was your—'

'My brother. I know.' He coughed into the glass. 'He was ten years older than I and had gone to sea before I really knew him. But his death was no excuse for the way my father behaved.'

Her eyes widened. 'Of course. Edwin, your nephew. He was your brother's son, wasn't he?'

'Yes. His mother died in childbirth. And as you now know, his father died at sea.'

'Would it be prying too much to ask why Edwin goes by the surname of Marsh then, not Cunliffe?'

He choked on the water he'd been swallowing. 'Why does Edwin do anything except to taunt or irritate? I imagine he thought it a marvellous prank to return here and demand he be known by his mother's, not his father's surname. I deliberately don't mention it, because that is what he wants me to do.'

Maybe it's more than a prank, Ellie? Maybe it's to try and avoid those angry debtors?

'I understand,' she said soothingly. 'By the way, someone mentioned the tale hadn't ended happily. I guess your father passing away in... in poverty was what he meant?'

He snorted. 'More likely they were referring to the final irony of my father's obsession with building the best lighthouse the world had ever seen. An obsession which meant he would only countenance having the most advanced light installed. And blast the cost! The design was so new, the makers had not finished putting it through the last of its tests. But, in his stubborn wisdom, Father would not be swayed. Nor would he wait.' Cunliffe threw his hands out. 'Shortly after it was put in commission, a technical fault occurred during a fierce storm and the lamp failed.' She shivered, part of her not wanting to hear the outcome. Cunliffe nodded. 'That's right. A ship foundered on the rocks.'

'That is so tragic,' she muttered, bowing her head.

He snorted. 'That is what comes of people acting irresponsibly, no matter their reason! I hold my father as the pinnacle of such dereliction.'

She looked up. 'To you, his passing away in debtors' prison feels like the hand of judgement striking him, perhaps?'

'No! Because he did not die there.' Cunliffe's tone became even more bitter as he grasped the lapels of his black jacket. 'I toiled to make money from the very moment I left to start my new life. Once I had secured enough funds, I paid his debt so he would be released.'

'That was very noble of you.'

'Ha! I did not do it for him, Lady Swift. I did it for me. For the family. So we would not have to endure the shame!'

She bit her lip, wondering if paying his father's debt had

been the original foundation of Mr Cunliffe's monetary problems. 'So your father was released and... and returned to Gwel an Mor?'

He nodded stiffly. 'By the time he was released, the prison had addled his brain. He idled out the rest of his days, never leaving the house or grounds. While I toiled away in the city securing my financial future, he toiled away in the gardens, apparently finding what to do I have no idea! I did not communicate with him once I left home. Nor did I return to Cornwall until I moved to Gwel an Mor upon my retirement. By then he was long dead.'

He strode to the door.

'Mr Cunliffe!' She had one question remaining she had to ask. He turned around reluctantly and waited. 'What happened to the lighthouse keeper at the time? I hope he wasn't blamed for the light going out?'

Cunliffe's hand fumbled with the doorknob as he snapped, 'He drowned.' The door slammed behind him.

'Gracious,' she said to the garland as it fell to the floor. 'The fisherman was right. The tale really didn't have a happy ending!'

36

Eleanor tugged her warmest cloche hat hard over her ears as she hastened beside Clifford to the furthest end of Lostenev's harbour. After speaking to Cunliffe, she'd telephoned Seldon immediately and then, an hour later, made the trip down to the village. She scanned the seemingly deserted harbour for any sign of her fiancé.

'Whatever Hugh's learned, I didn't expect him to meet us here,' she hissed to Clifford.

'Nor down there, my lady.' He gestured over the wall at the grey-wool coated figure pacing below.

She climbed backwards down the salt-pitted iron rungs, tingling as Seldon's muscular hands helped her gently to the ground.

'You'd better do that for Clifford, too, Hugh. Poor fellow's still got his arm in a sling.'

'Ahem! Not required, thank you,' her butler called in a horrified tone, despite his awkward one-handed progress after her. For the first time, she noticed he was all the more hampered by a waxed canvas duffel bag. She bit back her curiosity over why he'd brought it. Doubtless he'd reveal the reason later.

The three of them stood by an open rowing boat with one central plank for a seat and a small wooden box at the rear she assumed covered the retrofitted engine. The rope fenders rubbing back and forth along the mooring wall added a haunting tenor to the setting.

She looked up and down the deserted quay. 'This feels unexpectedly cloak and dagger, Hugh.'

Seldon ran an anxious hand through his chestnut curls made damp by the salty air. 'We're not hiding, Eleanor. I simply enquired around the village about the lighthouse as you asked, but the answer was unanimous. There's only one person who might know anything more about its history. And, blast it, that person is there!' He pointed out of the harbour to the open sea. 'The lighthouse keeper. Which is why I hired this.' He nodded down at the boat. 'The keeper's something of a hermit, by all accounts. Name's "Woon". It seems he never comes ashore.'

She peered across the water to the hazy, towering shape rising in the distance. 'Well, the sea's calm and at least we can be sure he'll be home.' At his expression, she slid her arm through his and stared into his deep brown eyes. 'Hugh, we'll be fine.'

'But I can't even come with you, blast it!'

She laughed. 'Good job too. You're a terrible sailor. You've no sea legs at all. Besides, I need you to go off and prepare for our return later as we agreed last night. Okay?'

'Not until I'm sure you'll be safe.' He tucked her scarf gently into her coat collar. 'Clifford?'

'One last check, sir.' Her butler nodded at the last plank he'd been checking then pulled back the wooden cover and leaned over the tiny engine. After a moment of fiddling with a slim brass rod and a flat lever, the motor started with a reassuringly healthy rumble. One finger behind his ear, Clifford listened carefully, then nodded. 'The fuel gauge reads full, spare oars present and correct. She appears perfectly seaworthy.'

'Eleanor, promise me you'll be careful,' Seldon whispered, stroking a lock of her unruliest red curls back under her hat.

'You too, Hugh. Just be where, and when, we said. Here, take Clifford's pocketbook. The sketch of the gardens I showed you before is towards the back. Leave now, then you won't fret watching him motor me out to sea.'

He held her hands. 'Are you *absolutely* sure you need to go? I mean—'

She shook her head. 'I'm not absolutely sure of anything, Hugh. If any of us were, I think we'd have found the killer by now. What I *think* is that St Clair was murdered because he stumbled on a secret long buried in Gwel an Mor's gardens. A secret our killer is also hunting. And a secret that was placed there some time in the past, as Addled Aida, the woman I met the first time I came to Lostenev, said. Well, Mr Cunliffe's father passed the last of his life a virtual hermit at Gwel an Mor, spending his every waking hour, it seems, toiling in the gardens. Why? I've no idea. Neither did Mr Cunliffe. Or so he said. But what I do know is that it's unlikely he wouldn't have stumbled across the secret in that time, *unless*—'

'Unless he was the one who buried it there?'

She nodded. 'Exactly. And Addled Aida also said something about "being like him, incorruptible amid a sea of wickedness". Clifford reckoned she was referring to the Lostenev Lighthouse. It is central to the tragedy that led to Mr Cunliffe's father walling himself up inside the Gwel an Mor estate in the first place.'

Seldon sighed. 'I can see your reasoning. And I have to confess, I've nothing better at this moment, so...' He leaned forward and kissed her on the lips. 'Just take care.'

After he'd climbed up the ladder and disappeared, she cast off and dropped nimbly into the boat.

As they motored past the harbour walls, the tranquil water was replaced by a choppy swell. After her childhood sailing years, she'd anticipated it and had positioned herself in the middle of the boat, with a hand gripped either side. Behind, at the tiller, Clifford was braced sideways, his knees pressed under the corner bracket, which served as the housing for the throttle lever and small brass compass. Their little craft rode up and over the crests like a dogged, sure-footed mule on a see-sawing, switchback mountain pass.

She drew in a deep breath of sea air and raised her voice to be heard over the engine and slap of the boat chopping through the water. 'We'll remember this Christmas more than most!'

'If we must, my lady!'

'Oh, nonsense. I won't believe for one moment you don't miss the adventuring life you lived with Uncle Byron all those years.'

'How could I?' he called back with a wink. 'It has never stopped since his beloved niece inherited Henley Hall!'

She laughed, looking up as something landed on her nose. A curtain of wet snowflakes slipped silently from the grey sky. She watched them settle on the water for the briefest breath before becoming one with the waves' white horses. The wind, at least, had the good grace to stay at their back, like an icy hand pushing them forward. To what, she couldn't guess.

'Lucky it's not foggy,' she called with a shiver as their tiny boat surged on into the open sea.

Twenty minutes later, she knelt up on the seat, keeping a firm grip on the top handrails. 'Excellent navigation, Clifford. The lighthouse is dead ahead. Remember, the safe channel between the rocks is around to the port side.'

He nodded. 'As mentioned by Mr Penrose.'

Arriving in the lighthouse's shadow, the landing was not as smooth as she'd hoped. The spray arcing over the bow caused by the narrowness of the channel soaked her and as she jumped out, she found the barnacle-encrusted rocks dangerously slippery.

Finally moored, with the ropes triple checked, she marvelled at the barren black rock rising in jagged lines up to the lighthouse. The last twenty feet to the door had been hewn into knee-jerkingly high steps with a thick hoary rope for hauling oneself up. She leaned back into the buffeting wind to stare up at the full height of the towering cone of granite. 'I'd hate to have been the builder, but it's incredible.'

'One hundred and twelve or fifteen feet, I estimate, my lady.' Clifford stepped up to show her his ingenious new addition. An etched glass protractor hinged into the bottom half of his compass case. 'Held to one's eye, it is a simple matter of counting the distance backwards until the forty-five-degree angle meets the highest point of any structure. I came up with it after our need to know the cliff height when we were examining the spot where Mr St Clair fell.'

She nodded appreciatively as she hammered on the battered wooden door. Pointlessly, Clifford's amused brow suggested, as he turned and tugged on a rusting chain which disappeared inside through a hole in the wall.

'If you would be so gracious, my lady?' He gestured at his bag. 'A selection of tongue-loosening gifts is within. I would suggest starting with the book, the brandy, and most definitely the pouch of tobacco.'

After a few minutes of no answer, Eleanor knocked even louder, and Clifford pulled on the bell even more vigorously. But still to no reply. With Clifford circling the base of the lighthouse to see if there was any life within, Eleanor knocked on the door once more and pulled the chain for all she was worth.

'Nothing!' she called to Clifford as he reappeared. He nodded.

'I'm afraid I have to report the same, my lady.'

She threw her hands out in frustration. 'He must be here, Clifford. Look!' She pointed to a chained-up rowing boat.

'I agree, but the gentleman either will not, or cannot respond.'

She glanced up at the lighthouse, brow furrowed.

Clifford hastily stepped into her eyeline.

'Categorically, no, my lady! The walls are practically sheer.'

She shrugged. 'Well, we didn't come all the way out here for nothing. The final key to this mystery lies inside that granite fortress and I intend to find a way in!'

Twenty minutes later, however, and she had to admit defeat. There seemed no other way in except the main door or scaling the outside to the small metal balcony that ran around the top where the light was housed. She caught Clifford's eye.

'The first is seemingly fruitless, my lady, and the second, seemingly suicidal.'

She sighed. 'You're right. Come on. We'd better return while we still have light.'

As they trudged to their boat, she glanced back, her lips puckering. 'Dash it! It seems the Lostenev Lighthouse isn't ready to give up its secret yet. We...' Her eyes widened. 'Clifford! Look!'

37

As Eleanor stood and stared, the lighthouse door swung open. A frowning face so thickly whiskered it might have belonged to a walrus poked out.

'Wrecked, yer be?' the keeper barked in a strained voice that sounded as if it were rarely used. He stepped out dressed in a double-buttoned navy work suit and cap.

As they hurried back, Eleanor shook her head. 'No, thankfully. I just wanted to hand over these Christmas gifts.' She held up the offerings. 'Season of goodwill, you see. Mr, er... Woon, is it?'

'Just Woon,' he said distrustfully, but his pale blue eyes roved hungrily over the gifts. He hesitated, then shrugged. 'Seein' as yer've come all this way, though Neptune knows why, yer may as well come in.'

She hurried gratefully over the threshold. A set of narrow iron stairs spiralled up the circular wall to the next floor, a sturdy grillework platform, through which she could just make out the steps continuing upwards. A trapdoor on one side of the circular floor was lifted up, revealing a pump handle and the top of a tank. Her voice echoed around the space as her teeth chattered.

'I've never been inside a lighthouse before. What a treat.' Her soaking and the century-old damp set off a fit of shivering. Woon cast a scrutinising eye over her before bolting what looked like a large sluice gate across the bottom two-thirds of the door. He picked up an oil lamp and turned up the wick.

'Follow me.'

The second level was a coal storehouse. He barely paused as he reached inside to scoop a small amount into a metal pail before climbing on ahead as easily as if he was walking down. On the third and fourth floors there was a confusion of tools, mechanical parts, wooden stepladders and mops and stacks of cloths. A few battered barrels, piles of rope and a pyramid of scratched and chipped glass bottles lay nearby.

'Ne'r one's had a message in, before yer ask. Collect every one as they floats by.'

As they passed the fifth floor, she heard Clifford mutter, 'Ah! The oil store,' and then they arrived at the narrowest door she'd ever seen. Inside was a tiny semicircular living room. The cast-iron stove against the wall radiated a hint of heat over a token piece of worn rag rug. Actually, everything was against a wall, she realised, there being little enough space for the three of them in the centre. The only seat was a wooden chair with curved arms, draped in a rough brown wool blanket. Two ancient chests sat on either side. A wire rack with a kettle, teapot and one pan hung above a dented metal bowl. She suspected the bowl might serve equally for washing the lighthouse keeper himself as the pots and pans.

'Sit,' he barked, holding the blanket out to her.

She pushed it away. 'Gracious, I can't make that wet. I'm sure you need it.'

'Odder'n mustard.' He glanced at Clifford, his heavy brows

knitted. 'Women be like the mystery of what lurks forty fathoms below the waves, huh?'

'Unquestionably so,' he said, clearly amused.

Woon thrust the blanket back at her, brooking no argument. She wrapped it gratefully around her shoulders and sat in the chair. He passed her an enamel cup of steaming, strong black tea, while Clifford pulled out his hip flask and added a warming dash to each of their cups. 'No sense starting in on your gift bottle, Woon,' he said nonchalantly.

Their host licked his lips and ran an appreciative hand over the brandy. 'If as yer say.'

'Have you been the lighthouse keeper here long?' she said.

He shrugged. 'Seventeen year.'

'Goodness. Without going ashore! Don't you ever suffer from cabin fever?'

'Nope. Busy all the hours. And I got me friends.'

'I thought you were the sole keeper?' Clifford said.

'I am. Rocks around know their names.'

'You've named each of the rocks?' she queried in amazement.

He frowned. 'Not me. Names has been handed down from keeper to keeper. But they're not all the company. The gulls stop often enough on the light's rail.'

'Seagulls?' she blurted out. 'I rather thought you'd need to catch them to eat being stuck out here.'

Woon's expression turned to horror. 'Eat seagulls? Why, their cries is the souls of men calling to be saved!'

She blinked. Something about 'the souls of men' Addled Aida had mentioned came back to her.

'And lost souls are rather a part of this lighthouse's history, aren't they? We learned yesterday about the shipwreck which led to this being built, you see.' Woon grunted in reply. 'In fact,' she continued, 'I was rather hoping you might be able to tell us what else you know of its history? Perhaps about the keeper at the time of the shipwreck? Tales are probably handed down like the wonderful rock names, I imagine?'

'That they be. But only to pass on to the next keeper. Ne'er anyone else. It's an unwritten code.'

She pursed her lips. 'It might help explain why two men are dead. Please.'

'Death comes. Like the sea,' he said matter-of-factly. 'In and out. Me, I'm goin' in with the fishes.' Reaching for the book she'd given him, he flicked open the cover, squinting at the print. 'Eyes is goin' rather for seein' small. The lamp's so fierce, it burns 'em out, see?'

'Ah! Then these will indubitably help.' Clifford pulled his hand from his inside pocket with his pince-nez at the ready. 'It can't be easy fixing the intricacies of the lamp's mechanism with reduced eyesight.'

Woon reached for them eagerly, growling as Clifford held them back. Staring at Eleanor, he leaned forward. 'Important enough, is it? Truly? For me to break the keeper's code?'

'Yes, Woon,' she said passionately. 'Two men have been murdered. And maybe more will be. I believe the key to catching the killer lies somewhere in the tale of how this lighthouse came to be built and the tragic story of its failure.'

At least I hope it does, Ellie. Otherwise we're on a wild goose chase.

Woon stared at her, his eyes focusing elsewhere. Finally, his lashes flickered. 'I'll tell.'

As Clifford made a fresh pot of tea and stoked the small amount of extra coal into the stove, Eleanor sat quietly through Woon's telling of the tale. As he neared the end, she grew restless.

Blast, Ellie! He hasn't told you anything new that helps. Perhaps your hunch was wrong after all?

Woon stopped speaking and shook his head sombrely. 'So,

finally there were a lighthouse. The old man's dream had become a reality. But a lighthouse without a light in a storm is worse than none. And the light had well and truly failed. Nothing the keeper could do would fix it. So, the ship were blind and foundered on the rocks and started to break up. But despite the fearsome storm, the lightkeeper set out and rowed to the stricken ship. The first time he rescued four of the crew and brought them back to the lighthouse. But on the return trip, the ship broke and went down as he was trying to help the remaining six crew off. The ones he'd already saved saw the sinking ship take the keeper's boat down with it and everyone on it.' He shook his head again. 'That was the second son the old man lost to the sea.'

Eleanor and Clifford shared a puzzled look.

'It can't be,' she said. 'We're staying with his second son, Mr Cunliffe, now. Though he must be in his sixties, he's very much alive.'

Woon ran his hand over his whiskers. 'He be the third son. The two oldest perished at sea.' He stood and opened the door, running his tongue down the inside of his cheek. 'Mind, it'll take a fair bit of somethin' extra to grease my memory into rememberin' any more...'

The route back was slower going as they were heading into the wind, which was now blowing the manes of the white horses into the air and their boat. The sea itself was almost inky black, the snow-laden sky menacingly grey above.

'At least we're on the incoming tide,' she called, shuffling to the rear of the boat to brace herself. 'So that should help.'

Clifford nodded. 'I would offer you some brandy to keep you warm, my lady, but it went the way of the rest of the contents of the duffel bag, as you know.'

She shrugged. 'Yes, and half the contents of your pockets.

But you did get to admire the lamp and all her workings while he told me the last of the tale.'

'Quite. However, the unrivalled magnificence of the lamp notwithstanding, I am curious to hear what he said.'

He feathered a lever on the engine and crouched down, steadying himself on the sides. 'I am all ears.'

'Right. You heard that our Mr Cunliffe was the youngest of three sons? Not two, yes?' At his nod, she continued. 'Well, the first, as you know, drowned before the lighthouse was built. In fact, his death inspired its building. And the second son, the mystery one we knew nothing about, was evidently something of a prodigal son, according to Woon. He got into bad company at a young age. Mr Cunliffe's father, or the "old man" as everyone seems to call him, considered him completely lacking in moral fibre. In fact, a disgrace to the family name. To cut the story short, he threw the boy out and disowned him.'

'A harsh lesson.' Clifford tapped the gauge beside him.

'I know.' She paused as the boat lurched in and out of a series of larger waves. 'But there was an even harsher lesson to follow. For the father. And son. The bodies from the ship that ran aground when the light failed washed up on the beaches over the next few days. The old man, Mr Cunliffe's father, went down to pay his respects. Only to discover the body in the keeper's uniform was' – she fought the lump that filled her throat – 'his second son. The one he'd disowned. He'd taken the job as keeper secretly to try and regain his father's respect after he'd reformed himself and returned to the area.'

'And I assume he chose the job of keeper because the lighthouse meant the world to his father?' At her nod, Clifford closed his eyes. 'Only the follies of men,' he murmured.

'I know. It's too tragic for words. Because, of course, by then, Mr Cunliffe's father was bankrupt after pouring all his money into the lighthouse. And in doing so, he'd neglected the last of his living family and the house and ended up being thrown into debtors' prison. It's helped me forgive our Mr Cunliffe, after knowing his past and that he paid his father's debt to get him out.'

The engine faltered momentarily. Clifford glanced at it and shrugged. 'Dirt in the fuel, I expect, my lady. And yes, what you learned goes some way to excusing Mr Cunliffe's behaviour. Unless, that is,' he said grimly, 'it transpires he *is* our murderer.'

She nodded. 'Whether it does or not, our trip out to the lighthouse has confirmed what we suspected after our discoveries in the garden. And what Penrose and Mr Cunliffe himself told us. The—'

The engine faltered again. Clifford's brow furrowed. She looked at him enquiringly.

Then it cut out altogether.

38

Still on his haunches, Clifford looked up from poring over the engine. His expression was grave.

'Tell me,' she said as she hung grimly onto the tiller, fighting to keep the boat at right angles to the waves.

'The fuel tank has been sabotaged, my lady.'

Without warning, they pitched into the trough of a fierce swell, throwing them both forwards and wrenching the tiller from her hand.

'Sabotaged?' she gasped, scrambling back up onto her knees. 'While we were at the lighthouse?'

'It must have been. Someone has punched a hole low down and then partially plugged it. With this.' Bracing himself against the engine casing, he held up an oily nail with his one free hand.

'Then quick! Hammer it back in and save the last of our fuel. We only need...' She faltered at his sober headshake.

'Too late. The tank is completely empty. Whoever did this, wanted us to reach the lighthouse—'

'But not return to Lostenev!' She groaned. 'And all the

while we were with Woon, our precious fuel was trickling away!'

He banged his fist against his forehead. 'While you were indulging over the lamp's mechanics, you fool man!'

She beckoned him firmly to shuffle over beside her. 'Clifford, beating yourself up won't help. Nor is it justified. Woon was still telling me the last of the tale when you came back down. Besides, it must have been the murderer who sabotaged the fuel. And whoever that is has proved deviously clever from the start. But they will not beat us!' she shouted defiantly into the wind.

Clifford bowed as best he could in the confines of the wildly rocking boat. 'Hollered just like his lordship, my lady.'

'Thank you. Now, grab the oars. We'll just have to...' She stared at the sides of the boat. 'Clifford?'

He nodded sombrely. 'Yes, my lady. Whoever sabotaged the engine also took the oars.'

She closed her eyes for a moment and then thumped the seat. 'Well, we'll just have to do whatever we can.' Her hand reached for the tiller again. 'Which isn't much, admittedly, given we're completely incapacitated.'

He blanched. 'You mean?'

'Yes. We've no steering without the engine. The rudder's hopeless. It's just flapping uselessly against the strength of the sea. It hasn't let me keep us' – they ducked as a claw of water arched over the side – 'facing the waves. They're coming broadside.' She rubbed her scarf's fringing over the caustic salt now biting into her tongue. 'It's only a matter of time before we capsize. Unless we can come up with something.'

'In which case, boots, my lady!'

She nodded, fumbling at her laces with freezing fingers, while Clifford did the same. Boots off, she cast around again. Knowing losing heart would only guarantee failure, she thought for a second. 'Ah! Here's one good thing, though. If the murderer was planning for us to run out of fuel with no hope of reaching shore, they underestimated your most infuriating habit.'

Despite the perilousness of their situation, his eyes twinkled. 'Hardly the time for squabbling, my lady.'

'I wasn't. I meant your natural tendency for doing everything at a measured pace. Anyone else with a full tank of fuel would have roared back from the lighthouse with the throttle set to maximum. Thanks to you, however, we have made it much further back than our saboteur could have guessed. We can't be more than' – she see-sawed her head, pointing – 'half a nautical mile away from that cliff. Now, we can sit here and hope to end up ashore or actually try to reduce the distance.' *Think, Ellie, think!* 'A sail from our clothes?'

He shook his head. 'We might be able to fashion a rudimentary one if we had an oar, but even then we'd have no way of securing it. If we tried holding it, it would be ripped from our grasp with the first gust.' He examined his pocket watch. 'The tide is coming in fast.'

'Well then, at least it will push us towards the beach.'

Ten minutes later, fingers numb from desperately grasping their seats to stay onboard, remarkably they were still upright. And her prediction looked like coming true.

'Clifford. We've halved the distance to the shore already.'

'Indeed. But we are starting to drift perilously close to those rocks, my lady.'

She nodded grimly. 'I had noticed.'

A swell caught them. They held on as the tiny craft reared up. As they slammed back down, the boat swung around.

'Brace!'

The wave punched against the side of the boat.

'We're going to roll!'

'Incoming!' Clifford shouted as the sea rushed into the bilges.

As the craft righted itself, she hung on grimly, the water rushing out again, threatening to take her with it. Gasping for breath, she stared down and then up at Clifford. His face told her he had the same thought. Only half the water had run back out. The bilges were still submerged. The next wave which caught them would capsize—

She was suddenly thrown from the boat. Submerged, her lungs collapsed from the force and freezing temperature of the sea. Unable to breathe, her father teaching her what to do if she fell overboard flashed into her memory. Forcing herself to remain calm, she waited until she was above the waves and sucked in as much air as she could. Her chest burned, but she was back in control. Her upbringing had left her unafraid of the sea, but she still held it in absolute respect. And awe, having seen first-hand just how deadly it could be. And now, as she was relentlessly tossed up and sucked down by the icy black swell, every wave seemed alive with malice.

But her greatest fear was for Clifford. With only one arm, he would be in dire trouble unless he could yank it free of its sling. Which looked impossible, as she was struggling with two good arms just to stay above the waves.

'Tread water!' she yelled as she spotted him behind her. Striking out as hard as she could, his head still disappeared twice before she could reach him.

'Elbow must be broken,' he gurgled. 'Won't extend.'

A fragment of wood floated past with a fender bobbing along behind it.

The boat must have hit the rocks, Ellie. And if we don't move, we will too.

'Your pocketknife. Quick!'

Her hands grasped for it below the surface of the water for fear he might drop it. Holding the knife, she grabbed the wreckage and sliced through the loop attaching the knotted rope fender to the wood.

'Press this to your chest,' she yelled. 'And stay as flat as you can on top while you swim one-armed.'

However, the tide had now become their enemy as it pushed them towards the same rocks where she could see the splintered bow of their boat trapped between two outcrops.

Swimming wide of it, she looked behind, spotting Clifford worryingly far off. She trod water until he caught up, then grabbed the fender rope and swam on, towing him behind her.

And then she realised all their fight with the sea might have been for nothing. The incoming tide had already covered the beach. Instead, they were swimming towards a vertical cliff face.

She knew, even if she could get a firm enough handhold on the slippery rock, it would be a near impossible climb, especially in the gathering gloom. And even if she could make it, Clifford couldn't. Not with only one arm. She glanced behind her.

'You go on!' he shouted.

'Together or not at all!' she shouted back.

Treading water in a circle, she desperately looked for an alternative to 'not at all'.

Then she heard it. At first she thought it was the blood pounding in her ears, but then she recognised it. A whooshing sound.

'This way!' she yelled, grabbing the rope again.

The entrance to the cave was hidden by an enormous boulder that must have crashed from the cliff into the sea aeons ago. Struggling not to be dashed against it by the waves, she swam around it and through the narrow opening.

Inside, the water was only three or four feet from the roof of the cave and still chasing in after them. She struck out for the highest ledge she could reach and scrambled on to it before helping Clifford up beside her.

'I am forever indebted, my lady,' he wheezed between

snatched breaths. 'Without that hemp fender, I sincerely doubt I would be here.'

'Yes, you would!' She coughed as she brought up mouthfuls of seawater. 'You're too fearful of the unchecked chaos I would wreak on polite society without your restraining influence to succumb to a mere ocean.'

His face broke into a tired smile. 'Perhaps.' The smile faded. 'I fear, however, my lady, we are not out of danger yet.'

She reached up and ran her grazed fingers over the barnacles pimpling the roof. 'You're right. This cave is clearly totally submerged at high tide.'

It was also almost pitch-dark inside. Her brows met in a deep frown as she stared at a spot further up the ledge. 'Then why does it make that noise?'

'What noise?'

'Strangely, it's quieter now than outside. But listen. It's like a... a sleeping whale snorting through its blowhole.'

He scrambled up into a hunched position, wincing as he hit his arm on an overhanging rock. 'Yes, my lady! I hear it now. It is the sound of the waves rushing in and pushing the air up the cave until it is forced out. And for it to be forced out—'

'There has to be an exit!'

He passed her his torch, which miraculously still worked. On all fours, as the roof was too low to stand, she crawled along the ledge and behind a protruding rock which looked like a hooked witch's nose. Ducking back around, she called to him. 'I think I've found the way out!'

Ignoring her icy, soaked clothes and wet stockings which were flapping past her toes like duck's feet, she clambered upwards, just grateful they were both still alive.

'Managing alright?' she called behind her after five minutes of climbing.

'Indeed, my lady.'

'It does feel easier than I expected. And far wider than

simply the erosion from an old water course.' She gasped. 'Clifford! My hand has just fallen on a chain. It seems to be shackled into the rock wall. Like the path we scrambled down on the cliffs.'

'As I dared hope a few minutes back,' he said in an uncharacteristically relieved tone. 'I believe, my lady, we are in an old smugglers' tunnel.'

'Thank heavens! Then it must come out somewhere. And frankly, I don't care where. As long as it just keeps going up.' She set off with renewed vigour, Clifford close on her heels.

The tunnel steepened, and after a couple of minutes, they were rewarded.

'I can see a shaft of dim light ahead! Come on!'

The last section felt much colder on her face and hands as the frosty December air outside rushed in. But underfoot, it was less hard. She looked down and saw damp earth.

'We must be almost there.'

The tunnel emerged onto a flight of rough-hewn steps. At the top, she fought through a thick curtain of tangled ivy and stopped dead.

'Clifford. It's the weeping mulberry tree. We're in Gwel an Mor's garden! Of course! That tunnel must be how the murderer got back and forth without anyone seeing them!'

He nodded. 'The first piece of the puzzle solved, at least.'

A bright light blinded her.

'How right you are!' a familiar voice said.

39

For a moment there was silence, then Eleanor smiled grimly. 'I know I'm right. Just as I know how surprised you are to see us. We were supposed to have perished at sea, weren't we? But here we are. And here you are. Though not in your role as an upholder of all things lawful, but in your role as a double murderer!'

Inspector Trevilick smiled thinly. 'You want to be careful who you go around accusing, Lady Swift. I'm the one who put St Clair and Brae's murderer behind bars, remember?'

'Then why, pray tell,' Clifford said smoothly, taking his torch from Eleanor and shining it on Trevilick, 'are you carrying a non-police issue weapon? That gun you're concealing badly is a John Rigby version of the Mauser C96 pistol. Your police gun would be a Webley revolver, would it not?'

Trevilick's eyes narrowed. He raised the gun from where he'd been pressing it to his leg and pointed the barrel at Eleanor. 'Drop that torch!' Once Clifford had obeyed, he continued. 'Too sharp a box of tools for your own good, you two. But not as sharp as myself, evidently. Seeing as I'm the only one with a working firearm.'

Blast it, Ellie. He's right.

He turned to Clifford with a smug expression. 'I know your mistress never carries a gun – something else I checked with Chipstone – and anything you're carrying will be wet through, from the look of your clothes. An unforeseen capsize, was it?'

She nodded. 'It was, strangely. And yes, we are completely unarmed. And shockingly dishevelled. You owe us for two sets of boots, by the way. Not to mention extra recompense to my butler for a month's loss of sleep due to the indecorousness of my appearance.'

Trevilick's moustache quivered. 'I saw your fiancé asking around the harbour and then your Rolls Royce coming down the hill and put two and two together.'

She caught Clifford's jaw tighten but flapped a discreet hand at him. 'Let me guess, Inspector, your infamous nose started twitching?'

He nodded. 'Hats off to you, Lady Swift. As I said, you're a smart one. Anyway, I realised you'd worked out the connection between Gwel an Mor and the lighthouse and knew that's where you were headed. And that once you'd spoken to the keeper, you would figure out the rest.'

'The "rest",' she said grimly, 'that led you to murder two men, you mean? In cold blood?'

He shook his head. 'I warned you, Lady Swift. You should have heeded my advice and left here with your butler and fiancé after your Christmas shindig in the pub. Then it would never have had to come to this.'

Eleanor's brain was working overtime.

Just keep him talking long enough, Ellie. Hugh must be here somewhere.

'A question, though. When I first arrived, why did you send that garden roller hurtling down the slope after me?'

He grunted. 'Because I knew you were going to be proper trouble the minute you started nosing around on the beach where St Clair's body was recovered. I wanted to see how much it would take to put you off. When the roller didn't do it, I knew I would have to be smarter.'

Clifford's fists balled. 'How was trying to poison her lady-ship with cyanide in the hothouse being smarter?'

Trevilick glanced at him, but kept the gun firmly on Eleanor. 'Simple. It bolstered the idea that a mad poisoner was responsible for the murders.' He returned his gaze to her. 'Something, after all, you should take the credit for, Lady Swift.'

The glint in his eyes made her shake her head.

'Mr Cunliffe was right! There never was any poison in St Clair's body, was there?'

Trevilick's lips quirked. 'No. But you handed me a silver spoon I hadn't even reckoned on by suggesting I arrange for a post-mortem.'

'My error, there. And for not realising you lied to me that cyanide was listed in the coroner's report.'

His heavy jowls shook as he tutted. 'Please! Lady Swift. Naturally it's in the report because it was found in the body. Well, in one of the samples tested.'

She slapped her forehead. 'Your men didn't return from Gwel an Mor with any glasses or bottles of St Clair's with traces of poison in, did they? You planted the poison during the post-mortem.' At his glib nod, another piece of the puzzle fell into place. 'And there never was any wheel mark along the cliff path, because St Clair's body wasn't carried in a wheelbarrow. He walked there. To meet you, not Cunliffe. And you pushed him over!'

Clifford tapped his chin thoughtfully. 'Then why were my calculations about where Mr St Clair's body was found still off?'

Trevilick laughed curtly. 'Don't feel bad. Once he realised he wasn't going to leave that spot alive, he twisted around at the last minute to try and make a run for it. So, I kicked him back-wards over the edge.'

Eleanor nodded. 'That would explain it. But tell me. Why *did* you kill him? I think I have a pretty good idea, but I'd like to hear it first-hand.'

Trevilick growled. 'Because he was ruining my retirement nest egg, that's why! There's a fortune buried right here in this garden, as well you know. A little canary sang long before St Clair showed up. He told me the truth about the supposed light-house disaster. The light never failed that night. The keeper was bribed to turn it off so the ship would founder. Because' – he licked his lips – 'it was secretly carrying a fortune in jewels. Once the gang had looted the remains of the ship, they transported the jewels up here via that smugglers' tunnel to wait until everything went quiet. Gwel an Mor has been a smuggling hideout for some time, as I'm sure you worked out.'

Eleanor was listening with only one ear. With the other, she strained to hear any sound from the garden.

Dash it! Where's Hugh?

But it seemed her face had betrayed her again as Trevilick's smug look returned. 'Looking for your fiancé? He might just have had a bout of car trouble!'

She mentally browbeat herself. Why hadn't she thought of that? If Trevilick had sabotaged their boat, of course he would have done the same to Seldon's car.

But what exactly did he do, Ellie?

She tried to keep her concern that Seldon might be hurt from showing.

'You interrupted yourself, Inspector. Why didn't the gang who took the jewels from the ship return for them?'

'If your butler moves one more inch out of my torch beam and into the shadows, I'll shoot. Understood?'

She glanced at Clifford, who stepped back into the circle of light.

'Understood, Inspector.'

'Good.' He turned back to Eleanor. 'Because, Lady Swift,

excise officers caught up with them while they were smuggling contraband. They were all killed in a shoot-out ten miles down the coast.'

She laughed dismissively. 'And you believed this fairy tale?'

He nodded. 'It's no fairy tale. I'd heard the rumour of the fortune years before and dismissed it. But the thief, the one who told me, he was the son of the gang's leader.'

'But why did he tell you, of all people?'

'Because I arrested him. So he offered a simple trade. His freedom for the whereabouts of the jewels.'

'But why hadn't he simply collected them himself?'

'Because, fool though he was, he was intelligent enough to know he'd never pull it off. He was a small-time petty thief, no chip off the old block that his father was cast from. Whereas me, in my position...'

'A position of trust!' Clifford muttered.

'Trust nothing!' Trevilick snapped. 'I've worked my whole life to rise up the police force. Just like my father did. And all I had to look forward to was a joke of a pension so I could eke out my last days in hardship as he had. So, I took my chance! The evidence against the thief was "misplaced" and I spent the next few months checking out the details he'd told me. I knew he hadn't spun me a yarn. I found the cave down there in the cove. And the tunnel hidden behind the witch's nose rock, just as he'd detailed. The best part he didn't know, though. Where it comes up, here, where we're standing, no one had touched in decades. So all I had to do was work out the clues as to where the fortune was actually buried.'

'Yet while doing so, you didn't even notice the other goings on in the garden?' she scoffed. 'What sort of detective are you?'

'An intelligent one, Lady Swift. Local history is in my blood as much as the next Cornishman. Two young under-gardeners left to their own devices? It was almost certain they'd be running some scam up here. I made sure to discreetly find out all about it.'

She bit her lip. 'Which is how you knew where to get the "evidence" when you needed it to plant on Brae's body?'

He nodded. 'And I received a tip-off that the handyman here was as bent as the rest of them. But I quietly squashed any investigation. I wanted this place left well alone.'

'Which was St Clair's innocent mistake,' she said sadly. 'The poor fellow only came here to make something of the gardens and himself.'

Trevilick gritted his teeth. 'By clearing, cutting and exposing! It was obvious he'd discover the tunnel entrance sooner or later. And find the clues to the whereabouts of the jewels. Or, even worse, destroy those clues without even realising!'

'So you got rid of him,' Clifford growled in disgust.

'That's right,' Trevilick said, far too matter-of-factly for Eleanor's stomach. 'I told him that Cunliffe was under a discreet police investigation I was heading up. Well, he was keen as a puppy to dish the dirt on Cunliffe, as Cunliffe had just sacked him without giving him a penny of his severance fee. And he was just as eager to share the trail of "oddities" he'd uncovered. "Oddities" he'd marked on his garden plan.'

She laughed mockingly. 'But when you asked him to hand that plan over, he told you he'd burned it.'

His eyes narrowed. 'It was a blow, I'll admit. Especially as I still had to kill him because he'd become suspicious. I couldn't risk him contacting someone higher up to check my story.'

She grimaced in disgust. 'And poor Tristan Brae? He stumbled on you coming out of the tunnel, I guess?'

'Yes. I knew if you kept digging you'd stumble on the truth sooner or later. Most likely sooner according to your Sergeant Brice. I needed to speed up my own search of the gardens.' He shrugged. 'I should have done something about those two under-gardeners earlier on anyway. But then Odgers fell right in my lap! The perfect scapegoat for both murders.' He waved the gun. 'Enough explanations now, Lady Swift. You just hand over those plant sticks.'

She reluctantly reached into her pocket. 'To go with the ones you've already stolen from St Clair's office?'

'They're the ones. And I know you and your meticulous butler will have reconstructed St Clair's original garden plan.' He smiled smugly. 'So, all I need to do now is add the writing on your two sticks with the writing on the four I have, compare it to the new plan you've made, and hey presto!' His expression darkened. 'Now, stop wasting time and hand them over. And the plan.'

She pulled the plant sticks out and held them up. 'What? These? They won't do you any good, you know. That thief lied to you. To save his skin. They aren't the last pieces of the puzzle as to where jewels are hidden in Gwel an Mor's gardens.'

He waved the gun threateningly. 'So, they're not, eh?'

'No, they can't be. Because there is no treasure buried here.' She shook her head, her expression turning grim. 'You see, Inspector, the only thing buried in this garden is *regrets*!'

A shaft of light split the night...

40

Trevilick spun around, pistol swinging wildly.

'What's that?'

She let out a sigh of relief. *Hugh! Somehow he's made it, Ellie!*

Her relief was short-lived as Trevilick recovered and swung the gun back on her.

Blast! That was your chance, Ellie. You can't expect Clifford to wade into action as normal with a broken arm.

'Inspector!' She made sure she had his full attention. 'Prepare yourself for a disappointment.'

He glared at her. 'Stop bluffing! I'm still the one in charge here!' He waved his gun again, but his voice lacked conviction.

'Of course you are,' she said soothingly. 'But surely you want to hear the truth, rather than spend the rest of your days fruitlessly digging and searching?'

He snorted. 'Nice try! But you can't fool me!'

'Unlike a petty thief did,' Clifford muttered.

Trevilick shot him an evil glance. 'Look at the state of this place!' He waved a hand around the gardens. 'Old man

Cunliffe could have never found the jewels, if that's what you're trying to have me believe.'

She shook her head vigorously. 'You're absolutely right. He couldn't have.'

Clifford nodded sagely. 'Inspector, when you telephoned Chipstone, did Sergeant Brice not mention if there was a seemingly impossible puzzle at the root of an investigation, her ladyship invariably deciphered it? Even when the greatest police minds had drawn a blank?'

'Yes,' he hissed through gritted teeth. 'But all I heard in my mind was what a bloody nuisance she was going to be to me!'

He jumped as a second shaft of light illuminated the sky.

He wavered momentarily. 'Listen. I don't know what game your fiancé's playing, but you've got one minute to hand over those plant sticks and garden plan or—'

She held her hands up. 'I'm only trying to save you the bother of, well, killing us, really. And all for nothing.' She hurried on. 'You see, you were quite right to be worried. St Clair did start to notice things as he progressed in clearing the garden in order to implement his grand new design. Odd things he recorded in his notebook. Anomalies which struck him, as an expert in landscape design, as inexplicably strange. Like a series of pots inscribed with letters and containing lanterns, each built into the walls of identical beds. Identical, except each was filled with a different plant. And presided over by a different tree. The arrangement of the beds to each other felt all the more odd to him, spread illogically as they were, to his mind. And not conforming to any of the usual patterns associated with an old Georgian estate like Gwel an Mor. It was all just too peculiar for him not to note it down for himself.'

Trevilick's eyes gleamed with greed. 'And you think you've worked it all out, do you?'

'No. I'm certain I have. Though to give you credit, you were part way there by realising the wooden plant sticks were a clue.

Those marking every flower and shrub bed staked around the garden are etched metal. St Clair used wood ones while exploring the gardens because he could paint over them and use them again if need be. Depending on what he worked out. Which I'll tell you in a second.' She'd got his undivided attention now. That was clear in the way his tongue flicked over his bottom lip repeatedly. 'You see, inscribed on each of those pots, St Clair found *two letters* which he noted down on a plant stick. And he also discovered, I think, why the pots are, in fact, lantern holders.'

A vein pulsed in Trevilick's neck as a third beam lit the dark. He hastily waved the gun for her to go on.

'Inspector, the letters on each pot, and St Clair's plant sticks, are the initials of the sailors who drowned when the light failed and their ship foundered. The ones who the keeper went back for, but who perished alongside him. They are beds of remembrance. A resting place for sailor's souls, not stolen stones!'

'I don't believe you,' Trevilick spluttered unconvincingly. 'They... they probably buried the treasure in six different locations so there was less chance of the whole lot being discovered. And the letters on St Clair's plant sticks point to each urn. And each urn marks a place where a portion of the jewels were buried!'

She shook her head. 'A good theory. But not correct. You see, Clifford suggested that we consulted with my own expert gardener at Henley Hall, Joseph, yesterday. And he confirmed my suspicions. Each bed is planted with a single plant; rosemary, sea lavender, hollyhocks, lily-of-the-valley, pansy and tulips. Each one is a symbol of remembrance. And each bed is presided over by a weeping tree; copper beech, linden, willow, cherry, fig and mulberry. And an urn. And the paths around those urns and beds all lead to one place. More specifically to the memorial Mr Cunliffe's father toiled his last days away to build in memory of his middle son whom he had disowned. Disowned, not knowing until it was too late that he was the lighthouse keeper who perished trying to save the crew that night.'

Trevilick jerked around as a fourth ray of light joined the others.

'You expect me to believe this... this nonsense, I'm hearing?'

'No. I want you to see it for yourself. Because Mr Cunliffe's father did all of this himself. In his final years. Isolated, with no money to pay for any help. It must have been back-breaking work with so much of the garden being rock. But I'm convinced he felt it was in atonement for forsaking his middle son. And for the sailors who died due to his hastily installing the faulty lamp in the lighthouse. When he knew, in his heart, he should have waited until it had finished its tests.'

A fifth lantern threw a piercing stream of light across the garden to where they were standing. 'You see, each lantern is a beacon for a sailor who died that night. A substitute for the lighthouse light that should never have gone out. Each lantern has enough fuel to burn all night. Cunliffe's father would have lit them every evening. Here!' Eleanor tossed the two plant sticks she'd kept back at Trevilick. Catching them with a snatched hand, he wrenched the four others from his pocket.

Keeping one eye on Eleanor, he glanced at each stick in turn as Clifford intoned, 'S.R. – Silas Rosman, L.L. – Lionel Lattimer, A.R. – Alan Ross, C.M. – Connan Marrack, V.T. – Victor Triss, T.G. – Tyler Greswyn.'

Trevilick's left eye twitched. 'Those are the men who went down with the ship?'

Eleanor nodded. 'And any supposed treasure on the boat would have gone with them or been salvaged by the locals long ago. If it ever existed.'

The space flooded with light as a sixth beacon lit up behind her.

'The only precious jewel in this garden is right in front of you.' She stepped aside to allow the last shaft of light to meet the others in a shimmering ring. 'The sundial.'

'What the—' Trevilick's face betrayed his disbelief. He strode up to the dial, his gun still aimed squarely at her.

She pointed at the dial. 'See for yourself. It's only when the beacons are lit that the indented sections stand out because of the opposite shadows they throw. So you can see it's actually an inscription.' Her finger followed the intricate pattern encircling the centre. She swallowed hard. 'Forgive me not my sins you suffered, beloved son. But know, I always loved you.'

Trevilick's eyes blazed as he stepped back, his eyes darting around.

She shook her head. 'It's over, Inspector. Even if you got rid of Clifford and me, my fiancé knows everything. And if he disappeared, you'd have half the police forces in England descend on Gwel an Mor, Scotland Yard included. And you'll never find him out there in the dark. But he'll find you.'

With unexpected speed, Trevilick lunged forward, bringing his gun barrel down on Clifford's broken elbow with a sickening crack. Spinning around, he let fly a flurry of bullets into the darkness and ran.

Jumping up off the floor where she'd thrown herself, she bit her lip rather than call out Seldon's name to make sure he was unhurt. She knew better than to give away his position.

She hurried forward. 'Clifford, are you alright?'

He stifled a groan, gripping his arm to his chest. 'Fine, my lady.'

'Thank goodness. But he's going to get away!'

'Not without a vehicle!' A bedraggled Seldon burst through the box hedging and pulled her to him. 'I didn't see any vehicle or tracks when I ran up here earlier.'

She gasped. 'You ran all the way from the village?'

'That wretch left me no choice.' He shook his head angrily.

'If only I could have got a shot off, blast it! But he was too close to y—'

She grabbed his arm. 'The car, Hugh! He's probably making for Mr Cunliffe's car!'

'But hopefully he doesn't know the shortcut through the grotto we found!' Clifford beckoned urgently for them to follow him.

As they finally raced across the lawn to the driveway, she could see the car parked outside the house.

The front door opened, light streaming out and illuminating—

'Trevilick. There he is!'

All three came to a dead halt. Seldon raised his gun and took aim. But before he could call out, Cunliffe appeared on the front step.

'What the devil are you doing here again?' he thundered. Trevilick ignored him as he yanked on the car door. 'Oh, no you don't!' Cunliffe raced down the steps and threw himself between the car and the policeman.

'Give me the key!' Trevilick shouted.

'No! I will not. How dare you come here in the middle of the night? Again! I—'

Trevilick grabbed him by the collar. 'I said give me the key! Now!'

The three of them inched forward.

'I still can't get a clear shot,' Seldon muttered in frustration.

Cunliffe pressed himself harder against the car. 'Take your hands off me. This is my house. My car. Now get out!'

He doesn't realise Trevilick's the killer, Ellie!

She glanced at the other two and without a word, they ran forward.

'Give him the key!' she yelled.

Cunliffe shook his head. 'No! A gentleman never yields to threats from a—'

Trevilick raised his gun and pressed it to Cunliffe's forehead. 'You three stop right where you are!' he yelled over his shoulder. 'And put that gun down. Now!'

They froze. Reluctantly, Seldon slowly laid his gun on the ground.

Trevilick smiled grimly and turned back to Cunliffe. 'Right, now give me the keys or—'

A sharp swish rent the air, followed by a dull thud. For a brief moment Trevilick looked confused. Then he fell like a stone.

Behind him stood Marsh, golf club in hand. He raked back the thick lock of black hair from his eyes and looked around the startled group.

'Did I forget to shout FORE?'

They were there in a flash, Seldon binding the unconscious Trevilick's wrists with his tie, while Eleanor grabbed Cunliffe's arms.

'Are you alright?'

Cunliffe looked at her dazedly, then turned slowly to his nephew.

'Edwin! You... you saved my life! I... I thought you'd... you'd rather like to have seen me shot.'

Marsh grinned. 'I thought it over. But, after all, we're family, Uncle Godfrey.'

41

'Ah! The thing is,' Eleanor said as she twirled the skirt of her emerald-green gown as her butler glided over to her in Gwel an Mor's drawing room. 'To the untrained eye, it might look as though I'm not packed and ready to leave.'

He raised a brow. 'The reason being, my lady?'

'Because I'm not. Not at all, in fact.'

His lips twitched. 'Heartening news. And quite the turn-around.' Deftly balancing the tray of drinks on one hand, he scrutinised her outfit. 'However, your gown is dry, and not caked in mud, sand, or seaweed. And you are even wearing shoes. An early New Year's resolution, perhaps?'

She laughed. 'No, you terror. Everyone else has made a special effort, so I have too.'

'Then a belated Merry Christmas, if I may offer such.' He passed her a sherry.

'You too. But it doesn't feel like the festive season is over yet. I've got back that delicious tingle which only comes this time of year.'

She glanced around the room, thinking the atmosphere was positively jovial for the first time since they'd arrived. But it couldn't be the decorations, she mused, even though the tree was shimmering with extra glass angels, each hugging a flickering candle between the spinning baubles. Or the fresh scarlet-berried holly and silver spruce looped by satin ribbon ties along the mantelpiece above the crackling fire. Or Gladstone, who was shamelessly enjoying the fuss as he paraded back and forth in his smart embroidered bow tie which had magically appeared with Flora and Clara. Not even Tomkins. To Eleanor's amazement, he had been the one to penetrate Marsh's customary indifference. The pair sat at opposite ends of the window seat, Marsh spinning marbles for Tomkins to skittishly pounce on.

No, she decided, it must be because they'd caught the murderer and all that unpleasantness was behind them!

She scanned the room. 'Wherever has Hugh got to, Clifford?'

'Your fiancé has been "borrowed", my lady. By Mr Cunliffe. They have just retired to the study.'

'Oh no!' She bit her lip. 'Poor Hugh. Whatever the conversation's about, he's going to find it hideously uncomfortable.' She lowered her voice. 'I know Mr Cunliffe doesn't approve of our getting engaged.'

She adroitly turned one satin-heeled shoe to trap a runaway marble from skittering past.

'Rather off!' Marsh said, ambling over with his hand outstretched.

'My playing for Tomkins' side?'

'No. That inspector blighter being the murderer. Had everyone fooled.'

His great-aunts slid in beside him in a rustle of lavender taffeta.

'Except you, dear,' Clara said breathlessly.

She laughed. 'Gracious, no. It was a team effort.'

Over at the drinks table, Clifford quietly shook his head.

Flora pointed a bony finger at her. 'So we won't go on, until you do.'

'Do what?' Eleanor whispered to Marsh, fearing she might be none the wiser if the ladies answered.

He folded his arms. 'Tell us how you knew.'

'That it was Trevilick? Oh, right!' She faltered as the door opened to reveal Cunliffe leading in her bemused-looking fiancé. He caught her questioning look and shrugged.

Flora tapped Eleanor's arm. 'On tenterhooks isn't very comfortable, dear.'

Clara nodded. 'Not at our age.'

Cunliffe seemed equally intrigued as he joined the line of expectant faces.

'Very well, then,' Eleanor said. 'The short version is that, as an experienced policeman, Trevilick covered his tracks almost perfectly. But he slipped up on three minor details. First, if poor St Clair had been killed at high tide, his body would have been washed away.' She hid a shiver that she and Clifford had very nearly succumbed to just such a fate. 'Which got me thinking later. Why didn't the murderer kill St Clair at that time then? It would have been such a gift to get rid of the body.'

'The answer?' Flora cooed.

'That someone would have soon reported him as missing. You, Mr Cunliffe, almost certainly, since he was in your employ. And your call would have instigated a thorough police search of the gardens as a matter of course. The very thing Trevilick didn't want to happen, but couldn't have stopped without arousing suspicion. And that gave me my first inkling that somehow Gwel an Mor's gardens were central to the mystery.'

Marsh's interested stare bore through her skull. 'And secondly?'

'On the night of poor Tristan Brae's murder, I noticed when Trevilick arrived he had dark rings around the bottom of his eyes. And his trousers.'

'Ooh!' the sisters twittered, clutching at each other's arms.

'I put the dark rings under his eyes down to lack of sleep, obviously. Something hard-working policemen never get enough of.' She glanced pointedly at Seldon. 'And, at the time, I put the dark rings around his trouser bottoms down to him having stepped in a large puddle in the driveway here. But later I realised there *were* no puddles that night. Everything was frozen. To the point even Brae's heavy bleeding only melted a little of the snow, and for a short while. So Trevilick must have got wet trousers from somewhere else.'

'Trousers, trousers, smartly set—' Clara started in, only to be hushed impatiently by the others.

Eleanor smiled at her. 'Then I remembered seeing exactly the same dark line on Clifford's usually impeccable suit bottoms, the first time we got caught in the sea.'

'Paddling with your butler?' Cunliffe quizzed with a twitch of his brow.

'We were checking the beach where St Clair's body fell, actually, and the tide came in. But when we found the smugglers' tunnel up into the gardens, I realised Trevilick had come back here the night Brae was killed. He must have got wet trousers, stepping out of his boat. And then Brae saw him creeping out of the tunnel. So there it is.'

'Three!' Marsh protested. 'You promised.'

She hid a smile. 'So I did. Well, at the police station, when I asked Odgers about the plant labels, Trevilick scoffed. He said the pilfering of a few wooden plant labels could hardly matter. But no one had said they were made of wood. All those set in the flower beds around the garden are metal. Which meant Trevilick had to be the one who had quietly taken them from St Clair's office. And then lied about it.' She paused for dramatic effect. 'Only the person hunting for something in Gwel an Mor's gardens would have done that. And that person was the murderer.'

She shook her head bashfully at the rousing round of applause. As it faded. Cunliffe raised his hand. 'Everyone. A moment of your attention.' He hesitated. 'I have—'

'No, no, Godfrey dear,' Flora said, fluffing her sister's identical lace frills. 'That won't do.'

Clara nodded. 'Ladies, we be, with gentlemen three.'

With a resigned shake of his head, Cunliffe tried again. 'Ladies and gentlemen, it has been an extraordinary Christmas. And not one any of us would wish to repeat, I'm sure. Except for one element.'

'More bubbles, Uncle?' Marsh said keenly.

'No, Edwin. I was referring to the visit of a remarkable young woman. Lady Swift. Or perhaps she might forgive me for presuming to call her Eleanor?'

He turned to her with such an affectionate look, she was momentarily lost for words. Recovering, she beamed.

'I'd love that. Genuinely.'

'Then, family, friends, please raise your glasses to the happy future of Eleanor. And Hugh, this exceedingly bright young man.' Cunliffe smiled at Seldon. 'And Eleanor's most-deserving fiancé.'

Her jaw dropped as the room burst into a cheer, including a flurry of woofs from Gladstone. Cunliffe wafted his family back to their places, leaving him alone with Eleanor and Seldon.

'I hope you didn't mind?'

'Quite the opposite. Thank you. But... I thought...?'

Cunliffe nodded. 'That I was an obdurate old fool. Too stuck in his ways to see that a difference in social standing between two people in love was no business of his. And you were right.'

'Gracious, that's... that's not what I thought at all.'

Cunliffe smiled. 'Byron always said your face gave you away. How right he was.' Seldon and Clifford shared an amused look. 'But I will admit to another lack of good judgement.'

Cunliffe reached up and patted Seldon on the shoulder. 'On behalf of my very good friend, Byron, I took this fellow into my study to assess his suitability as he has become engaged to you, Eleanor, Byron's beloved niece and ward. But, as I closed the door behind me, I realised it was entirely unnecessary. Another very fine fellow, and far more eminent judge, had already done so. And if he heartily approves, so do I.' Eleanor's eyes pricked with hot tears as he turned to Clifford. 'Good man. Byron was a lucky chap to have you by his side all those years. Gosh, how I envied that old warrior of adventure!'

Seldon squeezed Eleanor's hand gently behind his back. Uncharacteristically, even Clifford seemed to need a moment to regain his composure.

'Sir, if you will forgive my disgraceful overstepping, I am sure his lordship would wish I impart to you just how resolutely he would feel the same.'

Cunliffe frowned. 'About... me?'

'Indeed, sir. Facing off anyone holding a loaded weapon is not for the faint-hearted. It takes a certain... Byron spirit!'

Cunliffe beamed, but then shook his head. 'But if it hadn't been for my nephew, it would all have been in vain. Edwin is the one who should be proud at this moment.'

All eyes turned on Marsh. Uncharacteristically, he looked uneasy. Clearing his throat, he took a deep breath.

'Not quite, actually. As everyone else seems to be... confessing, I have a confession of my own...'

42

The room fell silent. Eleanor glanced around.

Whatever is he going to say, Ellie?

Cunliffe cocked his head questioningly.

Marsh cleared his throat again. 'The thing is, Uncle Godfrey. You and me. Well, we haven't always got on.' He chewed his lip. 'And, in truth, I wanted you out. In fact, I tried to think of anything I could to get you to pack your bags. Only...' He threw his hands out. 'I couldn't think of anything, blast it, so I just hoped you might be carted off to jail for... well, you know.' He glanced at his aunts. 'Alright. The truth is, I wanted you all out so I could sell this place and... well, make a new start. Or if I'm going to be horribly honest, probably make another poor start somewhere else.'

Cunliffe looked crestfallen. Eleanor and Clifford shared a mortified look.

This is no way for the day to end, Ellie.

Flora tutted. 'That's the trouble with nephews.'

Clara nodded. 'Big and small.'

Eleanor glanced at Cunliffe, noticing he was blushing from his neck up. Before she could speak to him, he raised his hand.

'I too have another confession. It has long been my intention to... to remove you all.' He pulled an official-looking sheaf of papers from his inside pocket. 'And this morning, I finally received the legally amended deeds to Gwel an Mor. The original clause no longer stands. These now state that none of you, nor the Liddicoats, have the right to reside here in perpetuum any longer.'

'Gone? Us?' Clara said with a pout. 'Because of the piano?'

'And the poems?' Flora huffed. 'We've only been making the best of it.'

'A bit off,' Marsh grumbled. 'Very, actually.'

Cunliffe nodded. 'It would be. But for this.' He marched to the fireplace and threw the papers into the flames. 'And to think I almost repeated my father's mistakes!'

With a squeal, Flora skipped over and embraced him.

'Godfrey, dear! You mean you'll get the piano tuned after all?'

Eleanor put her hand in front of her mouth to hide her laughter.

Cunliffe broke free of Flora's embrace and smoothed his waistcoat down. Eleanor frowned.

Why is he still looking so upset, Ellie? Of course!

Cunliffe shifted on the spot. 'I... I can't promise. About the piano tuner, I'm afraid.' He glanced at Marsh. 'And as for you, Edwin, my boy. I would dearly love to help you onto the right path. And pay off the debts I suspect brought you here and have kept you ever since.' He raised a hand as Marsh opened his mouth. 'But I haven't enough funds.' He put his hands in front of his face and took a deep breath. 'In fact, I shan't pretend any longer. The short of it is, we none of us are likely to be able to live here very much longer. I... I have debts of my own. I need to sell Gwel an Mor to pay for them.' He shook his head sadly. 'If there was any other way—'

Flora tutted. 'No, no, Godfrey, dear. That's far from the

case.'

Cunliffe stared at her. 'What are you on about, Aunt Flora?'

She tutted again. 'Lady Swift's man knows why. Don't you?'

The whole room stared at Clifford.

For one of the few times she'd known him, her butler seemed totally perplexed.

'Would that I could, Miss Flora. However—'

'Oh, but you do know!' Flora hurried to his side with Clara clamped to her arm. 'You know the rules, remember?'

Clifford glanced pleadingly at Eleanor. She shrugged.

Clara flapped her string of beads at him. 'There is a house with ivied walls, and mullioned windows, worn and old. And the long dwellers in those halls, have souls that know but sordid calls...'

Eleanor held her breath.

For a moment Clifford said nothing. Then he nodded slowly. 'And dote on gold!'

As Flora and Clara applauded, Cunliffe stared at him in confusion.

'Clifford? What is all this?'

'The painting of the cottage, sir, I believe. In the long passage.'

'It's worth a great deal now, Godfrey,' Flora said. 'It's by a fellow I used to know when I was at the Royal Academy. Terrible man. Wonderful painter. He gave it to me when we broke up as a sort of consolation prize. His works have simply soared in value these last years. No idea why, but that's the art world for you, dear.' At Cunliffe's disbelieving look, she patted his arm. 'It's perfectly alright. I don't mind if you sell it. I'm over him now and you have paid for us, and Edwin, since you arrived. So take it as Clara and my debt of gratitude.'

Eleanor slipped her arm into Seldon's and whispered, 'No fortune in the garden, but one right under their noses all the time!'

Cunliffe's lips flapped, but no sound came out. He shook himself. 'You're... you're sure, Aunt Flora?' At her nod, he held his hands out in exasperation. 'Then why didn't you say before?'

This time Eleanor couldn't hide her laugh as Flora looked in askance at Cunliffe. 'Because you didn't ask, dear.'

They all turned at a tap on the door. Mrs Liddicoat stepped in with a nervous-looking Dewi Odgers.

'Ah, Odgers.' Cunliffe beckoned him forward. 'Welcome back.'

Odgers gawped. 'I can stay, sir?'

'You've learned a hard lesson about the scam you were using my gardens for, haven't you?'

He stared at the floor. 'That be the truth, Mr Cunliffe, sir. Ne'er such a trick would I think to pull again.'

'Then it's settled.' Cunliffe looked down in surprise as Eleanor handed him a large sheet of paper, meticulously folded several times. 'What's this?'

Eleanor smiled. 'Clifford's pocketbook. Containing his plan of Gwel an Mor's gardens, section by section, which he completed this morning.'

Cunliffe spun back to the under-gardener. 'Then, Odgers, we might still talk about a landscape project after all! If rather more restrained.'

'I'd like to help with that,' Marsh said. 'Together, perhaps, Uncle Godfrey?'

'Of course, Edwin.' He turned to Mrs Liddicoat. 'You may rest assured that you and Mr Liddicoat may stay on, too. But, like Odgers, and Edwin,' he said sternly, 'you may continue in my employment only if you do not engage in any other illegal activities.' She nodded contritely. 'Good. That's settled as well. And, funds permitting, a little brightening up of your cottage may be in order.'

'Too kind, sir.'

'Oh, and I shall officially retire seagull from the menu.'

Mrs Liddicoat frowned. 'But I thought you loved it, sir?'

Cunliffe shuddered. 'It's positively foul! But it helped stretch the shillings seeing as Mr Liddicoat caught them on the cliffs for nothing.'

The housekeeper flapped her apron. 'Then you've saved me collecting so much comfrey to cover up the taste.'

She beckoned for Odgers to follow her out, but he stood frowning, his hat turning in his hands. 'There be no comfrey growin' in the kitchen garden, Mrs Liddicoat. That bed got left to the foxgloves to take over, two year back.'

Her hand flew to her mouth. 'Then what ninny left the metal plaque sayin' comfrey!'

Seldon nodded around the ring of the family. 'Your unintentional poisoner, it seems!'

'And we were so looking forward to eighty candles on our cake this year,' Clara said with a sigh.

Clifford gave them a reassuring look. 'Ladies, mild digestive discomfort is the worst that can result from the proportions of, as we know now, foxglove leaves I witnessed Mrs Liddicoat adding to the food from the jar marked "comfrey".'

Cunliffe heaved a sigh of relief. 'Thank goodness for that! And perhaps, therefore, we might also retire "comfrey" from the menu alongside the seagull, Mrs Liddicoat?'

She nodded and hastened out with Odgers.

Eleanor held out her hand to Cunliffe. 'I'd love to stay longer, but it's quite a journey back and as I'm driving the entire distance—'

Clifford turned to Cunliffe. 'Is there any way you would consider my continuing unofficially as a member of your household staff, sir? Perhaps just until my arm is mended well enough to drive—'

Eleanor's mouth dropped. 'You disloyal rogue!'

Over everyone's chuckles, she herded her butler out of the house and into the Rolls.

Seldon leaned in through the passenger door to help the scrabbling Gladstone up onto the blanket across Clifford's lap, while Tomkins bounded in and settled beside his best friend with a happy meow.

'Really, sir?' Clifford pleaded. 'Sporting their Christmas reindeer antlers? Not the most dignified of journeys for a butler.'

Seldon threw his hands out. 'You try taking them off. I chased them halfway around the garden before giving in.' He winked at Eleanor. 'Right.' He waved again to the family on the front step. 'Let's finish this festive season back home as planned. I'm only sorry I have to follow behind in my car and miss the entertainment of your endless squabbling.'

'I'll race you, Hugh,' she said impishly, tightening her grip on the steering wheel of the Rolls.

His face broke into a grin. 'But then I would have to arrest both of us for reckless driving.'

'And for prematurely ageing a butler,' Clifford muttered.

Laughing, she started the engine and trundled up the drive. At the top, she checked the rear-view mirror as she turned onto the road. And gasped.

'Clifford! I've just noticed there's a hamper on the back seat. Why didn't you mention it?'

He sniffed. 'Merely a small picnic for the journey to keep the lady fed. After all, only breakfast, brunch and lunch have been partaken of.'

'That's wonderful! What's in it?'

He lifted the lid. 'The finest only, of course, my lady.' His eyes twinkled. 'For starters, seagull sandwiches with comfrey relish. And then to follow—'

'Clifford!'

A LETTER FROM VERITY

Dear reader,

I want to say a huge thank you for choosing to read *Murder on the Cornish Cliffs*. If you did enjoy it, and want to keep up to date with all my latest releases, just sign up at the following link. Your email address will never be shared and you can unsubscribe at any time.

www.bookouture.com/verity-bright

I hope you loved *Murder on the Cornish Cliffs* and if you did I would be very grateful if you could write a review. I'd love to hear what you think, and it makes such a difference helping new readers to discover one of my books for the first time.

I love hearing from my readers – you can get in touch through social media, or my website.

Thanks,

Verity

facebook.com/veritybrightauthor
x.com/BrightVerity

HISTORICAL NOTES

CORNISH PIXIES

Anyone who hasn't read any *Harry Potter* or seen the films (does such a person exist?) may not be familiar with Cornish pixies (or piskies). They are magical little fellows who inhabit Cornwall and spend their time spreading mischief and general upset to anyone who comes across them. The little blue scamps in the *Harry Potter* books are quite close to the ones in genuine Cornish folklore who were supposed to be wandering souls stuck in limbo (which might explain their generally rather anti-social behaviour!). Disappointingly, Eleanor and Clifford never meet a real Cornish pixie, although Trevilick comes close.

DEVIL WORSHIP AND MR CROWLEY

Clifford is quite right as usual when he tells Eleanor that some Edwardians (and Victorians before them) were obsessed with the occult. He mentions Mr Crowley, who would definitely have been St Clair's inspiration if he had been a devil worshipper as Mr Cunliffe declared. Dubbed 'the wickedest man in the world' (which is quite a moniker to live up to) he preferred the nickname 'The Great Beast 666'. Along with W.B. Yeats and Bram Stoker (author of *Dracula*), he was a member of the Hermetic Order of the Golden Dawn. His fame grew after his death with the Beatles putting him on the cover of their *Sergeant Pepper* album and Ozzy Osbourne writing a song named after him. Jimmy Page of Led Zeppelin even bought his old house.

CORNISH LIGHTHOUSES

In Eleanor's time, Cornwall had some of the remotest manned lighthouses in Britain, some up to eight miles off shore. Sadly, they are all now automated. Some, including the Souter Lighthouse, were said to be haunted. And one, the Lizard, like Lostenev, was actually built by a private individual, Sir John Killigrew, who couldn't get enough money raised by public subscription. Mostly because the locals made such a lucrative trade from looting the ships that foundered on the rocks, they had no interest in a lighthouse ruining their livelihood. In fact, when the lighthouse was half completed, the locals tore it down. The most confusing thing about the whole affair, however, was that Sir John's family were themselves well-known pirates and smugglers. They reportedly regularly attacked ships in the area and looted ones that had foundered on the rocks when Sir John decided to randomly turn the light off for long periods.

LOST GARDENS

The gardens at Gwel an Mor are inspired by the wonderful Lost Gardens of Heligan in Cornwall. Maintained for hundreds of years on the Tremayne Estate, by the 1900s there were over twenty gardeners. Unfortunately, World War One intervened and only eight returned. Soon the estate itself struggled financially and the gardens were left to their own devices. In the 1990s they were rediscovered by the present owners who set about the mammoth task of restoring them. Oddly, the only items hidden in the Heligan gardens are eggs at Easter, which would get Mr Cunliffe's approval.

EGG COLLECTING

Mr Cunliffe's collection of eggs amazes Eleanor, but he would have been considered a lightweight in terms of real Victorian and Edwardian egg collectors. Many of them were fanatics, willing to risk injury, and even death, to get their eggs. Some were killed by native tribesmen as they scoured the globe looking for rare eggs, while others died falling from the tops of trees. One collector, Charles Bendire, climbed a tree and returned with the rare egg safe in his mouth only to find it stuck there. He thought nothing of insisting the egg stayed intact, even if they had to break his teeth to remove it. And their collections numbered in the thousands of eggs, Lord Rothschild's collection consisting of almost twelve thousand.

MRS LIDDICOAT'S SEAGULL RECIPE

Unfortunately (or fortunately depending on your viewpoint), it's actually illegal to eat seagull in the UK today. Also, it seems its flavour really is as bad as Eleanor finds. Most people who have eaten it (when it was legal to do so) have remarked on its oily, fishy taste (not surprising given its diet). Which is another problem with seagull. Being a scavenger, you can never be quite sure what it last ate! If it is legal in your country to eat seagull and you're willing to take the risk, Mrs Liddicoat recommends removing the intestines and soaking the rest of the bird for a minimum of eight hours in salted water. And then you're still better off with chicken. Whichever you choose, personally I'd leave out Mrs Liddicoat's unintended addition of comfrey. It is used by some people as a health supplement, but, like foxglove, it is also considered a poison, so best avoided.

CORNISH MUSIC AND INSTRUMENTS

When Eleanor and Clifford celebrate Christmas in Kerensa Come Quick, they are regaled by several instruments often used around that time in Cornwall. As well as the wonderfully named 'horse's leg' (a type of bassoon), they might also have encountered the 'serpent, (a sort of twisted bassoon crossed with a cornet), a 'flutina' (a type of early accordion), 'bones' (a type of, well, bone played in pairs), and a bass viol (a kind of Baroque cello). All of these were often accompanied by tin pans (actually tin pans) which would have added to the din noted by Clifford.

CORNISH CHRISTMAS CUSTOMS

As well as its musical traditions, Eleanor learns a few more of Cornwall's ancient Christmas traditions such as giving loyal customers a slice of Christmas cake and tot of gin (my local supermarket has never offered me this – perhaps I should switch?). Also the habit of young men (wassail boys) going door to door demanding food and drink (or money) in exchange for a song or more (much to Mr Cunliffe's horror). Clifford mentions 'guise' singing which is similar. One Cornish tradition Eleanor might not have wanted her staff to find out about was Innocents Day (28 December), where it was considered bad luck to do any kind of housework!

ACKNOWLEDGEMENTS

Thanks to all the team at Bookouture for their never-failing patience and professionalism in making *Murder on the Cornish Cliffs* as good as it could be. And possibly, even a little bit more.

PUBLISHING TEAM

Turning a manuscript into a book requires the efforts of many people. The publishing team at Bookouture would like to acknowledge everyone who contributed to this publication.

Audio
Alba Proko
Sinead O'Connor
Melissa Tran

Commercial
Lauren Morrissette
Jil Thielen
Imogen Allport

Data and analysis
Mark Alder
Mohamed Bussuri

Cover design
Tash Webber

Editorial
Kelsie Marsden
Jen Shannon

Made in the USA
Las Vegas, NV
08 December 2023